Mayfield's Law

OTHER BOOKS BY GRAHAM SUTHERLAND

Dastardly Deeds in Victorian Warwickshire
Leamington Spa, a photographic history of your Town
Leamington Spa, Francis Frith's Town & Country Memories
Around Warwick, Francis Frith's Photographic Memories
Knights of the Road
Warwick Chronicles 1806 – 1812
Warwick Chronicles 1813 – 1820
Felons, Phantoms and Fiends
North to Alaska
A Taste of Ale
Wicked Women
Fakes, Forgers and Frauds
Warwickshire Crimes and Criminals
Midland Murders
English Eccentrics
Edward's Warwickshire January – March 1901
Curious Clerics
Dastardly Doctors

Joint Author
Policing Warwickshire, a Pictorial History of the Warwickshire
Constabulary

Fiction
Mayfield (Part 1 of the Warwick Detective Trilogy)

Graham Sutherland can be contacted on:
graham.g.sutherland@btopenworld.com
www.talksandwalks.co.uk

To Brian
Policing was never like
this in our day — or was it?
All best wishes
from
Graham Sutherland

Mayfield's Law

Part 2 of the Warwick Detective Trilogy

Graham Sutherland

Spiderwize

Mayfield's Law

Part 2 of the Warwick Detective Trilogy

Spiderwize
3 The Causeway
Kennoway
Kingdom of Fife
KY8 5JU
Scotland UK

www.spiderwize.com

ISBN: 978-1-907294-87-7

To: Mo, Claire, Jo, Ally and Clara

PROLOGUE

February 1825

The young man ran through the dark street, so totally distraught, he had not noticed the swirling snow. Having left the *Three Crowns* in such a hurry, without stopping to put on a coat, he was oblivious to the cold for the time being.

He counted the houses on his right hand side as he ran. At last he found the one he wanted, opened the gate, ran up to the front door and began to hammer on it loudly and frantically.

Soon an upstairs window opened, and he could see what appeared to be a woman's shadow, silhouetted against a candle. "What do want?" she called in a quavering voice. "The doctor's not here!"

"But I need a doctor urgently," pleaded the young man.

"I'm sorry, but my husband's out on a call."

"When will he be back?"

"Not before morning. And that's provided the snow doesn't settle too much."

"Surely there's another doctor in town?"

"Well......... there's Dr Boyd....but ..." she answered reluctantly.

"Where can I find him? My wife's seriously ill, and I must have a doctor," he interrupted her.

"You'd be better off not using him," she cautioned.

"Don't you understand?" his voice had risen. "My wife's likely to die if she's not seen soon by a doctor. I must have a doctor to her. Please, where can I find him?"

"You really would be far better off without him. Believe me........."

1

"I'll take that chance. My wife will die if she doesn't get some medical help soon."

The woman shook her head. "But Dr Boyd........"

"PLEASE! Where can I find him?"

Mrs Wilton gave him directions, albeit reluctantly. By the time she had finished, he was off running in the direction of Dr Boyd's house. As he ran, the man counted the houses, before sliding to a halt, outside a rundown looking dwelling. A brass plaque on the wall, confirmed it was the residence of *Dr William Boyd*. Wasting no time, he hammered on the door, and continued until an upstairs window opened.

"What do you want?" called an imperious voice.

"Dr Boyd. Can you tell me where he is, please?"

"You want Dr Boyd?" The voice sounded amazed. "You must be a stranger here?"

"Yes, we're just passing through."

"Nobody in their right mind wants Dr Boyd. Go to Dr Wilton."

"I have, but he's out on a call. Please! Where can I find Dr Boyd? My wife's having difficulty breathing and she is likely to die without a doctor. You must help me. Please!"

"Wait."

After what seemed a lifetime, the young man heard the bolts on the door being drawn back. By now, he was starting to feel the cold, as the snow fell even heavier, settling on his shoulders and hair. As his body cooled, it provided no protection against the now biting cold. The door opened, and he saw a small, dirty, scruffily dressed man appear, who smelt strongly of alcohol, and stale sweat. From the way he swayed, the man was obviously drunk. Clearly he had been in that state for some time, and was generally unwholesome

"Please!" the young man pleaded. "Where can I find Dr Boyd?"

"Who are you? I don't know you?" The man stared at his visitor, holding his hand over his eyes, as he peered into the gloom and swirling snow.

"I don't live here. We're just passing through. Where's Dr Boyd, please?"

"You're talking to him."

The young man's heart sank and his worst fears were realized, as he saw the wreck of a man standing in front of him. Now he fully understood Mrs Wilton's reluctance to send him here. Dr Boyd was clearly an alcoholic, and in no state to treat anyone. But he had no choice. He would have to trust his beloved wife to this man, and just hope he was sober and concerned enough to treat her.

"What's wrong with you? You look alright to me," slurred Boyd.

"It's not me. It's my wife. She can't breathe properly."

"Where are you staying?"

"At the *Three Crowns* in Pope Street."

"I know where it is! I'll be there soon," Boyd snapped. He turned on his heel, went back inside and closed the door. For a moment, the young man was undecided what to do before he ran back to the Three *Crowns.*

Nearly two hours later, he was still waiting for Dr Boyd to arrive, as he held his dead wife's cooling hand. Even more distraught, he set off to find the missing doctor.

He did not have far to look before finding him, in the tap room of the *Barley Mow,* even more drunk than he was before. The room went suddenly quiet as he entered leaving the door open, and with snow swirling behind him. They watched as he approached Dr Boyd.

"You bastard!" he spat. "You drunken bastard! You apology for a human being! You're not fit to be called a man, let alone a doctor. You never came near us, and now my darling Mary is dead. Dead! All because of you."

The room went even quieter, if that was possible. All the drinkers watched, fascinated, as the drama unfolded before them. Boyd was lost for words, and although he tried to splutter an apology, no words came out. He blinked and looked up at the new widower: and was terrified by the look of pure menace he saw in the other man's eyes. Even in his drunken state, Boyd knew he had never seen such quietly suppressed anger, and he trembled.

The young man said nothing else, but he took a long, last withering look at William Boyd, before turning on his heel and walking out of the inn, through the still open door. The other drinkers fell back as he approached, and nobody attempted to speak to him. Although well used to Dr Boyd's drinking habits, they were shocked by what had happened.

The next morning, after he had made the necessary funeral arrangements, the young man went to the town's only solicitor, Michael Clarke, to see what action he could take against Boyd.

"How much money have you got?" was Clarke's first question.

"Only a few shillings."

"Then forget it. If you can't afford to pay for a prosecution, there's no way I'm doing it for free. By rights I should charge you for this consultation. But, this is on the house, because of your recent loss. Good day sir."

* * *

In the following days, the locals became used to seeing the strange young man wandering about the town, although he spent much of his time in the churchyard, by a freshly dug grave. There was no headstone, and her name was simply recorded as *Mary Gibbs deceased 4 February 1825,* in the church burial register. Her home town was shown as Rochester, and her husband's name was given as Roland Gibbs. Many years later, these details would prove to be false.

The grieving husband, the landlady of the *Three Crowns*, and Mrs Wilton, were the only people to attend Mary's funeral, apart from the vicar, who was clearly disinterested. He was, however, pleasantly surprised when Mrs Wilton paid for the funeral. She felt somewhat to blame for directing the young man to Dr Boyd, who had remained sensibly out of sight for the days following Mary's death, obviously terrified of meeting Roland again.

However, Boyd's worst fears were realized several days later, when he was forced to leave the security of his house, to buy some more alcohol. He was scared to see Roland following him to the *Barley Mow*. Neither man spoke. It was as if Boyd had ceased to exist, as far as Roland was concerned. Boyd started to relax when he saw the anger had gone out of Roland's eyes.

Considering the danger to be past, he now felt it was safe to resume his normal way of life. This included his weekly visit, on a Wednesday night, to the widow Ellen Hawkins, who lived not too far out of the town. Nobody knew what she could possibly see in him and assumed, rightly, that it was purely a financial arrangement.

On his arrival back in town, the following Thursday morning, Boyd was greeted by the news Roland Gibbs had packed up, and gone. All manner of rumours had abounded about the mystery couple, such as her being an heiress who had eloped, or that she was a foreign princess. None of them was correct.

Following his wife's death, Roland, aged about twenty, had kept himself to himself, and spent much of his time walking around the town, and the immediate countryside, coupled with visiting several of the taverns. Here he would sit morosely, making his drink last a long time. After a few attempts, nobody tried to engage him in conversation, which all added to the air of mystery about him. Now he was largely ignored by the locals, as he sat drinking his ale, and gazing wistfully into the fire.

However, they would have been surprised to discover, that far from being in his own little world, he was listening intently to their conversation. He was well rewarded for his patience, especially in the early days following Mary's death. Once they were used to him being there, he would listen to them talking about Dr Boyd. When he returned to his room in *The Three Crowns*, Roland made notes of the information he had discovered. In a short time, he had learned about the widow Hawkins, and began to make his own plans.

* * *

The following Wednesday, Dr Boyd set out for his weekly visit to Mrs Hawkins. It was a wild and stormy night, although the snow had gone, and he regularly took a swig from the bottle of brandy he carried.

"Dr William Boyd?" A quavering voice called. "Your time is up. Prepare to die."

The voice came from behind. Boyd swung round and saw a hideous flickering face looking at him. Panic stricken, he threw down the brandy bottle and spurred his horse into a gallop. A hideous laugh followed him.

"You can't escape me. Murderer! You let me die. And now, you must die!" The voice wailed after him.

Boyd kicked his horse hard, which made the animal put on an extra burst of speed. Man and horse hurtled down the narrow lane. In his panic and the dark, Boyd never saw the rope stretched out across the lane, between two trees. It caught him in the middle of his chest, and he toppled backwards out of the saddle, on to the ground, but his drunken state prevented him from being seriously hurt. Lying there winded, he was aware of someone kneeling over him.

"Help me. Oh help me. Please," he wailed.

"Just as you helped my darling wife?" hissed the man, known in the area as Roland Gibbs.

Boyd screamed as he recognized his tormentor. "I'm so sorry. So, so sorry," he wailed. "Please don't hurt me."

"I'll give you a chance," said Roland quietly. "Which is more than you gave my beloved Mary. Would you like a chance?"

"Oh yes. Please. Please. I'll pay you and do anything you want."

"Here it is. This is the deal. If you can escape from here, you can live. Understand?"

"Oh yes! Oh yes!" Even as he spoke, Boyd began searching round with his hand for a stone or branch, just anything he could use as a weapon. But there was nothing. Suddenly he had become very sober.

But, even as he pondered over Roland's offer, he felt the other man lift his head up, and slip something over it. Too late he realized it was a rope. Before he could react, the rope had tightened round his throat, and his body was slowly being pulled upwards. Soon he was gasping for breath and clawing at his throat, which loosened the rope a little, enabling him to draw in some welcome air.

"Now you know how my wife died. She couldn't breathe," hissed Roland, as he pulled the rope a little higher, cutting off Boyd's air supply again.

Soon Boyd was standing, and the rope was still rising, although not yet supporting the whole of his body weight. "Please, no," he gasped, although he knew his plea would fall on deaf ears.

Soon he was standing on his toes, clawing at his throat, and fighting the pain in his throat: the shortness of breath: and the growing pain in his calves, from being in this position. His body was raised higher, and he slowly strangled.

Once Boyd had stopped kicking, Roland took out a bottle of brandy, from his saddlebag, and uncorked it. He tipped as much of the contents as he could, into Boyd's mouth, and the rest of it over the dead man's clothes, before dropping the empty bottle nearby. Lastly, he pulled the rope higher, and tied it to another tree.

"Enjoy hell," he said. "No doubt I'll see you there sometime. Make room for some more doctors and solicitors. I'm going to make their lives such a misery, they'll be glad to die."

He stood and admired his handiwork, for a few moments. Then remounting his horse, he rode off without a backward glance.

Widow Hawkins had a lonely night, and missed the money.

* * *

Two farm labourers found Boyd's body next morning, on their way to work. The general feeling was he had taken his own life, out of remorse for Mary Gibbs' death. That was the verdict of the coroner at the later inquest, although he added a rider to the effect Boyd had done so, *whilst suffering from temporary insanity, brought about by drink.*

Nobody had noticed the remains of a pumpkin, a few yards away from where Dr Boyd had been found. Even if they had, some wild animals had chewed it, so the cut out face and candle grease would not have been noticed.

By then, Roland Gibbs was miles away, already planning the next part of his revenge. But first, he would need some money, although that would not be a problem. In spite of his youth, Roland was well on the way to being a successful criminal: a man of many parts: and his Mary had been a willing partner.

Not for them small time pickings: no, they aimed for much bigger ones, and had become very proficient at all manner of frauds, and thieving of one sort or another. And now he had added murder to his talents. Surprisingly, he found he had felt no qualms about killing Boyd, and making him suffer in the process.

He would need to think very carefully about taking on another partner. Nobody could replace his Mary.

CHAPTER ONE

The Theatre June 1841

Superintendent John Mayfield sat at his desk, trying to do some paperwork, although his mind was not on the task. Nearly thirty-one years of age, John was tall, slim but wiry. He had grey eyes, fair hair, and sideburns, otherwise he was clean shaven.

Now he relived the events of the previous night, time and time again, trying to work out what had gone wrong. It had been their mutual decision to go to the theatre, although he had been given complimentary tickets, by the theatre manager, or so he thought.

Nobody else had known the programme had been changed, until the very last minute. So, how could he have known? It had not been his fault. He just did not know the answer. And, much more to the point, what could he do to put it right? Harriet had not been available to see him, when he called earlier that morning.

* * *

Yesterday had been a pleasant, late June evening, warm without being too hot. He had booked off duty early, gone upstairs to his new quarters, changed and called on Harriet Foxton. As he expected, she was not ready, but his friend, Dr Thomas Waldren, her uncle had greeted him. When John had arrived in Warwick the previous year, Thomas and his wife, Sarah, had been the first to befriend him.

Thomas was some twelve years older than John, and not quite so tall. He was broadly built, with twinkling blue eyes, and sported a moustache and sideburns. His one time dark hair now contained more than a few grey streaks. He and John sampled some wine, which Thomas had just purchased. John found Thomas in a jovial mood, and it was the first time the two had met for a while.

After John's first few hectic days in Warwick, the previous year, his appointment, as superintendent of police, had rapidly been confirmed, and the Watch Committee could not speak highly enough of him. Since he had seen Kate Whiting and her family leave on the train to London, his relationship with Harriet had grown. Both enjoyed being in each other's company, and they shared several common interests.

Slowly, John had found himself falling in love with her, and he was fairly confident she felt the same way about him. From time to time, she still teased him about Kate, and any other women he had known, but it was all done in a good natured way.

He would never forget how Harriet had saved his life on two different occasions, and that knowledge seemed to strengthen their feelings for one another. Yet, at the same time, he felt the ghost of her dead husband Edmund, still hung between them.

Whilst Harriet had saved John's life, Kate had saved his career, and he knew she loved him deeply: and, if he was honest, he felt the same way towards her. But Kate was already married, and to a local criminal, which meant their love was doomed from the outset. So it had been for the best when she and her family left Warwick.

"What are your plans for tonight?" Thomas interrupted his thoughts.

"I've got two complimentary tickets for the theatre. It's a double bill. The first one's called *The Husband,* and the second one is *And the Dog came Too.* I've no idea what they're about, but...." he shrugged.

"I don't know either of them. If they're any good, let me know and I'll take Sarah tomorrow, especially as I've got the evening off. And that reminds me, Sarah keeps nagging me so much, that I'm taking on an assistant. She says I work too hard and don't take enough time away from the surgery. You know what she's like?"

John chuckled. "I know the feeling only too well. Mathew nags me just as much. But I know he's right."

Mathew Harrison was John's sergeant. Whilst John was the chief of police for Warwick, his entire force only had six men, which included Mathew and himself.

"I'm very lucky having him as my deputy, and I have every faith and trust in him," John continued. "But, who's this new assistant doctor?"

"A Richard Gilson, who will soon be finishing a voyage as a ship's doctor, and he is looking for a practice back on land. I saw him in London, just before he sailed, and he hopes to start with me in a few weeks time."

"And I expect he'll be good looking and have all the women, in town, swooning away at his feet."

"Who will have all the women swooning away at his feet?"

Both men turned, and smiled as Harriet came into the room. She looked as radiant as ever, with her long copper red hair hanging down in ringlets, from a centre parting. The long rich blue dress she wore, complimented her attire completely.

"My new assistant, who starts in a few weeks," replied her uncle.

"And is he good looking?" Her green eyes twinkled mischievously at John.

"And pray, madam: just why would you want to know that?" he bantered back. They all laughed.

Thomas poured his niece some wine, and the three of them talked for a few minutes, before John and Harriet left for the theatre. Redman, Thomas's butler, opened the door and John took Harriet's arm in his as they walked out, into High Street.

The first play entitled, *The Husband*, was a most amusing farce, which had everybody laughing. In the interval, John and Harriet sat having a glass of wine, gazing happily into each other's eyes, oblivious to anybody else in the foyer. Several people knew John and nodded as they passed. After a while, they saw he was deep in conversation with Harriet and holding her hand, and they made no attempt to engage him in conversation.

John had never felt so close, and so attached to any other woman before, who was not his mother. He was summoning up the courage to ask her to marry him, when the bell went for the second play. And then it all went wrong.

The audience filed back into the theatre, sat down and waited for the next play to begin.   When all was quiet, the theatre manager appeared, from behind the stage curtains. "Ladies and gentlemen," he cleared his throat. "I very much regret to tell you that, due to sudden illness of the cast, earlier on today, we cannot now perform *And the Dog Came Too.*"

He held his hands up to still the outburst of voices which greeted his announcement. "However, we are lucky in having a member of the Company who is a writer, and she has just written her first play. Ladies and gentlemen, do sit back and enjoy *The Card Player.*"

There came a round of applause, but John felt Harriet stiffen alongside him, and she took her hand out of his. Her late husband, Edmund, had made a very successful living as a card player in Australia, which ultimately led to his murder. It became ever so clear, in the first few lines, that this play was set in Australia, and involved a card player called Edmund with a red headed wife, called Harriet.

It was just too coincidental to be true. John glanced, appalled, at Harriet's face, and saw it had gone white. Suddenly she stood up, left her seat, and pushed past him. Luckily they had end seats, so not too many people saw them leave. John followed her out of the theatre, and by the time he caught up with her, she was in tears.

"How could you?" she cried. "How could you take me to see that?"

"I didn't know the programme had been changed. I'm just as appalled as you are." He took her arm.

She shook off his hand and said nothing else. He walked home with her, but she still refused to speak to him. When they arrived, she rang the bell and stormed inside the house the moment the door was opened. John was not invited in, and the door was closed firmly behind her. What had started off as such a pleasant evening had ended in disaster.

After a sleepless night, John rose early and went on duty. He waited until 8.0'clock before returning to the theatre. Here he discovered the acting company's manager was staying at the nearby *Globe Inn,* on the other side of the road.   John crossed the road and went to the inn, where he had no difficulty in discovering in which room the man was staying.

Somehow he was not surprised to find him still in bed. After knocking loudly, an unhappy Percival Devereux was woken. He opened the door and peered sleepily at John.

"Yes?" he queried insolently, yet at the same time, looking lasciviously at John. The man clearly had little or no time for the new police.

"Good morning. I suppose I should thank you for the complimentary tickets for last night's performances, but I'm damned if I will." John struggled to control his rising temper, only too aware of the leering way the manager kept looking at him. "I want to know where I can find the writer of *The Card Player,* that you produced last night?"

"Afraid I can't help you there. She's already left for London."

"Who was she?"

"What's the problem?" he yawned in John's face, clearly bored by the whole affair.

"Just answer the question," snapped John. "It's a police matter, and you could find yourself in a lot of trouble, and possibly end up in gaol, if you don't give me an answer."

John doubted if he could do that, but the man was deliberately annoying him, and it was time to fight back. "And," he added menacingly. "If you do, with your rather obvious sexual tendencies, I can easily arrange for you to have a hard time."

It was a petty and idle threat, but it did the trick.

"Yes, alright," the man gulped. "She told me her name was Mary Anne Peters."

"How long had she been with you?"

"Literally only a few days. When she heard about the cast all going sick yesterday, she offered me her play, called *The Card Player.* She had a man with her, whom she said was her husband James. Did you see the play?"

John nodded. "Only the first few minutes."

"You were probably wise to go. It was a lousy play. She played the part of Harriet and he was Edmund. She said they'd done it before and knew all the main parts. It was easy for me to find a couple of players for the supporting roles."

It seemed the cast of *And the Dog came Too* had all been taken ill during the previous day, with severe stomach pains and vomiting. Strangely nobody else had been affected. John thanked Devereux curtly and went to leave, but the man stopped him.

"What complimentary tickets were you talking about? As if I would send you any." The contempt in his voice made John believe he was telling the truth.

John was puzzled. It now seemed obvious someone definitely wanted him to take Harriet to the theatre. But, had he known the play would be called *The Card Player,* there was no way he would have gone: even more so, when the names of the main characters were introduced. It was just too coincidental and, as all his men knew, he did not believe in coincidences.

Someone wanted them to see it, and that someone had to be Mary Anne Peters, or whoever she was. Somehow he doubted it was her real name. It was just too convenient for the cast, of the scheduled play, to have been taken ill so suddenly. That same Mary Anne Peters, assuming she had really written the play, knew about Harriet's husband and had been determined to cause mischief. But why had she done so?

Concerned about Harriet, he went straight up to High Street. Redman, looked uncomfortable as he told him everyone was out, including Harriet. John left a message asking her to contact him, as soon as possible, on a matter of some urgency. As there was nothing else he could do, he returned to his office and tried to do some paperwork, but his thoughts kept returning to the previous night.

* * *

It was late afternoon before he was able to concentrate on a piece of new legislation, and then his train of thought was interrupted by a knock on the door.

"Come in," he called.

"Dr Waldren to see you, guv'nor," announced Constable Samuel Perkins, and he made way for Thomas. Like the rest of John's men, Samuel usually called him *guv'nor,* as opposed to *sir.*

Samuel, now more popularly known as Sam among his colleagues, was one of John's original constables. He was tall, thin, and looked no older than a child. However, as several people had discovered, to their cost, his looks totally belied his fighting skills.

John stood up to greet his friend and offered him a chair, opposite his desk. He could see by Thomas's face that he was upset, and had a horrible feeling it was to do with the previous night.

"John, please don't blame yourself for what happened last night." Thomas came straight to the point.

He explained how Harriet had been restless for a while. It seemed there was some business, which needed her attention in Australia, and she had been putting off doing anything about it. Both he and Sarah, had been out for most of the day, so it was only a few minutes ago when Thomas had returned and found a letter waiting for him.

In brief, he explained Harriet's letter informed them she had decided to return to Australia. It seemed she had been preparing to do so for several days, having already purchased her ticket, but not telling anyone. Last night's play had finally decided her.

John sat back stunned. Just when he thought they were getting somewhere, this had to happen. If only they had not gone to the damned theatre. If only he had taken her somewhere for dinner, and then asked her to marry him. Would it have made any difference? He voiced his thoughts to Thomas, who shook his head.

"I don't really know. Somehow I think she would still have gone," he said, slowly. "I know how you were close and I hoped you would make a go of it, and that might still be case, but........" His voice tailed off.

"You are not optimistic?"

Thomas shook his head. "God knows it's what we would all want. But....and it is a big but.....Edmund's ghost will always be between you. I don't think she'll ever put him to rest...I'm sorry my friend."

"How long will she be away?"

"I don't know." Thomas replied hesitantly.

"She's not coming back, is she?"

"I don't think so." Thomas shook his head. "She made it clear in her letter, that you should not expect her to return, and you should find someone else."

Both men were silent for a while.

John broke the silence when he told Thomas what he had discovered from Devereux, and raised his concerns about Harriet's welfare. Thomas was silent for a moment.

"That's interesting. I was called out to the players who were taken ill yesterday afternoon. From the way they described their symptoms, it's possible they had gastric fever, but...I don't really think so. In fact, now I have had time to think about it, I believe they could have been poisoned."

"Poisoned?"

"Yes. Not fatally, but just enough to make them very ill, and unable to act."

"Which would be just the opportunity, this Mary Anne Peters wanted, to put her play on instead. It's just too coincidental. It had to have been planned, but who is she? And why is she out to spite Harriet? Or has she done it to get at me through Harriet?"

Thomas had no answer.

"What you have said explains a lot, but who is Mary Anne Peters? It would be more understandable if it had been me she was getting at, although I don't know why. Meanwhile, I will get her description circulated, for what it's worth." John paused for a moment.

"If only we hadn't gone to that damned theatre," he continued. "But it explains why I was sent the complimentary tickets. Although Harriet might be safer out of the country...."

"Or possibly in even more danger," interrupted Thomas. "And we may not be able to warn her. There is just one chance of making her change her mind about going. You!"

Thomas continued. "I know her ship sails early tomorrow morning, but I don't know what it's called. If you get a train from Coventry, you should be able to get to the docks in time. Go to her John. Make her change her mind. Do it for both of us, and for Sarah. Here, you may find this useful in trying to find her."

He handed John a miniature portrait of Harriet, which was an excellent likeness. "I know she's a striking woman, but not everyone will recognize a verbal description. A picture will be much more use."

"But......but what about my work here?" John faltered, knowing he was only making a token resistance.

"Tish! That's not a problem. I'm not chairman of the Watch Committee for nothing: I've given you a special job to do, and that's all anyone needs to know. And, in any case, you'll be back soon. Mathew's more than capable of looking after things here, whilst you're gone."

John needed no second urging. After he had quickly changed out of his uniform, and left instructions for Mathew, Thomas drove him to Coventry railway station and watched as the train departed. He prayed John would be successful.

But, it was not to be.

About halfway to London, the engine blew a valve and came to a sudden stop. John and several other passengers walked along the track to the nearest town, and continued their journey by coach. However the night became very foggy and the coach had to slow down from a steady trot to a slow walking pace.

Then it lost a wheel when the coachman drove off the road, in the fog. By the time John arrived at the docks, and discovered which ship he needed, Harriet had been at sea for several hours.

Ruefully, he began the long journey back to Warwick, knowing he had failed in his mission. The only consolation was Harriet could be back in England in less than a year, provided she was going to come back, but that could not be guaranteed.

At the time, he never realized this would not be the only occasion when he would miss a boat.

On arrival at the coach terminus, he learned there were no available spaces, on any coaches until 6.30 the following morning, and he was obliged to spend the night in London. Possibly he might have caught a train to Coventry, but he preferred to use the coach, which would take him directly to Warwick.

For a while he thought about looking up some of his former Metropolitan Police colleagues, but decided he would not really be very good company. He spent the night on his own.

It was a very sorry looking, and sorry feeling John who boarded the coach next morning. His head hurt from the drinks he had taken the night before, and his stomach felt decidedly queasy. He was glad he was on the outside and not sat in the stifling misery of the coach's smelly, stuffy and claustrophobic interior. And, if he was honest, he preferred travelling by coach to using the train.

CHAPTER TWO

Laura Grant

By the time the coach had left Banbury, in the early afternoon, John felt decidedly better. Apart from himself, there was now just one other passenger on the roof: a young woman. John was only vaguely aware of her presence as he took out Harriet's miniature portrait, and studied it again.

He was sad she had not even left him a letter, although Thomas said she promised to write from Australia. It might have helped him understand. But he knew he would have to wait months for such a letter, assuming she actually wrote. Thomas had warned him how she would not be returning for some years, if she ever came back at all. The saddest and unkindest part of all was she had instructed Thomas, to tell John not to wait for her, but to find himself another woman. That had hurt him.

John lowered the portrait and stared up into space, still unable to grasp he would probably never see her again; and even if he did, how would she feel for him after such a break? Also, would he still feel the same about her? Perhaps he ought to consider going to Australia himself. After all he was an experienced policeman, and had little doubt he would have any problem in finding a suitable position over there. But, even so, could he guarantee Harriet would still want to resume their relationship?

"She must mean a lot to you?" It was the young woman who spoke.

"Yes. She does," he replied, and turned to look at her. He saw she was smartly dressed, with a dark complexion, framed by jet black hair, held back in a bun. Her eyes were a deep dark brown, and although they twinkled, he saw a degree of concern in them. For reasons he could never explain, he handed her Harriet's portrait, which she took from him and studied admiringly.

"She's very beautiful, and I think you must love her very much: and yet, you're very sad." She gave him back the portrait.

John told her about his abortive visit to London, and the reasons for it. She nodded sympathetically. "Do you think she will come home?" he asked, suddenly wanting some female advice.

"Who knows? Possibly, but I feel she's not going to............" The woman stopped, unsure of how to finish the sentence. Although she had no idea of who her fellow passenger was, she felt attracted to him, and even jealous of the unknown Harriet. "Did you ever tell her that you loved her?"

"I think I only realized it a short while ago."

"But, did you ever tell her?"

"I was going to."

"So you never did?"

"No. And now it's probably too late, isn't it?"

"Probably."

"By the way, I'm John Mayfield," he introduced himself, somewhat belatedly.

"Miss Laura Grant," she replied, and they shook hands. "I'm a schoolmistress, and I have just purchased a small school in Warwick."

"That's where I work." John smiled and thought for a moment. "Have you taken over Miss Logan's premises in Mill Street?"

"You are well informed."

Laura wondered what he did for a living, but he was not very forthcoming about his work, and she did not like to ask. However, if he worked in Warwick, then he would almost certainly live there, or very close nearby, and their paths should cross again. She hoped the elusive Harriet would stay in Australia. They spoke about various topics, both connected with Warwick and elsewhere, for the rest of the journey.

All too soon, she thought, the coach clattered to a halt outside the *Green Dragon,* in Warwick Market Place, where John helped her down and unloaded her luggage. Seeing her standing for the first time, he saw she was quite tall with a slender, willowy figure. Although he kept thinking about

Harriet, he knew deep down, and had done so for a long time, how Edmund would always have come between them.

Perhaps he should take Harriet's advice: do himself a favour and forget about her. For a few fleeting seconds, the memory of Kate Whiting flickered across his mind. How they had wanted each other so badly, but never had the opportunity. Perhaps it had all been for the best. Sadly he knew, however much they had wished it, she really could not come into his life. That had been their painful decision. She had to stay with her family.

They also knew it would have been impossible for Kate to return to Warwick. Apart from already being married, she had acted as a whore to help put an end to James Cooper's criminal enterprises. That had resulted in several innocent men and women losing their jobs, which had not made Kate very popular. Also, James Cooper still had some friends in Warwick, and her life would be at risk.

From John's point of view, if he brought Kate back to Warwick, there would be no chance of her ever being accepted in society. It would not take the Watch Committee long to find an excuse to dismiss him.

On the other hand, he might just enjoy getting to know more about Laura. Hopefully, she had no ghosts to haunt her. Had he known women better, he might have realized she was having similar thoughts about him.

John hailed a cab, and the driver brought it over to them.

"Good evening, Mr Mayfield, and ma'am," said the driver, touching his hat. Laura was clearly impressed. This Mr Mayfield was obviously well known in the town. Whilst she could have asked the cab driver what he did for a living, she decided to wait and try and find out for herself.

John watched the cab disappear, noticing how Laura gave him a small wave, then he picked up his own small case, and strode across to the police station. Caleb Young was in the charge office and he leaped to attention when John entered.

"All correct, guv'nor," he said, in the time recognized greeting. "How was London, if I may ask?"

Caleb had not been one of John's original men, but he was his first replacement, and very reliable. He was tall and sturdily built, with a shock of dark hair and brown eyes. Like Sam, he had been keen to be a policeman, and was a quick learner.

"Smelly and dusty, and a mug of tea would go down very well, thank you." John smiled, knowing how the younger man was trying to find out what he had been doing in London. He had used the same tactics himself, many times over the years.

After having enjoyed the tea, he went upstairs to his own quarters, changed and went round to tell Thomas about his failure to get to London in time and bring Harriet back.

* * *

Although sad at John's failure, Thomas and Sarah realized it had not been his fault, and, they knew he was probably even more distraught than they were.

"You know, John," said Sarah, gently. "It might just be for the best. I don't think Edmund's ghost would ever have gone away. I know it seems hard, but she might just have been cruel to be kind."

Sarah was short and a little on the plump side. She had dark hair, always kept in ringlets, and blue eyes. Harriet was her late elder sister's daughter, whom she and Thomas had adopted.

They talked about Harriet for a while, before John made his excuses and went to leave. Thomas went with him to the front door. For a while, they stood on the front doorstep.

"I've been thinking about Harriet possibly being in danger, though God knows why," said Thomas.

"Possibly to get at me," answered John. "I upset quite a few people over the Cooper affair. Perhaps it's one of his friends and now he's succeeded in driving Harriet away. Hopefully, she should be safe."

He was not to know, then, how close he was to identifying the reason for Harriet being targeted at the theatre.

Soon after his arrival in Warwick, John had been responsible for the ruin of James Cooper's criminal enterprise. Whilst Cooper had never been brought to trial, one his accomplices, Charles Pearson, had been hanged. Yet, as he would ultimately discover, the threats did not come from Cooper's friends, but from a totally different source.

"I'd like to think you're right," replied Thomas, without any real conviction. "But I have already sent her a letter, via a friend of mine, who'll get it on a clipper for me. So she should get it when she arrives in Australia. It's just to warn her."

"That's probably wise."

The two friends talked for a few more moments and John went to leave. Thomas took his arm. "Please don't tell any of this to Sarah. It would only cause her more distress."

"I quite agree."

* * *

Next morning, John received a letter, addressed to him and marked *personal*. He opened it and read:

Mayfield

I do hope you enjoyed my play? And what about the lovely Harriet, did she think I played her well?

Now, now, now, no swearing please. But I don't think you'll ever see her again. Gone to Australia has she? It's a long voyage and who knows what might happen on the way?

And now, you bastard, you know what it's like to lose someone you love. You destroyed my future and so now it's your turn to suffer. Think of the long nights ahead without your Harriet. When you do, then you'll know how long my nights are without my beloved.

See you in hell one day.
Mary Anne Peters.

He needed no confirmation about the letter being genuine, although he doubted *Mary Anne Peters* was the writer's real name. Whoever she was, she was well informed: too well informed for his liking. What made the pill even more unpalatable, was the fact he did not have the slightest idea who she was, or even why she was tormenting him this way. The only good thing was, he now knew he was the mystery woman's target, and not Harriet. She had just been used as a means to an end to get at him.

For a while he reflected on who the mystery woman might be. The name *Peters* meant nothing to him. Clearly she was connected to someone he had dealt with over the years. Possibly it might be someone he had sent to the gallows, and there been a few of those, whilst he was in London, and also here, he reflected ruefully.

Or, more likely, he thought, could it be someone who I have had transported? There had been no shortage of those over the years. On reflection, it was a mammoth task to try and work out who it might be, and even then, with no guaranteed result, especially if the writer was using a false name.

CHAPTER THREE

More new arrivals.

In the following weeks, John told Mathew Harrison and Sam Perkins what had happened. They were saddened and angry, having known Harriet, whom they both liked. Mathew, who was John's only sergeant and also his deputy, was happily married, with two growing sons both eager to join the police. He and Sam had been with John from the very beginning.

Samuel, now more usually called Sam, only looked like a young teenager, and belied his true age of twenty-five: and he was more than capable of looking after himself. He was also extremely fit, and enjoyed a fully growing romance with Lucy Penrose.

She had come to Warwick, in the wake of the James Cooper affair, and was a superb artist. Employed in a free-lance capacity, the Bank of England had employed her considerable talents in drawing the scenes of Cooper's crimes, and Sam had been appointed as her escort. Now they were talking about marriage, and her moving to Warwick to be with him.

Robert Andrew, who was John's other original officer, Caleb Young and Ben Underwood, made up the rest of his staff. In time they all knew about Harriet going back to Australia, and how miserable her departure had made John. Their happiness did not seem fair, whilst John suffered, so they decided to try and do something about it, should the opportunity arise.

Both Mathew and Sam had been aware of the new schoolmistress, Laura Grant for a while, and made some enquiries about her. Most importantly, they had discovered she was a single woman, with no obvious suitors on the horizon. Mathew was still trying to find an excuse for them to meet one another, unaware they had already done so. Then fate took a hand when

24

Laura came into the police station, one afternoon in late August, to report someone having broken one of her windows.

Sam was in the station at the time and recorded the incident. He promised to send a constable round to look at the damage, as soon as he could.

"I'll go," announced John, as she left, having recognized her voice.

Sam only just managed to suppress a grin. His guv'nor always had a knack of finding attractive women. Perhaps this meeting with Laura Grant might be just what he needed.

"I know the address, in Mill Street," continued John as he picked up his kepi, and went to leave the station.

"Shouldn't you let her get back home first, guv'nor?" chuckled Sam, safe in the knowledge John could not have heard him, as he had already left the station. He had not gone a moment too soon, as Sam could not hold his grin any longer.

John walked out into the late afternoon sunshine, crossed the Market Place and headed off towards Mill Street. He acknowledged the wave from the driver of the *Crown Prince* coach standing by the *Green Dragon*, and was only vaguely aware of its passengers disembarking, as his thoughts were on Miss Laura Grant, in Mill Street.

Sam need not have worried about John arriving too early. Initially John had seen Laura heading home, and he had started to follow her. But, as usually happened when he was in town, people stopped and talked to him. Some wanted advice, whilst others were content just to pass the time of day with him. When he finally arrived in Mill Street, Laura had been home some time. With his heart beating, John rang the doorbell. It was answered by a middle-aged woman. Clearly he, or rather a policeman, was expected.

"It's the..... police, Miss Grant," she called. Somehow she had struggled over the word *police*, but John was well used to that.

"Bring him through to the kitchen, please, Abbie," came Laura's reply. In the background he could hear children's excited voices. They sounded happy. John took his kepi off and followed Abbie into the kitchen.

Laura had her back turned to him, and she was speaking to several children, who were clustered around her, gazing in a suddenly hushed awe at the policeman. "I'll be with you in a minute," she called, without looking at him. "I must just finish this lesson."

"That's quite alright, Miss Grant."

Recognizing his voice, Laura spun round. At the same time her ears and face reddened. John saw she was up to her elbows in flour and there was even some on her nose.

"Why......why.......Mr Mayfield? What are you doing here?" Then she realized he was in police uniform. "I didn't know you were....you were a policeman."

Her pupils had all gone quiet looking curiously and a little apprehensively at John. He smiled and waved to them. One or two waved back, but the others just stared at him. All of a sudden he was tongue-tied. Laura Grant was just as attractive as when they had first met. In fact, he thought, even more so with the flour on her nose.

"I've come about your broken window," he said at last.

Quickly Laura dismissed the children and sent them out to play, promising to continue the lesson on baking, another day. For a while the children moved quietly, still overawed by John's presence. However, as they moved outside into the garden their chattering grew. Laura was aware how Abbie was watching the interaction between her and John. Abbie's face was impassive, and she gave no clue as to what she was thinking.

"Would you make us some tea, please Abbie? And bring it into my study." Laura quickly wiped the flour off her hands and nose.

Abbie nodded, not exactly thrilled by the idea. She was far more interested in what Laura was going to say to the policeman. Obviously they had met somewhere before, and she wanted to know where. Laura took off her apron, led the way into her study and John followed. She offered him a seat, which he took. For a moment, neither of them spoke.

"About this window?" John cleared his throat. "I've come about the broken window."

"Does my broken window really warrant a visit from the superintendent of police?" Her eyes smiled back at him. "I heard you ran the town, but I never realized you were a policeman: and, not just any policemen at that. But the chief!"

John was saved from replying as Abbie brought in a tray bearing a pot of tea, complete with china tea cups, milk jug, two tea plates and a large fruit cake. "Will there be anything else, Miss Grant?" she sniffed.

"No thank you Abbie. We won't be too long as I have to give another lesson in a few minutes."

Abbie sniffed and turned to leave the room. John did not see the knowing smile she gave Laura. With Abbie's departure, the silence returned.

"Well no," John broke the silence. "I didn't only just come about the window. I wanted to see how you were getting on, and how you like Warwick. And to see you," he confessed.

She reddened again, yet pleased he was showing an interest in her. Since arriving in Warwick, she had not had any time for socializing, and realised how much she missed having company. For a while they talked about various matters, and forgot all about the tea and cake. In the distance, a bell rang.

"I'm so sorry," said Laura, standing up. "But I've got to go and give a lesson. I have enjoyed talking to you. Oh!" she gasped as she saw the tea and untouched cake. "Whatever must you think of me? I've forgotten to pour the tea."

They both laughed, and John realized it was the first time he had done so since Harriet left. He stood up. "I know it's forward of me," he said. "But there's an art exhibition at the Court House next Wednesday evening. Can I take you to it?"

"Oh I'd love that, Mr Mayfield."

"It's a date then. Only, please, my name's John."

"And mine's Laura."

Later, they both realized neither of them had made any further mention of the broken window or Harriet.

* * *

When John had walked through the Market Place, the *Crown Prince* was unloading its passengers. One of whom was a man using the name of Giles Bradford. He had seen the police superintendent pass by the coach, and acknowledge the driver. For a few moments he was unsure of himself, and had contemplated running.

Moments later his nerves calmed and common sense took over. This policeman would not know who he was, so why draw attention to himself by running away? And, even if he did, he would not know where to go. As Bradford felt his heart start to calm, he saw the policeman walk away from the coach. Bradford picked up his luggage and went into the *Green Dragon*, where he had already made a reservation.

Mickey Cassidy, the landlord, met him, and led the way upstairs to his room. He saw his new guest was only about five feet six inches tall, but well built, with a pockmarked face, fair hair and dark blue eyes. Although he could never say what it was, something about him disturbed Mickey. The landlord was a good judge of character, and he knew Giles Bradford was not what he pretended to be, and would need to be watched. This man radiated danger.

Had Mickey been a fly on his guest's bedroom wall, sometime later, he would have been even more wary. Once he had unpacked, Bradford took out a small revolver out of his pocket, and carefully checked it. He was not a man to take chances, and it would be several days before his partner, Jacob Harding, arrived. Once he was satisfied with the revolver, Bradford put it back into his pocket, and left his room. Carefully he locked the door behind him, and went out into the town.

He spent some time in the Market Place, carefully studying the location of *Jersey's Bank,* and in particular, the small empty premises next door to it, which adjoined the Old Square. This was why he had come to Warwick.

Bradford and his partner spent much of their time travelling around the country, seeking out banks which had empty premises next door to them. When one was found, Bradford contacted the agent handling the lease. If the premises were suitable for their needs, he paid out for three months rent in advance. Once he had the keys in his possession, Bradford would send for Jacob Harding, who came and joined him. After he had arrived, they would set up an office in the premises next door to the bank.

In order to appear legitimate, their business sold insurance and gave financial advice. For the most part the advice was real, but the insurances were frauds, usually practiced on solicitors, doctors and other affluent members of society.

If he was honest, Bradford knew it was risky, but he enjoyed outwitting these so-called clever businessmen, especially doctors and solicitors, whom he detested. Usually they both managed to cheat a considerable sum of money out of their victims before leaving town. But that was only part of their business.

The main reason, for being next door to a bank, was to rob it.

With everything timed just right, they robbed the bank, defrauded several of their clients, and left town before anyone knew what had happened. By the time the victims realized how they had been robbed, the thieves had disappeared without trace. Meanwhile, Bradford and Harding would have changed their identities, and moved to another part of the country, where they laid low for a while, before looking for another bank to rob.

After an early supper, Bradford retired to his room, carefully locked the door, opened his document case and took out some plain paper. Laying it flat, he began to sketch, from his excellent memory, the lay-out of the Market Place, paying special attention to the location of *Jersey's Bank* and the probable offices for *Bradford & Harding Investments*, which would be admirably sited next door. By the time he had finished, the plan was beginning to take shape, and he would add to it in the following days.

Next morning, he made his way to the agents handling the empty shop's lease, where he was greeted by an extremely nervous Peter Poole. He was a young man, wearing spectacles, who had only just started in the office, and Giles was his very first ever client. Quickly studying the man's age, Bradford soon guessed why he was so nervous, and decided to play hard to get.

It was not spite that made him do this, but if he could get the lease for less than the asking price, then it would mean a greater profit. As the expenses were shared with Harding, the more money he saved, the better would be their financial return. However, he would not necessarily tell his partner, about any reductions he had achieved in the rent. And, as this would almost certainly be their last criminal venture together, the more money he made, the happier he would be.

"I'm not quite sure it's what we want," he told Poole, after only the minimum of formalities."

"Oh!" Poole's face fell.

"However, I would like to see the premises, so I can make a proper assessment."

Poole quickly grabbed the keys to the premises, and his hat, before taking Bradford round to the empty shop. However, on arrival, his hands shook so much he dropped the key whilst putting it in the lock.

"Allow me," smiled Bradford.

He bent down, picked up the key, inserted it in the lock and opened the door. A grateful Poole led the way in, after having explained to Giles how he was his first client.

The premises were in a reasonable condition, but Bradford took his time examining everything, writing notes in his pocket book, as he did so. He spun it out deliberately, maliciously enjoying Poole's discomfort. The ground floor consisted of a medium sized room, opening on to the Market Place, which would be used for the main reception area. The hallway led to a smaller room, which would be their own individual office, offering some degree of privacy for their clients.

A door led out into the small kitchen and from there, to the outside privy and into the yard which ran along Old Square, with a small wicket gate at the rear, leading into New Street.

Having checked out the ground floor, they moved upstairs to the living quarters. These consisted of two small rooms plus another general sitting area. A further small staircase led up to the attic. Bradford took great pains to contain his impatience. He was fairly certain the premises were ideal, but it would all depend on what the cellar had to offer.

"What about the cellar, Mr Poole?" he asked.

Poole took him back downstairs to the ground floor, found and lit a candle, before opening another door under the stairs, and leading the way down. Bradford was grateful to find the cellar ceiling was not too high, but standing in the doorway, his heart sank when he saw the wall on the left-hand side seemed to have been cut out of solid rock. If the other side, nearest the bank, was the same, then the job was off. They would never be able to cut through it. Barely daring to hope, he turned to the other wall.

Relief flooded through him and he nearly sighed with pleasure. The wall, between the cellar and the bank, was made of bricks. But, he had to be sure it was not just a facing.

"Why is this wall made of brick?" he asked pointing at the bank wall. "And the other one is made of stone?"

"Because this all belonged to the bank many years ago. When they sold it off, they kindly put in a brick wall to block them off, so this cellar could be used by whoever rented the shop," Poole smiled.

It was the answer Bradford had wanted to hear. He left the premises with Poole and took him across to the *Rose and Crown.*

After suitably plying the young man with food and some wine, he negotiated a very successful rent and, paid him the first three months in advance. Poole went off extremely happy and Giles put a suitable price into his pocket book, which was considerably higher than what he had just paid. This would be for his partner's benefit.

It had been a good morning's work.

CHAPTER FOUR

At Sea

Harriet realized too late she was wrong. Going back to Australia was proving to be not such a good idea. Having had time to think about the matter, she now knew it had been a big mistake.

True she had been upset by the play, but to blame John for taking her to see it had been wrong. Its last minute substitution had taken everyone by surprise. And quite clearly, he had been just as upset as she had been. Although it had not occurred to her at the time, it had done so whilst she was at sea. Just who had put the play together, loosely based on her and Edmund? Had it been aimed at both of them? Or at John? Or at her?

Now, as the *Elizabeth of Napton* slowly battled her way off the West Coast of Africa, she had finally come to her senses. The problem was she loved John, and she knew he felt the same about her. But he had never said as much. Possibly, no almost certainly, she had felt he was going to propose to her, on that night at the theatre: but she had not given him the chance.

Edmund had played a big part in her life, but he had been dead for some time: and no matter how much she wished, she knew he could never come back. Whilst she liked to use him as an excuse for not re-marrying, it had not worked with John. Deep down, she knew Edmund would never hold it against her. Their love had been too strong for that. He might not have approved of John's profession, but it was the man she loved, not his job.

She had purchased the ticket for the *Elizabeth of Napton*, some weeks earlier, but had never meant to use it. All she had intended to do was to push John into making a commitment, not necessarily of marriage, but at least to declare his love for her. As he had not done so, she had intended to force the issue and threaten to leave Warwick and return to Australia.

The opportunity arose when the visit to the theatre had occurred, which had so upset her. It gave her the excuse, for deciding to leave, or at least go through the motions of doing so. If only, he had said he loved her, but it had not happened. Ruefully, she realized she had never given him the chance, and had left without even saying goodbye.

Having left Warwick, she began to have second thoughts, and was keen to see if he would follow her. Harriet had left a note for Thomas and Sarah, in which she asked them to tell John, where she was going, and hinted she might never come back to England, let alone Warwick. It was the same note in which she had suggested John forgot her and found somebody else.

Harriet reasoned that would have been all that was needed, to send John after her, and to talk her out of sailing. Whilst her reasoning was sound, she was not to know her letter had not been seen until much later in the day.

Although she had waited at the quayside, and was the last passenger to board the ship, John had not appeared. As Harriet reluctantly mounted the gangplank and watched it being removed immediately behind her, she knew he would not be coming. Angry, hurt and feeling betrayed, she retired to her cabin and had not surfaced for several days.

There were only two unattached males on board, and they both went out of their way to be friendly, and for a while she flirted with them. At one stage, she had come close to going further than just flirting, when she happened to speak to another family on board.

On asking where they had come from, she was told Coventry. Then she remembered they had arrived at the quayside only minutes before she boarded the ship.

"You were a little late arriving, on the quayside, weren't you?" she asked, beginning to experience a sudden doubt.

"Oh yes," replied the wife. "Our train broke down and we had to get a coach. But we were lucky. We heard the coach that left before us, still hadn't arrived, when we did. Goodness only knows when it got to London."

"And there was a man on it, who was in such a hurry to get to London," added her husband. "He said he was a policeman and was on urgent business."

"What did he look like?" continued Harriet very quietly, now feeling very cold. "I really do have a very good reason for asking." Yet, she knew what their answer would be.

They described John perfectly.

Barely able to contain her tears, she ran back to her cabin. From time to time one or other of her new suitors came and knocked at her door, but she told them to go away. How could she have been so stupid and doubting, not to have believed John would have come after her? If only she had waited. Slowly, the full impact, of what she had done, began to dawn upon her. Apart from leaving Warwick, and John, she had sent that message, via Thomas, to the effect she would not be coming back, and advising John to find somebody else.

Tears began to trickle down her cheeks as she sobbed, until at last she fell asleep. Sometime later she became aware of someone else being in her cabin, and was not surprised to find it was Edmund.

"You've made a right mess of things, haven't you?" he chided.

"Yes," she answered miserably.

"You really do love him, don't you?"

"Yes." Her answer was quiet. "I'm so sorry."

"Don't be," he smiled. "He's a good man and will make you happy."

"Don't you mind?"

"Good Lord no. We loved each other, but ...." His voice tailed off.

"What shall I do?"

"Write to him. Tell him you love him. Tell him you've buried me. Tell him you'll come home just as soon as you can. Have the letter ready to give to a passing ship. Leave this ship at Cape Town, and get back to him as quickly as you can."

"Oh Edmund, my love. Thank you so much. As ever, you still give me good advice." She reached out to touch him, but he had gone.

Suddenly she woke, acutely aware she had been dreaming. Or had she? Whilst she just did not know what to believe, her mind was now made up.

She would write to John and explain what had happened, beg his forgiveness and ask him to wait for her.

Then she had a horrible thought. What if John had taken her at her word, found somebody else, and was already married by the time she returned? The thought prodded her into action. Swinging her legs out of the bunk, she went across to the small desk, sat down, took out some paper, and began to write.

As Harriet did so, she noticed the sea was not nearly as calm as it had been. The ship was now rising and falling quite steadily, and seemed to be increasingly so. In the next few hours, the storm increased and conditions on board became more and more uncomfortable as time passed. Harriet was lucky in being a good sailor, and she did not suffer from seasickness, which was more than could be said for most of her fellow passengers, whom she could hear retching. They had all been instructed to stay in their cabins, and not to move about the ship, or attempt to go up on deck.

The night moved into day, but there was no let-up in the weather. As far as Harriet could tell, the ship was being blown along by the storm, which seemed to her, to be an easier option than sailing against it. Once there came a terrific crash, as something hit the deck heavily. It was followed by much shouting and the sounds of running feet.

After that had happened, the ship no longer seemed to be sailing in a straight line, but spun round from side to side, clearly out of control. As night fell once more, the storm began to ease, and by dawn, it had ceased. Harriet seized the opportunity to go on deck for a breath of fresh air and a little exercise.

She was greeted by the sight of a sorry looking, totally grey-faced exhausted crew, dragging themselves about the deck. A quick glance towards the mast confirmed her worst fears. It had gone. Clearly that had been the crash she had heard.

"Why aren't these men being fed?" called Captain Archibald Banks.

"The cook's too ill," came a tired reply.

"Then find somebody else!"

"There is nobody else," another tired voice replied. "Everyone's working the pumps, though God knows, that's a losing battle. We can't stop the water rising."

"Let me do it," called Harriet. "I know where the galley is. If nothing else I'll get a fire going and make some tea."

"But you're a passenger, Mrs Foxton," objected Banks weakly.

Harriet ignored him. Catching hold of a sailor, who looked slightly less exhausted than the others, she persuaded him to lead her to the galley. Between them they re-ignited the galley fire and soon had a kettle boiling. Slowly she brewed some tea and made sandwiches, which she distributed to the crew, including those working the pumps.

She was appalled to see how high the water was in the cargo hold. In spite of the men working the pumps, the water was obviously rising. For the most part the men accepted the food and drink with deadpan, exhausted and hopeless faces, which slowly became more animated. Lastly, Harriet took some tea and sandwiches on to the bridge and gave them to Banks.

Gratefully he took them and Harriet sipped her own tea with him. The man was totally exhausted. "I expect you're glad that's over?" she said, for something to say. He made no reply, but pointed out to sea behind her.

She turned and was aghast to see evil black clouds, interspersed with forks of lightning, headed their way. "Oh God! We're in the eye of the storm?" she asked, already knowing the answer. He nodded.

"We've got a bit of time," Banks replied. "But I fear the worst is yet to come. And we've no mast and the water's rising." He bit into his sandwich.

"Where exactly are we? Do you know?"

"I know." His voice was grave. "We're off the West Coast of Africa, and that makes us almost certainly close to the Skeleton Coast. It's probably the most inhospitable region on this Planet. And, if we end up wrecked there, I doubt any of us will survive." He finished his sandwich and tea.

Tossing the tea leaves over the side of the ship, he faced the lower deck. "Jump to it, now men!" he bellowed. "The storm will soon be here. We'll run with it while we can and then....." He did not finish his sentence.

The crew looked at the approaching storm, and Harriet saw many of them cross themselves. Suddenly she missed John even more dreadfully, than she had done before. Slowly the realization hit her: she would probably never see him again. She felt the hot tears run down her cheeks. How could she have been so stupid?

"I think you'd better go back to your cabin, Mrs Foxton," instructed the captain.

"What are our chances?"

"Very slim. I suggest you get prepared to abandon ship." She looked overboard at the ever mounting waves hurling themselves at the ship. At the same time the increased wind buffeted her and she looked at him. "In this?"

He shook his head. "No, I'm hoping the wind keeps this way as it will blow us towards the coast. It's our only chance. Luckily the wind's blowing that way."

"To the Skeleton Coast?"

"Aye." The captain nodded grimly. "Hopefully we'll be blown through the reefs and onto the shore. Otherwise, we take to the lifeboats and God save us. If you land safely, head south. Just keep the sea to your right. And who knows, God willing, you might end up in the Walvis Bay settlement."

He decided not to tell her how the chances of survival were virtually nonexistent.

Harriet returned to her cabin. Firstly she took off her dress and put on a shirt and a pair of trousers. No doubt some of the women on board would object. But it made more sense to get out of a flowing dress, which would easily weigh her down, if she had to swim. Next she put on a belt, complete with a gun holster, into which she put her revolver. As an afterthought, she tied some cord to its trigger guard and the other end to her belt. Then she put all the ammunition she had, into a waterproof pouch, which she also tied onto her belt, and tucked in a hat as well. If she succeeded in landing safely, the sun would be unmercifully hot, especially as she had such a fair complexion.

That reminded her. She had not lived in the Australian Outback for nothing. Quickly she opened her case, and tipped its contents onto her bunk. With a small cry of triumph, she grabbed the two large water canteens she had packed, back in Warwick. How that all seemed a lifetime ago! Without wasting any more time, she left her cabin, went to the water butt in the galley, and quickly filled the canteens. She had just got back to her cabin, when suddenly the ship gave a lurch and seemed to settle deeper into the water.

"EVERYONE ON DECK!" A loud cry came from the deck. **"PREPARE TO ABANDON SHIP!"**

The cry was greeted by wails and screams from the passengers, who now realized what was happening. Harriet slung the canteens over her shoulders and went to the cabin door. Taking a last look round the cabin, she saw the letter she had been writing to John. Crossing back to the desk, she picked it up, folded it and wrapped it in some oilskin before putting it inside her shirt, next to her heart.

"You'll probably never get this now my love," she said wistfully. "But, if I should die, then your name will be next to my heart. Oh John. I do love you so much. How can you ever forgive me for running out on you?"

On deck, the passengers and crew huddled, trying to find some protection from the driving rain. In the distance, she could see white breakers and assumed, rightly, they marked the reefs just off the shore. But, a quick look overboard confirmed how the ship would be unlikely to get through them.

"MAN THE LIFEBOATS!" ordered Captain Banks, but it was already too late.

There came a shuddering crash as the ship hit some sunken rocks and began to break up. Two of the four lifeboats were immediately swept overboard. The others were launched, but they were quickly swamped by the fear struck passengers and swept over the reef, where they broke up. Harriet hesitated, unsure of what to do. She was joined by Captain Banks and a few crew members.

"We can't stay here, lassie," he said. "We must get off or be sucked down by her."

The wind whipped his words away, and his face was a sickly pale greenish colour in the flashing lightning.

"Grab that!" He pointed to a wooden packing case, floating at their feet. Only now did Harriet realize the sea was rising up her legs. She did as instructed.

Moments later she was afloat and being borne towards the white breakers on the reefs. Already she was starting to feel cold and her hands had difficulty in holding onto the packing case. Frantically she looked around for something she could tie herself on to, but there was nothing.

First one of her hands, and then the other released their hold. As she slipped off the case, into the sea, Harriet saw she was through the reef, and in much calmer water. Although she could see the breakers, which were hitting the beach, were not that far away, she felt so tired.

After the earlier coldness, she began to feel warmer, and tried to swim towards the shore. But it never seemed to get any nearer. Dimly she saw a whitish light hovering over the beach. It was a man holding a lantern.

"This way Harriet," the man called in a familiar voice. "This way!"

"John! Oh John! You've come to save me. I should never have left you."

But she saw it was not John who stood there. It was Edmund.

"Come on Harriet!" he called, smiling as he did so. "It's not far now. You can make it. Come to me, my love!"

"Oh Edmund!" she cried, and stopped swimming. "Oh Edmund! Where's John? Oh I do love you John. John!" Her hand went to where she had put John's letter.

Harriet's eyes closed as she sank, and the waves broke over her.

CHAPTER FIVE

The Bank Manager

G iles Bradford had several busy days. Having obtained the keys to his new property, he went back to it for a much closer inspection. He was not too worried about the living accommodation. Provided everything went to plan, they would not be staying very long. Where he concentrated was in the cellar.

Having equipped himself with several candles, he lit some of them, and began to inspect the cellar in minute detail. Firstly, he saw it had a stone slabbed floor, which might cause a problem but, on the other hand, it would be easier to clean. The ceiling was not too high, which meant the overhead road would have deeper footings.

His thoughts were confirmed after he had spent some time listening, but he could only hear the faintest of noises from traffic using the Market Place. The cellar was well sound proofed, and if they muffled their chisels, there would be little or no chance of them being heard outside.

Next he concentrated on the dividing wall between the cellar and the bank. He saw the mortar had been in place for some time, and was quite crumbly in parts. It should make removing the bricks much easier, and replacing them should be fairly simple.

The only possible snag concerned what was on the bank's side of the wall. Hopefully they would get straight into the vaults. He knew there was a risk the bank might have reinforced this wall. If they had done so, then the project could not be continued. However, knowing how most banks operated, Bradford was confident that it was unlikely, but he would soon know.

* * *

Some days later, he presented himself at *Jersey's Bank* and requested an interview with Albert Quinn, the manager. It was given reluctantly. "How can I help you?" Quinn demanded in his most superior tone. "It had better be important. I only deal with important clients."

Quinn was fifty-eight years old, with a long face and a small nose. He was balding rapidly, and what little remained of his once black hair, was now grey. Being a little on the short side disadvantaged him when dealing with his staff, and some customers. By nature he was a bully, and always affected a superior attitude when dealing with most people.

"It is," smiled Bradford. "On behalf of my partner, who will be arriving soon, I have taken the lease on the property next door, where we shall be operating as financial investors and insurance agents. With your bank as our neighbour, it seems only logical to use your services."

His face completely belied his true feelings for the man in front of him. He would let him have his day, happy in the knowledge it could not last much longer.

Quinn's attitude immediately changed. "By all means," he simpered. "We can soon set up an account for you."

"That's fine, but from time to time, in our business, people want to invest not just money, but jewellery or title deeds, and other securities."

"That's unusual, isn't it?"

"It happens. Sometimes these other items can be valued at several hundred pounds. So, I wonder what the position is regarding the use of safe deposit boxes?"

"The bank operates such a service."

Quinn felt self-satisfied. He was beginning to feel this interview was not going to be a waste of time. Already he was mentally calculating how much he could charge, as opposed to what the bank would actually receive. His creditors were starting to pile on the pressure, and making noises about informing the bank's directors how their manager had gambling habits.

"Excellent, but...er....um...please forgive me," Bradford could also be ingratiating when it suited him, as it did now. "But how secure is your system? Is it possible I can take a look, just to satisfy myself? Only, you see," he continued, only too well aware of Quinn's delicate financial situation. "Unless I can be absolutely sure of your security, my partner will insist on us using another bank."

"Oh I don't think there will be any need for that." Quinn fought down his rising panic. "Let me show you."

Both men stood up, and Quinn led the way to a locked door at the far end of the bank. He selected a key from his fob, inserted it into the lock, turned it, and opened the door. Once it was open, he stood to one side and beckoned Bradford to enter. Quinn followed him, locking the door behind them, before leading the way downstairs.

Every few feet a gas light hissed, giving the two men flickering shadows on the other wall, as they passed. At the foot of the steps, Bradford saw an iron door, which Quinn opened and locked again behind them. They were in the vault.

Bradford heaved a silent sigh of relief. The wall adjoining his cellar was also made of brick, and had not been reinforced. As a bonus, it was fairly uncluttered, apart from some shelves. But on the other side of the vault stood a cabinet, fixed to the wall, containing numerous locked drawers, secured with expensive padlocks.

"That's where we keep the safe deposits," announced Quinn proudly, as he pointed to the drawers. "Each one is locked."

"Who has the keys?"

"There's only one per box, and that's kept by the depositor."

"Are there any master keys?"

"Oh no: I couldn't open any of them, even if you tried to rob me." He gave a nasal laugh, which made him sound like a braying donkey.

Inwardly Bradford winced at the noise coming from this loathsome man. Although locked, and without any spare keys, he was not worried about getting into the safe deposit boxes. Apart from being a presentable looking businessman, his partner, Jacob Harding, was also a very skilled locksmith. No lock had yet been made which he could not open, and this made him a valuable asset to their business.

Pleased with what he had seen and learned, Bradford thanked Quinn and the two men returned upstairs. Once back in the bank, they shook hands, and

Bradford left, quickly returning to the *Green Dragon*. Back in his room, he quickly took out his plans of the Market Place and wrote in the approximate measurements of the bank vaults. He had a good eye for measurements, and they almost matched those in his own cellar.

Next he wrote a short letter to Jacob Harding, which simply said:

It's on. Get here as quickly as you can. GB.

It had been another good morning's work, and everything was progressing as planned. He left his room soon afterwards, and gave the letter, now sealed in an envelope, to Mickey Cassidy to send on the next mail coach.

After which, he went in search of a sign writer to come and do some work in his new premises.

* * *

Albert Quinn watched Bradford leave, before returning to his office. As Bradford knew full well, Quinn was a very worried man. For some time now he had become addicted to gambling on horses, and sometimes on cards. As a way of making money, it was a resounding failure. It was doubtful if he even knew what a winning racehorse looked like, let alone how to bet on one. And, when it came to playing cards, he was just as hopeless. For a man to whom handling money was his life, Quinn was totally inept at managing his own financial affairs.

He sat for a few moments, staring into space, before unlocking a drawer in his desk, and taking out a small notebook. Although he knew the figures by heart, nevertheless he opened it, and read them again. It made no difference, how often he read them: they never seemed to go down: if anything, they only increased.

But his gambling debts were not all he had to worry about. Whilst he might owe money to some influential people, his debts were not a criminal matter. True, he had on occasions given away the financial secrets of some of his clients, to their rivals, in return for an occasional debt being written off, but these were few and far between.

However, that was not the case in the methods he used to pay off his more pressing creditors. If ever there was a full audit carried out on the bank's accounts, his various little frauds would almost certainly come to light. When they did, that would mean him appearing at the Assizes.

The only good thing was, even if his frauds were discovered, he might not necessarily be incriminated. He had disguised his handwriting and made it look like Bernard Hamlyn's, his chief cashier.

Hamlyn was forty-one years old, and stood just over six feet tall, which did not endear him to Quinn. He was thinly built, and stooped from having spent most of his working life poring over ledgers in the bank. His hair was prematurely grey, and like Quinn, he was unmarried.

Quinn detested Hamlyn, knowing the feeling was entirely mutual. He feared, rightly so, how the other man had eyes on his position as manager. Henry Jersey, the bank's owner, had hinted as much, but true to his devious character, had put nothing in writing to that effect

The fact Quinn might be sentencing an innocent man to transportation, did not unduly worry him, because that was his nature. Albert Quinn only considered himself. He would have been more worried about Hamlyn, had he known his chief cashier, already suspicious of him, had commenced his own audit. It was a slow business which could only be carried out, when Quinn was not around. That, in itself was difficult, as the man was always first to arrive, at the bank, in the morning, and the last to go home.

However, there was a reason behind Quinn's apparent hard working routine. He had to wait until no members of the bank's staff were on the premises, before he could carry out his frauds. It was necessary for him to have full access to all the ledgers, without any member of staff being aware of what he was doing. Initially Quinn had only taken very small amounts from a few accounts, but as his debts grew, he had to take more money: and more often.

With a deep sigh, he locked his notebook away, and rested his head in his hands. If only he could stop gambling, but he knew there was no chance of that happening. True, he would charge this man, what was his name? Oh, yes, Bradford, more than the official bank fees. It would help a little, but it was only a drop in the ocean.

What he needed was a robbery at the bank, with money taken, and all the ledgers thrown in for good measure. He chuckled at the thought of Henry Jersey having his precious bank robbed. It would serve the fat little podge right.

Slowly the idea began to grow in his mind. Could it be done? And, if so, how? He cursed himself for not having used the time when the property next door had been empty. Now it was too late, and the man Bradford had taken it over. For a brief moment he wondered if Bradford could be persuaded to join him in robbing the bank, but quickly dismissed the idea. For a start he did not even know the man. And, if he was an honest man, he could cause Quinn a lot of trouble. No, he needed to think of another way. His thoughts were interrupted by a knock at his office door.

"Mr Quinn? Mr Quinn?" he recognized Hamlyn's voice.

"What is it?" he snapped. How that man annoyed him.

"I thought you should know, Mr Jersey's in the Market Place and headed this way."

Quinn grunted his thanks and stood up. He smoothed his cravat and tailcoat, before going to meet his employer.

Henry Jersey, never a patient man, was well-known for having a very short temper, and today was no exception. He had inherited the bank from his father, having been founded by his grandfather. Jersey knew when he was onto a good thing. *Jersey's Bank*, being one of only three such businesses in Warwick, was by far the most prosperous and he enjoyed the revenue it generated for him.

Whilst he had inherited Quinn, he did not like the man. He had far more trust in Bernard Hamlyn. When the right moment arrived, he would have no hesitation in dismissing Quinn. For a while he had thought about promoting Hamlyn in his place, but he was coming under family pressure, to find employment for a nephew. Somewhat begrudgingly, he had to admit Quinn seemed to do a good job, and he seemed to live at the bank, almost unnaturally so.

On arriving at the bank, that afternoon, he was in an exceptionally evil temper. He had just had a confrontation with Constable Ben Underwood, for allowing his horse to foul in Theatre Street. The constable had instructed him to clear up the mess, but Jersey had refused, and had tried to browbeat Ben. Surprisingly, it had made no difference, and Jersey found himself being reported for the offence.

Hamlyn had seen him arrive and immediately recognized the danger signs. He quickly warned the other cashiers, and studied his thin face in a nearby window. The thin face, which stared back at him, seemed much older, than his actual age. After smoothing his grey hair, Hamlyn stood up straight, to his full height, adjusted his cravat, and went to greet his employer. Having gone by Quinn's office, he opened the front door of the bank.

"Good afternoon, Mr Jersey."

Jersey ignored him and made his way towards Quinn's office, just as the manager was appearing. "I want a word with you, Quinn!" he snarled.

A pair of steely blue eyes glowered at the manager. They were made even more fearsome by a surrounding bald head, red face and a bulbous heavily veined drinker's nose. Like Quinn, Jersey was not very tall, but he was rather fat.

"General Spencer tells me there's something wrong with his account." He pushed his way into Quinn's office. The manager followed him and closed the door.

"Yes, I know all about it," replied Quinn, using one of his ready made excuses. "There's been a delay in meeting a bill of exchange, in London. It should be cleared by the end of the week."

For a moment Jersey seemed lost for words. "Well don't let it happen again."

"I wouldn't have let it happen, had I known, but he's actually one of Hamlyn's clients."

Jersey looked at him sternly. "Be that as it may, but let me remind you, the running of this bank is your responsibility. If you can't do it, I'll get Hamlyn to take over."

He stressed each point by poking Quinn in the chest. Just of late, something was bothering him about Quinn, although he could not say what it was.

After Jersey left, Quinn sat down and began to shake. So, it had started. How on earth had General Spencer discovered there was a problem with his account? He never came into the bank and rarely accessed his account, which was one of the reasons why Quinn had used it. He knew he could soon put the matter right, but he would need to choose, very carefully, which other account to manipulate.

It would mean another late night.

* * *

Three days later, when the *Telegraph* coach arrived at the *Green Dragon,* only two men alighted from it. One was a man in his early fifties. A formal black morning coat covered his thin body and made him look taller than his six feet, and a black top hat sat on his thick grey hair. His slight stoop, blue eyes, friendly face and soft voice, gave Jacob Harding, which was the name he was using just then, a benign, almost beatific appearance, which encouraged people to trust him.

It was a wonderful asset for a confidence trickster.

As the coach came into the Market Place, Jacob Harding saw his partner, Giles Bradford waiting for him. Both men waved to each other. Harding climbed down stiffly, and gratefully, from the roof of the coach. It had not been a good journey, having rained most of the way.

"Give me the train any day," he greeted Bradford.

"You're just a little too early. It opens here next month," chuckled the other man. He was only too aware of his partner's dislike of coach travel. "But we couldn't wait till then."

"Then that'll cost you dinner."

"My pleasure."

Bradford took one of the cases and led the way, still chuckling, into the *Green Dragon.* Harding picked up the other one and followed. Although not exactly chuckling, he was glad to be off the coach, and also excited at the prospect of the *joint project*, as his partner liked to call their latest plan.

* * *

The other passenger waited on the coach until Harding had descended, and greeted Bradford, before moving. He idly watched the banter between the two men, as he climbed down. Already his cases had been put on the ground by the guard.

Dr Richard Gilson gave him a coin tip, and looked at his new surroundings. He had arrived to take up a possible partnership with Dr Thomas Waldren. Looking around, he had expected Thomas to be there to greet him. Instead, he saw a thin man, formally dressed in black, standing by a carriage. A liveried footman stood by the carriage horse, holding its reins.

"Excuse me, sir," said the thin man. "Would you be Dr Gilson?"

"I am."

"Welcome to Warwick, sir. I'm Redman, Dr Waldren's butler. The doctor sends his apologies, but he has been called out, so I'm here instead. Please, would you care to step into the carriage?"

Whilst Redman was speaking, the footman handed the reins to him, and quickly loaded Gilson's luggage, then he climbed back on board and recovered the reins. As they drove off, Laura Grant was just crossing the Market Place and she waved to Redman, who waved back. She could not help but notice the good looking, well built man, with long brown hair, who was sat in the carriage, and blushed slightly as he raised his hat to her.

Their eyes met and he smiled, as she saw him studying her intently. Laura felt her heart lurch, and her face go red. Clearly he was smitten, but so was she.

Whilst she liked John, Laura could not help but feel he still thought about his Harriet. Consequently, they were friends and nothing much else. Perhaps she had expected too much, but she wanted more than just friendship from him. Having assumed, rightly, that Redman's passenger had to be the new doctor, she started to think about how she might make John jealous. Hopefully, that would spur him into action

Reluctantly, Richard turned back towards Redman, as Laura moved out of sight. "Who was that most divine looking woman?" he asked.

"That was Miss Laura Grant, a local school mistress."

"And how do I get to meet such a handsome woman?"

"I should point out, sir," Redman replied coolly. "Miss Grant is a very good friend of Superintendent Mayfield, who is Warwick's chief policeman."

Richard smiled. Policeman or no policeman, Laura Grant would be a very worthwhile challenge, and he would enjoy getting to know her. Clearly Redman did not approve, but that was not a problem. Still, he might just have to bide his time a little, before making a move. If Redman knew her, then so did Dr Waldren. At the moment Richard could not afford to upset him for the immediate future. He needed to build up a friendship and trust with the man.

The carriage soon stopped outside the Waldren's house. Richard was invited indoors, where he was greeted by Sarah, in her usual friendly manner. After he had been shown to his room, and his luggage delivered, Richard quickly unpacked and rejoined Sarah downstairs. Whilst they waited for Thomas to return, she quietly questioned him.

She soon discovered he was almost forty years old, and single. He told her how he had been married once before, but did not enlarge on it. In fact, he hinted quite strongly he was not yet ready to marry again, although he enjoyed female company.

Richard explained how he had just completed a return voyage, as a ship's doctor, to Brazil. Prior to that, he had practiced at Oakham, in Rutland.

Unfortunately, the owner of the practice had died of heart failure, which resulted in the widow selling up the surgery, and he had insufficient finances to purchase it outright.

Before that, he had been in Bury St Edmunds, where he had fallen out with the senior partner in the practice. He did not elaborate, but blushed slightly, intimating it had something to do with the partner's younger wife, and Sarah was too polite to ask.

By the time he had finished, Sarah was entranced by him. His tall well built body, dark twinkling eyes and brown hair, clearly made him a lady's man. No doubt he would appeal to many of the surgery's female patients, especially those with eligible unmarried daughters. If only she had not been

married, and was just a little bit younger, she would not have minded getting
to know him much better.

"I saw a Miss Grant, I think Redman, said her name was, on the way
here," he said innocently.

"That would be Laura Grant. She's very friendly with John Mayfield,
who's one of our best friends. You'll no doubt meet them soon." Sarah
stopped and looked intently at him. "I think I can see what you are planning.
She's a lovely woman, but I'm not sure she's for John......"

Sarah told him all about Harriet, and how John seemed to have attached
himself to Laura very much on the rebound. "He still hopes Harriet will
come back, just as we all do. But, I wouldn't want to see him hurt. Do you
understand?"

Richard was acutely aware how her voice had taken on a steely tone, and
he made a mental note not to cross her. "Of course," he smiled. They talked
about other matters, until at last Thomas returned.

* * *

Over the next few days, Richard sat in on surgeries, which Thomas held, and
then he began to take his own. It did not take long for Thomas, to realize
many of his female quickly preferred to see the younger doctor. He confided
to Sarah how pleased he was with Richard, and thought he had made the
right decision.

"It's early days, yet," she reminded him cautiously. "You both agreed to
have a six months trial, and I think you must do that."

* * *

By now, a sign writer had painted the name....*Bradford & Harding Insurance
and Financial Investment Agents,* on both a hanging sign and the front
window of their premises. Bradford placed an advertisement in *The
Chronicle*, which was the local newspaper, advising people of their
forthcoming opening date, and inviting them to visit the office, where

refreshments would be supplied. Having now established a deadline, they had their offices repainted, fully equipped and ready for the big day.

Their opening, in early September was a success, and they were visited both by numerous townspeople and others, who wanted to discuss their financial needs, with a view to either taking out insurance policies or making other investments. Bradford took the opportunity to introduce his partner to Quinn, who had received a personal invitation to the opening.

"I've been thinking, Mr Quinn," said Bradford, taking the bank manager to a quiet corner. "You must get clients who are looking for investments outside the bank."

"That's true."

"If you care to steer them this way, we would make it very worth your while, in commissions. What do you say?"

"I'm sure Mr Jersey would not permit it."

"Does he need to know?"

"Well no, I suppose he doesn't."

Quinn could hardly believe his good fortune. People were always asking him for advice about how and where to make more risky investments. The bank's policy was to refer them to London: But not any more. It was all going to change where Albert Quinn was involved.

Another visitor was Thomas Waldren. For the previous few days, he had not been feeling very well. It was nothing too serious, and hardly seemed worth worrying about, but it had concentrated his mind on the fact he was not immortal. Perhaps, he reasoned, it would be a good idea to arrange some sort of life insurance policy, which would leave Sarah financially secure in the event of his death.

Bradford was only too happy to arrange to see Thomas as soon as possible.

* * *

Quinn might not have been quite so happy, had he known Hamlyn knew about his invitation to the grand opening of *Bradford & Harding,* and seized the opportunity to carry out more of his personal audit of the bank's ledgers. These were kept in Quinn's office and only allowed out under his personal supervision. Hamlyn had heard Jersey's comments about General Spencer's account, and knew Quinn's excuse was untrue.

Hamlyn had personally arranged for the payment, and knew it had not been delayed. Now he needed to get to the ledgers. The trouble was trying to find a time when Quinn was not in the bank, which he always seemed to be. So discovering the invitation was too good a chance to miss.

After several minutes searching, he found the original transaction and the supposed one. By carefully checking on the various sums of money, supposedly paid out, after Jersey's visit, and re-grouping them, he came up with an identical sum of money. Although it looked like his writing, on closer inspection he could see it was not.

He sat back with a smirk of triumph and waved his fists over his head. "Got you!" he said to himself. "Try and blame me, would you, for your embezzlement? And now you're going to pay for the way you've treated me over all these years, you miserable old bastard."

* * *

Next morning, Friday, Quinn came in early as usual, but he was surprised and apprehensive to find Hamlyn was there before he was. To make matters worse Hamlyn was sitting in his office, with the ledgers open.

"How dare you sit in my office!" It was a statement rather than a question. Quinn paused for breath. "You're finished at this bank and I'll see you never get any references."

He stopped, suddenly unsure of himself, as Hamlyn only smiled at him.

"Oh no, Quinn. I've discovered your little game. Embezzlement they call it. I think you'll be the one without the references, other than your having have spent some time in Australia, by courtesy of Her Majesty."

Quinn's eyes bulged and he felt his head pound. "What...what...are you going to do?"

"That depends on you. I could go to Mr Jersey or I could go the police. Or....I could say nothing...but for a price."

The bank manager sat down heavily. "What do you want?"

"I'll settle for £5 now. And then £5 a month until I decide to call a halt."

"You can't do that. I don't have that sort of money."

"Not doing too well at cards are we?" Hamlyn smirked at his former tormentor. "Then you'll have to some more embezzling, won't you."

"NO!"

"Too bad. Then I'll go across to the police station right now. Good-bye Quinn. Enjoy Australia, provided you can survive the time in gaol and the voyage." Hamlyn stood up and turned to go.

It was a mistake.

Quinn hurled himself at the other man. Catching Hamlyn off guard, they both crashed to the floor. The manager, still having the advantage of surprise, was the first to recover, and his hands went round his chief cashier's throat. Hamlyn quickly realized there was no way Quinn would ever let him leave the premises alive.

By now Hamlyn was on his back with Quinn kneeling over him. Try as he might, he could not break Quinn's desperate grip around his throat, and there was a roaring sound in his ears. From somewhere he recalled a story his soldier father had told him, about being in a similar position. Summoning his last strength, he jabbed a thumb into Quinn's right eye.

He heard his attacker call out in pain, and at once the pressure eased on his throat, as Quinn removed his hands to nurse his injured eye. Hamlyn pulled himself away, staggered to his feet and made for the office door, but Quinn caught his foot and pulled him backwards. In doing so, Hamlyn fell against the desk, and he clutched at it to slow his inevitable slide back to the bank manager.

His clawing hands caught hold of the heavy glass inkwell on the desk, just as Quinn pulled him back onto the floor. Once again Quinn had his hands round the cashier's throat and he began to squeeze. Using the inkwell, Hamlyn hit him on the left hand side of his head, with all the force he could muster. Ink spilled over Quinn's face.

Quinn grunted, gasped with agony. Then he clutched at his head and chest, before he fell to one side. The pressure eased round Hamlyn's throat, and he pushed himself away from under Quinn.

Slowly Hamlyn stood up, gasping for breath and looked down at Quinn. The manager lay still and he could see no obvious signs of life. Putting down the inkwell, he knelt over the fallen man and put an ear to his chest.

There was no sound of any heartbeat.

"I think you've killed him," came a voice from behind.

CHAPTER SIX

Later the same day

Hamlyn spun round, and saw Bradford standing behind him. He recognized the man as having been in the bank recently, and knew he was from the office next door.

"The door was open, so I came in. I was looking for Albert Quinn," continued Bradford. He paused, and pointed at the body. "And it seems I've found him."

"It was self-defence."

"Quite probably, but is that what I will tell the police? They may not believe me and might even think I'm involved myself." Bradford gave a slight forced smile.

"If you saw what happened, then you've got to tell them. Otherwise, if they think it's murder, I'll hang." Hamlyn's voice rose in panic.

"Undoubtedly, and that's probably for the best."

Suddenly Hamlyn moved towards Bradford, with the inkwell still clutched in his hand. His intention was obvious, but Bradford made no attempt to retreat. Putting his hand in his pocket, he produced a revolver, and pointed it at Hamlyn. "Don't even think about it. You'd be dead, just like him, before you got anywhere near me. Now, put it down and let's talk about this."

Faced with no alternative, Hamlyn lowered the inkwell and his shoulders sagged. He knew when he was defeated, but his brain was working overtime. Why was this man unwilling to agree to the fact he had only acted in self-defence? And, why did he want see Quinn, at this early hour? Slowly he sat down at Quinn's desk and put his head between his hands.

"That's better. Now, let's talk this through. You have just cost me a lot of money by killing Quinn. So what are you going to do about it?" Bradford lowered his revolver

"What are you talking about? How have I just cost you a lot of money?" Hamlyn was genuinely puzzled.

For a moment Bradford hesitated then he decided to take a chance. He had come so far, and knew Quinn could have been blackmailed quite easily. Whilst he did not know Hamlyn, he knew he was in a very good position to demand his help.

"I'll tell you. Quinn was going to help me rob the bank, but thanks to you, he can't. So, you'll have to help us instead."

The silence became electrified as Hamlyn struggled to understand what Bradford had just said.

"Rob the bank? Rob Mr Jersey's bank? Quinn was going to help you rob the bank?" There was a note of total disbelief in his questions. "I don't believe you. Why should ....Oh my God." He broke off as the thought hit him.

Bradford allowed himself a slight smile. "You've got it. To settle his gambling debts. And, I wouldn't mind betting he's been helping himself to the bank's money as well. Am I right?"

Hamlyn nodded slowly. What was he getting himself into?

"Now with him out of the scheme, you will have to take his place."

"No! Never!" Hamlyn pushed his chair back and stood up. "I'll go and tell Mr Jersey all about it, right now."

Bradford stood to one side, with his arms folded, smiling wryly. "Fine," he said. "But just think for a moment. How will you explain your part in the late Mr Quinn's death? Eh?" He raised an eyebrow.

"And don't look to me for assistance," he continued relentlessly. "I'll merely say I heard shouting, after all I was only next door, and found the door open. Then I saw you hit poor, defenceless Mr Quinn, from behind with the inkwell, and you'll swing for his murder. See you in court." Bradford went to leave the office.

"Wait. Please wait," pleaded Hamlyn. "If I agree to help you, will you help me?"

"Of course," Bradford smiled.

"When will ....will....the robbery happen?"

"Two to three weeks time. When I'm good and ready. Are you going to help?"

"Do I have any option?"

"What do you think?" Bradford smiled, but it was a cruel, heartless smile. "What is it to be? The gallows or the robbery?"

"Not the gallows. I'll help you, but only because I have to. I want none of the takings."

In the next few minutes, they arranged Quinn's body so that it appeared he had tripped over the mat, and hit his head on the corner of the desk. Hamlyn took the inkstand, put it back on the floor, making it look like Quinn had fallen on it, and in doing so, had hit his eye.

Bradford looked quizzically at Hamlyn's throat, which was starting to show the bruises, from where Quinn had tried to strangle him. "Put your muffler on!" he instructed. "Pretend you've got a sore throat. It'll sound real enough, as your voice is starting to get hoarse. And, it'll hide the bruises." He took a last look round the office, before they both left and closed the door behind them.

"Now act normally. Wait until someone has to go into Quinn's office before the body is found. Then, send for the crushers. Do you understand?"

Hamlyn nodded miserably, knowing it would be a long morning, regardless of when Quinn was found. That would happen soon enough when a clerk needed one of the ledgers. Already his throat was hurting and he felt he was going to be sick. Whilst he was unhappy at being a party to robbing the bank, he did not want to hang for killing Quinn. Transportation for the robbery was by far the lesser of two evils. But, perhaps he could *Turn Queen's Evidence.*

"I know what you're thinking," Bradford interrupted his thoughts. "*Turn Queen's Evidence,* and testify against me for the robbery, and you might just get away with it. But, they won't let you turn for murder. Remember! I'm your only hope. Just be prepared to work all night on a Saturday, and all day on a Sunday. That's all you have to do. And, you'll qualify for a share of the takings. I'll see you later."

"You can keep my share. I couldn't possibly do that to Mr Jersey. I'm only helping you because....because......of...." his voice faded and he just pointed at Quinn's closed office door.

After Bradford left, Hamlyn moved to his own desk and tried to concentrate. In due course the various clerks arrived and started about their work. It was a long morning and almost noon before somebody needed one of the ledgers. There had been some comment about Quinn not having made an appearance: his absence suited everyone. They all preferred it when he was out of the way.

It was a junior clerk who went and knocked on Quinn's door. Hamlyn waited, pretending to be engrossed in his own work. The clerk got no reply, and knocked again. Still there was no reply, so he made his way to Hamlyn, and asked for advice.

For a brief moment, the chief cashier almost said he knew there would be no reply, but checked himself just in time. "Try knocking harder on the door again," he sighed, with apparent exasperation. "And call his name. If he doesn't answer, open the door and go in. We need the ledgers and I'm busy at the moment."

The clerk obeyed and returned to the door. Having knocked he called out Quinn's name. When he did not receive any answer, he opened the door and went in. Hamlyn watched him out of the corner of his eye, and waited for the reaction. It came seconds later.

"Mr HAMLYN! Mr HAMLYN!" the clerk shouted, as he ran out of Quinn's office and promptly vomited over the bank's floor. His cries brought all business in the bank to a standstill.

Hamlyn jumped to his feet. "Whatever is the matter? And get that mess cleared up!" he said sternly, and pointed at the vomit.

All the clerk could do was point into Quinn's office with one hand, whilst he held the other over his mouth. Vomit trickled through his fingers. Hamlyn went to investigate, carefully stepping over the vomit, and stood in the doorway. Quinn's body had not moved since the last time he had seen it, but it still gave him a shock. It was only with difficulty he managed to stop himself from also being sick.

Hamlyn backed out of the office, and closed the door behind him. "Someone go and fetch a doctor and the police," he instructed.

* * *

As it happened, Caleb Young had just left the police station, when a frantic bank clerk saw him. Quickly he told the constable how Mr Quinn had been found dead in the bank, and would he come. Having discovered a doctor had been summoned, Caleb wasted no time in following the clerk into the bank.

It was the first time he had been inside the building, and he was impressed by its marble floors and walls. But he had no time to study them any further, before being shown into Quinn's office. One look was sufficient to tell him the man had met a violent death, after having apparently fallen against the corner of his desk and onto an inkwell.

He wasted no time in ushering everybody else out of the office, and sending a clerk for the guv'nor, who he knew would want to get involved, although he was due to be at the railway station in a few minutes. At the same time he cursed. This morning would see the grand opening of the Railway coming through Warwick and linking the town with London and Birmingham, and Caleb too had wanted to be there.

* * *

John Mayfield was to be part of the official opening ceremony, at the new railway station. Dressed in his best uniform he had wanted to take Laura with him: but she had politely declined, saying she was already going, but with all of her pupils. However, she promised to see him there. When he did not arrive, Laura felt let down. It was not the first time he had cancelled seeing her, pleading necessity of work.

But then, she saw the new doctor was there, and moved the children nearer to where he was standing. Laura blushed when she saw him openly admiring her.

Slowly she inched her way closer towards him. He really was a good looking man, and she found herself attracted to him, just as she had been on the day he arrived. She was also aware of Richard slowly making his way towards her. So far she had never had the opportunity to speak to him, other than just passing the time of day. This was too good an opportunity to miss.

In the distance they all heard the sound of a railway engine's whistle, warning of the train's approach. The town band, resplendent in all their finery, heard it and carried out the last tuning of their instruments, before looking at their conductor. He looked back at them, with his baton raised. As the train came into the station, he gave the signal for the band to start playing.

There came an excited shriek from Laura's children, and the pupils from the other schools, as the train puffed its way into the station. Whatever tune the band was playing was totally lost, as the noise of the engine drowned everything else. Moments later all the children held their hands over their ears and screamed. Laura, along with many adults, did the same. Great clouds of smoke and steam filled the station.

The great engine stopped, and the band could now be heard playing *See the Conquering Hero Comes.* They ceased playing and an expectant hush fell, as the town mayor and two railway officials made speeches. When they had finished, the band played the *National Anthem* and the great engine continued on its way.

When the smoke and steam had finally cleared, Laura looked for Richard Gilson, but he had gone. She could only assume it had to have been something of great importance. But she was not pleased that he had gone without speaking: and John had never arrived.

* * *

John had been on the point of leaving for the railway station, when he was told about Albert Quinn. Waiting only long enough to change out of his ceremonial uniform, into an ordinary working one, he hurried across to the bank. Already a small crowd of people had gathered outside, and he had to push his way through them.

He was not in the best of moods. Firstly Laura had been reluctant to go with him to the station. The children would not have made any difference, and he would have been quite happy to have them there. However, this death at the bank meant he did not even get to the ceremony. But, as he knew only too well, such was police work.

If he was honest, he had the distinct feeling Laura was cooling towards him. Perhaps it was his fault? But he just did not know. Deep down, he still missed Harriet dreadfully, and was longing to hear from her. He had written her a long letter, in which he poured out his love and his hopes for the future with her. Although he had posted this letter several weeks ago, he knew there was no prospect of receiving any answer for many more weeks to come: if he ever received a reply. Possibly, no, more likely probably, Laura was aware of all that, and was keeping her distance.

On entering the bank, he was shown into Quinn's office, where he saw a stranger kneeling over the body. The man was clearly a doctor.

"May I enquire who you are, sir?" John asked.

The man looked up. "Ah, Mr Mayfield, I presume? We meet at last. Dr Richard Gilson at your service, sir," he replied with a grin. "However, please forgive me if we don't shake hands, just yet." He held up his bloodstained hands.

"Why you and not Thomas?" John returned the grin.

"Sadly, Thomas has not been very well lately, and he is resting at the moment, and Sarah would not let him come. In fact I was at the railway station, watching the arrival of the first train, when I was called. So Thomas has been left at home and I came on here in his place."

"The station is where I should have been. Ah, so be it. What have we got here?"

Any further conversation was prevented by the arrival of an angry Henry Jersey.

"What the devil's going on?" he demanded, storming into Quinn's office. "I want you police out of here. The doctor can stay and treat Quinn, but you others can get out. You're not wanted here."

"I'm afraid there's nothing I can do for Mr Quinn. The man's dead." Richard stood up, and looked Jersey straight in the eye.

"Dead? Dead? But he can't be!"

"I assure you he is," Richard snapped back.

"Well do what you have to do and then get the body out of here."

"I cannot do that. This man has met a violent end. Whilst it looks like an accident, it might not be so. He cannot be moved until the coroner has been informed, and given his permission."

"And that makes it my business," added John, struggling to keep his temper. "Please will you get out and leave us to do our job."

"I want you out of my bank now! And take that...that.....thing with you." Jersey pointed at Quinn's body.

"Mr Jersey," John said quietly, standing at his full height, and leaning slightly forwards on his toes. For those who knew him, this was not a good sign.

"I will tell you just once more. Kindly get out of this office now. It is possible a crime has been committed here. If it has been and you continue to interfere with my investigations, then I will have you arrested and charged with obstructing me in my duty. Do you understand?"

Jersey started to protest, but he saw the cold look in John's eyes and thought better of it. This policeman had a reputation for being hard, and he was known to be at his most dangerous when he spoke quietly.

"You haven't heard the last of this, Mayfield."

"Good day, Mr Jersey. You can have this office back just as soon as we have finished."

John called Caleb over, and together they began inspecting the office, starting with Quinn's body, and moving outwards. Richard watched them.

"What do you think?" asked John.

"Well guv'nor, it looks like he's fallen and caught his head on the side of the desk."

"Doctor. What do you think?"

"I agree, or at least, on first appearances, I'm inclined to agree, with your constable."

"But you're not sure, are you?" continued John.

"It's the injury to this eye which bothers me. If he hit the left side of his head on the desk, why does he have an injury to his right eye?"

John nodded in agreement.

Caleb was on his knees examining the floor, near to the inkwell. "Guv'nor, if he knocked the inkwell off the desk, then it should have marked the floor somehow. But there's nothing. No marks at all. Not even any spilled ink. But, there is ink on the left side of his face: so why is there none on the floor?"

Both John and Richard joined Caleb on the floor. From there they looked back at the desk. Richard saw the scratches first.

"Look at those, Mayfield. They look fairly new. Somehow the deceased strikes me as a tidy man. These scratches aren't in keeping with the rest of his office: Could they have come from the inkwell?"

"Possibly, but the lack of ink on the floor worries me. It's almost as if the inkwell has been placed there, and has not fallen. It just doesn't feel right. How soon can you carry out an autopsy for me?"

"Later this afternoon. I should have the preliminary results by this evening, if you care to come round. Can you arrange for the body to be moved to High Street?"

"Of course. Constable Young will go and arrange that. I'll wait with the body, for continuity of evidence purposes, in case we discover this isn't an accident."

Left to himself, John quickly sketched how the body lay. He marked in the rug, inkwell and desk, before he took another look at the scratches. They were obviously very recent. Picking up the inkwell, he put it on the scratches and found they matched. So, some force had been used, he mused, to cause such damage. Yet, there were no marks on the floor.

After Quinn's body had been removed, John questioned all the bank staff, but none of them could add anything else to what he already knew. Albert Quinn always came to work long before anybody else, and was the very last to leave, regularly working late into the night. This information intrigued him.

In John's experience, people with such working habits, often had guilty secrets to hide. If Quinn had been embezzling from the bank, and had been challenged about it, could there have been a fight? He decided to wait until the results of the autopsy before proceeding any further.

* * *

Hamlyn had been a bundle of nerves, and continually wrestling with his conscience, whilst John was asking his questions. He was genuinely upset at Quinn's death, but so was everybody else. Hopefully the policeman would put his nerves down to the shock of what had happened.

At last Quinn's body was removed, the police left, and the bank returned to normal, or what could be classed as normal given the circumstances. Hamlyn wanted to warn Jersey about the proposed robbery, but he was unsure how to go about it. Perhaps, if he made a full confession to his employer, then Jersey would help him. At last, having decided what to do, he went across to the owner's office and knocked on the door.

Jersey looked up as Hamlyn came in. "Ah Hamlyn, I was just about to call for you. I want you to act as temporary manger, until I can bring somebody else in."

Hamlyn was stunned. He was only going to be a temporary manager? Until a new man arrived? And then returned to being chief cashier? "But," he protested. "You always said I should be the next manager here, after Mr Quinn."

"Did I write anything down, saying that? No, of course I didn't. Now see here, Hamlyn, you're a good cashier, but you're not really bank manager material." He held up his hand, to silence the other man's protest. "No my mind's made up. The job'll go to my nephew. He'll start a week on Monday. If you want to leave, I'll fully understand and give you a good reference. In fact, it'll probably be best if you finish next Friday, before he arrives."

Jersey returned to the letter he had been reading, when Hamlyn had appeared, and ignored his chief cashier.

For several seconds, Hamlyn stood absolutely still, as his brain registered what he had just been told. He was not going to be the next manager, and had effectively been dismissed! Silently he turned on his heel, left Jersey's office and returned to his desk. Only now, he had no intention of warning Jersey about the impending robbery. In fact, any lingering doubts he might have had, were gone.

When the bank closed, Hamlyn was the last one to leave. Once he was sure none of the clerks was still in the Market Place, he locked up the bank, and went next door to the *Bradford & Harding* offices. The partners were not particularly pleased to see him. Bradford took him into a small office at the rear. Harding followed, closed the door and stood in front of it, with his arms folded.

"You shouldn't be here," admonished Bradford.

"Nobody saw me come in. But you need to know: there's been a development. I've been told to leave next Friday, by that miserable old bastard Jersey, just so he can bring his nephew in: and after all my loyal years working for him."

Bradford and Harding looked at one another. This was a development they had not expected. In spite of what he had said, Bradford knew it was now far too late for him to go to the police, and report what had happened. That would have meant his being arrested as an accessory after the fact. Hamlyn now represented their only chance of pulling off this robbery. The only alternative was to call it off and that was not an option.

"So," continued Hamlyn. "The robbery will have to be carried out this weekend, or not at all, if you want my help. And I've changed my mind. I do want a share of the takings. It'll serve the old bastard right."

Bradford relaxed. "Welcome partner," he smiled and shook Hamlyn's hand. Harding followed suit. "We've got a lot of work to do."

* * *

John spent the afternoon thinking more and more about Quinn's death. He discussed it with Caleb, and later with Mathew Harrison, his sergeant. Mathew was a big man, with a round face and broken nose. His dark eyes forever twinkled from a framework of a dark bushy moustache and sideburns. Like John, he too had previous military experience. John could not have wished for a better deputy.

Using the blackboard and chalk he kept in his office, John reproduced his sketch of how the dead man lay. No matter which way they looked at the sketch, it seemed to corroborate the suggestion he had died following his fall. Hopefully, Dr Gilson would be able to assist, provided he had finished the autopsy. Finally, John could wait no longer, and he and Caleb went to see Richard.

On arrival, John asked Redman if Thomas was any better.

"I don't really think so, Mr Mayfield. He got out of bed for a while this afternoon, but he's had to go back again."

Redman showed the policemen into the drawing-room and went to find Richard.

He soon appeared, and John saw he had a thoughtful look on his face.

"I think you may have a problem here," he announced without any preamble. "There's little doubt he had a heart attack and that's what killed him. But....I think you'd better come and see for yourselves."

They followed him into Thomas's laboratory. There was only one body there, and Richard took them straight over to it. "The problem is the eye injury," he explained. "The inkwell has sharp corners and if he struck his eye on one, then I would expect to see more injuries to the actual eye. But look!"

He bent over Quinn's body and pulled back the body's right eyelid. "Do you see what I mean?"

John nodded. Quinn's eye looked more bruised than cut. True there was some blood visible. "You think there should have been more damage if his eye had had hit the inkwell?"

"Yes. Now look at this."

Richard picked up the inkwell and held it close to Quinn's eye. Both policemen saw no part of the inkwell matched the injury. "There's no doubt it was a heart attack which killed him, but this inkwell did not cause that injury to his eye. Yet it almost certainly caused this injury to his head, which would probably explain the ink on his face."

All three men studied Quinn's ink stained face.

"And that's not all," Richard continued.

He pulled back the sheet further which covered the body. They saw several bruises on Quinn's chest. "And I believe these were caused before he died. But, look at his knees."

Richard pulled the sheet back further, and they saw abrasions on Quinn's knees. "I don't think these were caused by his going to church. So do you see what I mean by your having a problem?"

"Do you think he could have been in a fight before he died?"

"Almost certainly. But I can't see a court accepting that idea without other corroboration."

"Guv'nor," interrupted Caleb. "The chief cashier, Hamlyn, was wearing a muffler, and he spoke with a hoarse voice, saying he had a cold. Do you think he could have been involved?"

"Could be. But even if he has got marks on his throat, it doesn't mean to say he was in a fight with Quinn. He could say he had been attacked elsewhere. But, you make a very good point. Start making some discreet enquiries about Hamlyn and Quinn. Find out how they got on with one another etc, and see what we turn up."

Caleb left and John stayed talking to Richard for a few minutes before going up to see Thomas. His friend did not look too bad, he thought, but neither did he look too good.

It was late when he finally left, and he thought about calling on Laura. But a look at the time convinced him he would not be popular calling at such an hour.

In fact, Laura had stayed up quite late, hoping to hear from him. St Nicholas Church clock was striking midnight, when she realized he was not coming. Very disappointed, she went upstairs to her bedroom, wondering why she even bothered with him.

She really ought to make the effort to meet the new doctor.

CHAPTER SEVEN

The Robbery

Hamlyn thought Saturday would never end. Try as he might, he just could not concentrate on his work, for thinking about the coming hours. He had already found an excuse to go down to the vaults, and listened. All he could hear was the very faint rumble of carts travelling round the Market Place, and nothing else. There were no sounds to be heard from the market stallholders calling out their wares. And he had no doubt his two partners would have made similar checks from their cellar.

At last the bank closed for the day. Although he was last to leave, Hamlyn made sure he left with all the other clerks. Having said good night to them, he made his way round to New Street, to the rear entrance to the *Bradford & Harding* offices. They had left the gate unlocked for him, and he passed through, closing it behind him, but in his nervousness, he forgot to bolt it, as he had been instructed.

After tapping gently on the ground floor window, the back door was unlocked. Quickly he went inside and heard the door being bolted behind him. For a moment he thought about going back to bolt the gate, but decided it would not be necessary.

The three men ate a quick supper, without any alcohol, and then moved into the cellar. Since moving in, Bradford had repainted it, with the exception of a slightly larger than body sized patch, on the wall adjoining the bank. It was here where they started work.

Harding produced a long metal chisel and held the point against some mortar, in between two bricks. The other end of the chisel was wrapped in thick cloth. Only when he was satisfied, did Bradford begin to swing the short hammer he held, onto the muffled end of the chisel. Ideally he would have preferred to use a long handled one, but the confines of the cellar did not allow enough room for him to swing it.

He made a few tentative strikes on the chisel, with ever increasing force, just to see how much noise it made. There was very little, and the work began in earnest. They changed positions every five minutes. One man held the chisel, whilst another used the hammer, and the third man rested. It did not take long for them to discover that the mortar was much harder than it looked, and several hammer blows were needed just to remove a single piece.

To make matters more complicated, they discovered it was a double thickness wall, with space between the bricks, when at last the first one was removed. It took some time until the hole was big enough for the three of them to climb through into the bank vault.

Once they had managed to get into the vault, there was little they could do, until Harding had opened all fifty-seven deposit boxes. Although he had a rough model key to work from, which had come from the padlock on the *Bradford & Harding* box, it would still take time to open each box. For their plan to succeed there had to be no signs of a forcible entry.

Harding had provided himself with a variety of similar key blanks, but as he knew from experience, a master key was totally out of the question. All the boxes would have individual keys, and padlocks, specially made for them. Whilst not an impossible job, it was time consuming, especially at first. Once he had an idea of the general pattern of the keys, it would get quicker.

Whilst he worked on the boxes, Bradford and Hamlyn started to clean up the bricks they had removed. These would be needed for replacing, in the wall, as another part of the plan. Once again, the hardness of the original mortar slowed the work down.

"Got you!" snorted Harding, triumphantly, interrupting their work, as the first padlock was sprung open. Ignoring it, he moved onto the next one and started all over again.

Once the bricks had been cleaned up, Bradford and Hamlyn moved onto their next task. On the bank's wall, nearest their office side, a set of large wooden shelving had been fixed. These held all the old ledgers for the bank. Each shelf had to be unscrewed, and fresh preparations made for it to be re-fixed, but this time slightly further along the wall. The idea was for the shelves to cover up the new mortar, when the bricks were replaced.

This was a job Hamlyn would have to do, early on Monday morning, before the staff arrived and the bank opened. Firstly he would tidy up the mortar on the new bricks and then replace the shelves. They had it all planned, and with the newly prepared holes, for the screws, it should not take him too long.

Yet they were not fooled. The risk of their being discovered depended, on nobody needing access to a deposit box, until Wednesday at the earliest. By then the mortar would have dried and nobody could say it had been a recent robbery. With a bit of luck, it would all be blamed on the late Albert Quinn.

By mid-afternoon on Sunday, the bricks had been cleaned, the shelves prepared and more than half the boxes opened. So far, none of the boxes had been emptied. Bradford now produced a set of scales and set about weighing the contents of each box. He only removed money and any other valuable objects he found. These he weighed and put into the first of several sacks.

Next, he opened another sack he had with him, which held pebbles. From here he weighed out a similar amount of pebbles, which he put back into the empty box, and re-locked it. As he explained to Hamlyn, this way the boxes would still weigh the same as when they were last inspected, so there should not be any early suspicions arising from any sudden audit check.

His real masterpiece though, was not to re-lock the box with its proper padlock, but to use one of the others. The idea was for more delaying tactics in the event of someone coming to check their box. Hamlyn had already explained how such checks only happened about every two or three months. Most of the clients, who went down to the vault, did so to open new boxes, and that was not a regular occurrence.

"What about this one?" chuckled Harding. "It belongs to a *Bradford & Harding*, and contains a bag of sand."

"We take it, of course and claim for two gold watches and fifty guineas. Let's not be too greedy!" answered Bradford.

"Poor Mr Jersey," announced Hamlyn in a solemn voice, before collapsing with laughter. "Serves the old bastard right!"

"Language!" chided the other two, also laughing.

It was past midnight before the last box had been emptied and re-filled with pebbles. Wearily the three men climbed back through the hole in the wall, and into their own cellar. Next they replaced the bricks they had taken out, on both sides of the cellar and cemented them back in. Once they were in place, Hamlyn put a quick coat of matching paint over them. Finally they set about lifting some flagstones in their cellar, in order to dig a hole in which to hide their takings.

* * *

William Beech, or Billy Beech, as he was more commonly called, was on his way home. But he was not in the best of moods, having had a poor evening. Billy was an habitual thief, who always kept an eye open for anything that could be stolen. He was a tall, very thin man, in his mid-forties, who had spent a large part of his life in one gaol or another. Luckily for him, or so it seemed at the time, he had never been in court for a serious enough offence to warrant him being transported. His back bore the scars from where he had once been flogged, but he looked upon such punishment as an occupational hazard, and accepted it as such.

Known as a *snakesman* in the criminal underworld slang, Billy specialised in climbing, and he could squeeze through any bars which were more than six inches apart. This was why he had never been convicted of burglary, only petty crimes. Nobody believed he could have climbed and passed through such small gaps.

He had only been released from the County Gaol the day before, and was already up to his old tricks again. Earlier that day, he had seen Mathew Harrison watching him, and knew he would have to take care. The big police sergeant was the one person who bothered him, because he knew Billy's real talents, and was determined, one day, to arrest him.

After an unsuccessful foraging in the Butts and Northgate Street, Billy made his way down New Street, loosely heading in the direction of Monk

Street, where he lived. As he passed the rear of the *Bradford & Harding* offices, he tried their rear gate, more from habit than for any other reason.

Much to his pleasant amazement, the gate opened, because Hamlyn had forgotten to bolt it. After quickly looking round and making sure Constable Andrew, whom he had just seen in Church Street, was not watching him, he pushed the gate open and went through, closing it carefully behind him.

As Billy expected, on trying the rear door, he discovered it was locked, but undeterred he looked around and noticed a small upstairs window was open. Several moments later, he was climbing the drainpipe towards it. Just as he moved across to the window, his jacket became caught on something. But, giving it a quick pull, he felt it tear. Later he would discover he had torn a piece of the material from it. Now he had freed himself, it then took him only a matter of seconds, to climb through the window. Once inside, he stood still and listened.

He heard voices coming faintly from downstairs, and he tiptoed quietly towards them, not knowing what he might find.

Arriving on the ground floor, he first looked for the rear door, which still had the key in it. After unlocking and unbolting it, he pocketed the key. Being a cautious person, he liked, wherever possible, to have an escape route planned. And, if he kept the key, he could always use it to lock any pursuers in the building. As he removed the key, Billy heard the distinct sound, of a trowel and mortar being used on bricks, coming from the cellar.

Curious to see who could be laying bricks at this hour, and wondering how he could turn it to his benefit, Billy quietly crept down the steps, and very cautiously looked round the last bend, ready to flee at an instant's notice.

He saw a pile of small sacks on the cellar floor and two men, who he did not know, lifting flagstones. Clearly that was where they were going to bury the sacks. A third man was smoothing off some mortar, in between bricks on the bank side of the cellar. Billy nearly gasped in surprise as he recognized Bernard Hamlyn from *Jersey's Bank*.

Having lived for most of life depending on his wits, Billy quickly worked out what had happened. *Jersey's Bank* had just been robbed. Now, he wondered, how could he turn this knowledge to his own advantage?

Knowing how the bank would not believe him, and having no great love of such places, his natural target had to be the robbers. And there was no doubt which one of the three he would target: it had to be Bernard Hamlyn.

Billy carefully retraced his steps upstairs, and went to leave the building. In passing, he noticed an open door, leading into one of the offices. On the desk, he saw a silver plated pen tray. Going into the room, he picked up the tray and slipped it into his pocket. As he had not been disturbed, and he wanted to keep his visit a secret, for just a few more hours, he would not use the back door. So he returned the key, re-locked the door and drew the bolt across. Quietly he went back upstairs and climbed out of the window.

Minutes later he was walking briskly down Friars Street, making his plans for the morning. Back at his home he found a pen, some paper, and started to write. Whilst he was not well educated, he could read and write, after a fashion, although it took him some time.

Much later, having written his letter, he returned to the bank, posted it through the letter box, and walked away smiling to himself. How he would love to see the look on Hamlyn's face when he read it, later that morning.

* * *

Thomas Waldren now realized he was not a well man. Apart from the ever increasing stomach cramps he was experiencing, he had started to vomit. For a while, he thought he might have contracted typhoid, but the symptoms did not quite agree. Next he thought about cholera, but with the same result. He had spent most of Saturday night, in either cold or hot sweats. On Sunday morning, Sarah asked Richard to take a look at him.

Richard gave him a thorough checking, but admitted he was at a loss to diagnose any illness. He took various samples for analysis, but added he was not very hopeful, about discovering the cause of the problem. Nevertheless, Sarah was grateful to him for having tried. Just before he left, Richard suggested that a second opinion might be a good idea. Whilst Thomas considered such an idea to be a waste of time, Sarah agreed to think about it.

During the late morning, Thomas received another visitor: Dr Julius Hopper, who also the coroner, came to discuss a forthcoming inquest. He was perturbed to discover Thomas was not well. Having been briefed by Sarah, he also gave him a thorough checking and took away several samples.

On his way out, he saw Richard and discussed Thomas's condition with him. Julius was saddened to discover the new doctor was also concerned about Thomas's mystery illness, and they agreed to share notes.

Although Julius said nothing to Richard, he was convinced the symptoms seemed familiar from somewhere, although he could not say why or where. But, the thought bothered him so much, he spent the next three days searching through all his old case notes, but he never found what he was seeking.

By now, Thomas had already made some tentative enquiries about obtaining life assurance for himself, and decided to make the effort and go and see Messrs Bradford & Harding in the morning. They made a great play about specializing in providing such cover for doctors and other professional people. He would get John to take him, knowing the premiums would not be a problem, as he had more than enough money, in a safe deposit box, at *Jersey's Bank*. Some of it could be used to pay for the first premiums straight away, and thereby secure the policy.

In the early evening, he was aware of the front door bell being rung. Several minutes later, Redman came into his bedroom, and handed him a letter, which had just come by special delivery. Thomas opened it and began to read.

When he had finished, he was white with shock, and he read the letter a second time. But it still read the same. Ringing the bell on his bedside table, he sent for Sarah, and also instructed a servant to go and find John Mayfield, and ask him to call at once.

* * *

John had spent a fairly profitable day. Very little crime had been reported, recently, and he had been able to devote some of his time in studying Quinn's death in more detail. He had not been at all surprised when Dr Julius Hopper called to see him, in his capacity as coroner. For a while they discussed Quinn's death, and Julius agreed to adjourn the inquest, to give John more time to continue with his investigations.

"There's another matter, I would like to discuss with you," continued Julius. "I'm worried about Thomas Waldren. He's not at all very well, and I'm seriously worried about him."

"I know he's not very well, but didn't realize he was that bad."

"And that's what's bothering me. I've examined him, but can't find anything specifically wrong. I know young Gilson's of the same opinion." He paused and chewed his bottom lip.

"His condition reminds me of a case I read about, oh several years ago now. I can't remember where it was, but it resulted in the strange and unexplained death of the victim." He paused for a few moments. "I need to find my notes. But, if I'm right, and I hope to God I'm wrong, then Thomas is being poisoned."

"POISONED?"

"It's only a suspicion at the moment."

"Does he know?"

"No: and I don't want him to just yet." He held up his hand, as John was about to speak. "No, let me finish. If he is being poisoned, then it has to be by somebody in his household, from Sarah downwards."

"Surely not by Sarah?"

"I'd like to think not. But you must have come across cases of wives murdering their husbands?"

John nodded. "What are you going to do?"

"Firstly try and find my notes, and secondly, send the samples I have taken from him, to a friend of mine, who will know exactly what to look for."

After Julius had left, John sat and thought. Not for a moment could he believe any suggestion of Sarah poisoning her husband. Yet, he had known it happen, when a loving spouse had murdered the other. He just hoped Julius was wrong. His thoughts were interrupted by Caleb arriving. The officer was excited and his face was aglow, so John needed no telling he had found out something about Quinn.

"The man was heavily in debt," Caleb said. "He was a regular card player, often out at Barford. By all accounts, he owed somewhere in the region of £55, and his creditors were pressing him hard for payment."

"£55? That's way above what his bank salary would have paid him. Well done. But, would it have been enough for someone to have killed him? That way they would never have got their money, would they?"

"No, guv'nor, but what if they had just come to frighten him and it all got out of hand?"

"Good point. We need to do some more digging."

They discussed the case for a few more minutes, and Caleb left. Almost immediately he returned, with one of Thomas's servants.

"Can you come and see the master at once, sir?" the man asked.

Thinking about Julius Hopper's suspicions, John sprung to his feet, grabbed his kepi and quickly left the police station with the servant. On arrival, he noticed how Redman looked very solemn and immediately feared the worst. Having discovered where Thomas was, John ran upstairs and into the bedroom.

His first thoughts were ones of relief when he saw Thomas was still alive. Then he noticed how he was holding a sobbing Sarah. Thomas held out the letter, he had recently received to John. Not knowing what to expect, he unfolded it and read.

NAPTON SHIPPING OFFICE
ROTHERHITHE
LONDON

Dear Dr Waldren

It is with great sorrow that I write this letter. I am aware your niece, Mrs Harriet Foxton, was a passenger on the Elizabeth of Napton, which was sailing to Australia.

Following a severe storm, off the West Coast of Africa, a Royal Naval vessel was patrolling along the Skeleton Coast, when it discovered a ship's wreckage and the remains of four lifeboats, all of which bore the name of Elizabeth of Napton, the vessel on which your niece was sailing. The crew found several bodies nearby, and a search of the nearby beaches revealed no traces of any living persons.

Therefore, it has to be assumed, in the absence of any evidence to the contrary, that the vessel has been lost with all persons who sailed on her. I deeply regret I cannot hold out any hopes of your niece having survived.

The remainder of the letter was just a blur to John.

The totally unbelievable had happened. Harriet was dead. His Harriet was dead and it was all his fault. For one of the few times in his life, tears came to his eyes, but he quickly wiped them away. John was lost for words. What could he say or do?

"Don't go, John," whispered Sarah. "We all know she meant a lot to you just, as you did to her"

"Oh, why didn't I tell her I loved her? Why? Oh Why?"

The bedroom door opened quietly and Richard slipped into the room. "I've only just heard," he said solemnly. "I know just how much she meant to all of you. Is there anything I can do?"

"There's just one thing," answered John. "I was supposed to be seeing Laura Grant this evening, but I can't go now. I wonder, could you get one of the servants to go and tell her what's happened please?"

"There's no need for that," replied Richard. "I'll go and tell her myself."

"Thank you."

* * *

Several minutes later, Laura heard a knock at her door, and thought it would be John. Abbie opened it and saw the new doctor standing outside.

"Is Miss Grant at home?" he asked in his most charming manner.

"Wait here whilst I go and find her," she sniffed.

Richard was only too happy to wait. He still could not believe his good fortune. Mayfield had given him just the opportunity he desperately wanted, and he was not going to miss this opportunity.

"Is John alright?" cried Laura as she ran into the hallway.

"He's fine," came his smiling reply. "It's just that he cannot get away from the police station tonight, and he has asked me to come and tell you, and see if you'd be happy with my company instead?"

Laura blushed, uncertain of what to do. Now that she had the chance to be with the new doctor, she was unsure.

"I'd actually arranged for him to have supper here with me tonight."

"It would be a pity to waste it." Richard's eyes twinkled and he knew she was hooked.

"That would be a nice idea. Do come in."

His lies had worked. Now all he had to do was use his considerable charm, and woo her away from Mayfield.

He had no qualms of conscience about having lied to her.

CHAPTER EIGHT

Monday

John slept badly that night. In fact, he barely slept, spending most of the time tossing and turning in his bed. Every time he closed his eyes, he kept reliving his last night with Harriet. If only he had just plucked up enough courage to say how much he loved her, then she might not have gone. If only that train had not broken down. If only the coach had not gone off the road. If...if...if....such a small word, but so often with such great consequences.

Briefly he thought about Laura, and hoped she had understood why it had not been possible to have dined with her last night. It was just too soon after learning about Harriet.

Possibly this was how it was meant to be. Harriet had already been lost to him, if she had ever been there in the first place. Hadn't she always been married to Edmund, even after his death? If that was so, then John realized he would have stood no chance of becoming a permanent part of her life. Then just as he was thinking along those lines, he began to wonder: might she have come back?

Perhaps she had only gone to teach him a lesson. But, what had she told Thomas to tell him? To find someone else? No, she had not been going to come back. Anyway, it counted for nothing now. Harriet was dead. What was the term? Oh yes......*Lost at sea!*

Much as he wanted to hope, against all hope, that she might have survived, he knew it was unlikely. From his army days, he knew the Skeleton Coast was one of, if not the most inhospitable place on Earth. It was the one posting everyone dreaded. He had been lucky: his troopship had only called in at Walvis Bay for a few days. But it had been long enough.

No, if the alternative was to be cast up, and die of heat and starvation, then it would have been kinder all round for her to have drowned.

He would make the effort to see Laura tomorrow, and explain it all to her. It would have to be later on, as he had arranged to take Thomas to the *Bradford & Harding* Offices, to arrange for some insurance policies. Thomas did not want Sarah to know, so John was going with him, instead of her.

* * *

Sarah had a poor night's sleep. She too was haunted by the tragic news concerning Harriet. Although she said nothing, she had not been too happy about Richard going to see Laura. Whilst she did not doubt his abilities as a doctor, she did not trust him where women were concerned. Somehow, he was just too forward, when dealing with members of the opposite sex. True, he always behaved impeccably towards her, and generally speaking, she liked him, but......? Something about him bothered her, especially where women were involved. It was called it woman's intuition, but she did not want to see John hurt again, especially so soon after the devastating news about Harriet

He had taken Harriet's departure quite badly, especially with his own failure to get to her ship in time, but he had seemed to be getting over it. Now he was building up his relationship with Laura. Sarah knew he had not seen too much of her recently, but as she knew only too well, from being a doctor's wife, that was the nature of John's job. Her deepest wish was to see John married, and with Harriet now gone, she thought Laura would probably make a good wife for him, but would he see her that way?

John was very good at hiding his emotions, and that had been his main problem with Harriet. Sarah hoped he would not make the same mistake with Laura. Richard could pose a threat to their relationship, especially as she considered the new doctor was just seeking another conquest, and not any form of commitment with Laura.

Sarah believed once Richard had got what he wanted from Laura, he would drop her and move on. But, with John in his current fragile and emotional upset state, it could well end his relationship with Laura. The girl would have to be given some advice.

With her niece's death, Sarah now had none of her family left alive. Harriet was her much older sister's child, and they had looked after her for a number of years. In many ways, Sarah had always been more like an older sister to the girl, than an aunt. Only ten years separated them.

When her mother died, it was only natural Harriet had stayed with Sarah and Thomas. Her father had been killed in Spain, fighting against the French. Unable to have any children herself, Sarah wanted to see John settle down, probably with Laura, and have his own family. When that happened, she knew that would be the nearest to being a grandmother she would ever get.

* * *

Thomas also had a bad night's sleep, not only because of Harriet, but he was now becoming quite worried about his illness. Spending any amount of time out of bed was making him feel giddy, and he was eating next to nothing. Based on his own medical knowledge, he was having serious doubts as to whether he would actually survive. Hence why he decided it was so important to arrange these insurance policies.

The fact he was ill should not be a problem, as almost every insurance company never required any medical examinations to be carried out. If they did, then the word of the agent was normally sufficient. And, he had no reason to believe that *Bradford & Harding* would be any different. All he needed to know was how much money they wanted.

* * *

Richard had spent a very pleasant evening with Laura, even with Abbie acting as chaperone. Laura had also enjoyed the evening, and was very taken by the new doctor. What had started off as a way to get her own back on John, had turned out not to be quite so simple. When Richard had offered to visit her again, the following afternoon, Laura had jumped at the idea. Only now, lying in bed, did she begin to have second thoughts. Should she or should she not carry on seeing him?

She thought John's excuse, of working late, sounded weak and somehow not true. Possibly he was having another fit of conscience and thinking about his Harriet again. If only he could get that woman out of his system for good, then there would be a chance for the two of them. Meanwhile, she decided, she would see Richard again.

Laura had no idea of the real reason why John had cancelled their evening together.

* * *

Hamlyn had slept very well, mainly because he had not had any sleep the previous night. Consequently, he was in a very cheerful mood, as he opened the bank, on Monday morning. He watched as the staff all entered, before moving into Quinn's office. Jersey had made it quite clear his nephew would be starting the following Monday, and Hamlyn was determined to be gone before he arrived, and not be around to explain the bank's systems to him. Let the new manager's uncle show him what to do. Meanwhile, he would enjoy sitting at Quinn's desk, albeit for just a few days.

But first he had a job to do. Telling the staff he was going to check some of the old ledgers, he went downstairs and into the vaults, carefully locking the door behind him. In the next twenty-five minutes he made up a small amount of mortar and faced off the new brickwork in the vaults. Then he moved the shelves into their new position, and screwed them to the wall, using a coin in their slots. He was very grateful for the holes they had made for the screws, the previous night. Once the shelves were in position, he stacked the old ledgers onto them.

As other members of the bank's staff came into the vaults so rarely, he had every confidence nobody would even notice they had been moved. Casting a quick glance round, he was satisfied there was nothing immediately obvious, to indicate the vaults had been entered during the week-end.

Quickly he cleaned his pen knife, which had been used to face the bricks, and put it back into his pocket. After closing and locking the door behind him, he returned upstairs, and went back into Quinn's office, feeling very satisfied with himself.

He enjoyed just thinking of the shock Jersey was going to experience, once the robbery was discovered. It would serve the old bastard right, and the chances were it would ruin him. Still chuckling, he found an envelope, addressed to him personally and marked *Pryvitt n connfidenchul.*

For a fleeting moment, he thought Jersey might have changed his mind. But, even if he had done so, it was too late. The idea quickly faded when he saw just how illiterate the writer was. It had certainly not been written by the bank's owner. Hamlyn opened the envelope, took out the letter and started to read. Moments later, his good humour vanished.

deer mr hamlin

u dont no me, but i no u. so wen i say i saw u in the seller larst night bricking op the wall i wos very interested. even more so when i saw the sacks being berried. i reelly did see u. u shoodnt ave left the gate unlocked.

now i reckon u just robbed the bank. for the moment yore secrets safe, but i suggest u diskuss it with your partners. becos i want £250 from u to keep quiet.

Put it in a ole in the wall, in st mary churchyard, by the gate to the college. go 6 paces from the gate and the stone is 5 rows op. put it there toonite between 11 and arf past

if u fink i not telling the truth...what appened to the pen tray in the orfice.

After Hamlyn read it again, he found the contents were still the same. The fact the writer had stated how he was the one bricking up the wall, really left him in no doubt.

They had been seen, and all because he had forgotten to bolt the gate. His partners would have to be told, especially as they still held his share of the proceeds. Why did this have to happen, just when everything was going so well? He knew they would not be best pleased.

Having made an excuse to the clerks, he left the bank, and quickly went next door. It was not exactly a warm welcome.

"What are you doing here?" snapped Bradford. "I told you to stay away. This had better be urgent."

"It is," Hamlyn replied unhappily as he handed over the letter.

"Is this some sort of joke?" Bradford asked after he had read it.

"I don't think so."

Harding now entered the office and asked what was going on. Bradford gave him the letter, which he quickly read.

"Funny," he commented, after he had read the letter. "I can't find my pen tray."

"You useless bastard!" cursed Bradford. "I told you to lock the gate?"

"I thought I had," came Hamlyn's weak reply.

"I ought to top you here and now."

"Easy, Giles," said Harding. "Killing him won't solve anything."

"You're right. But, you slip up just once more, and that's it. Understand?" Bradford jabbed Hamlyn in the chest, who nodded meekly in reply.

"What are we going to do?" whined Hamlyn.

Further conversation stopped, as the bell on the front rang, telling them the door had just opened.

"Out the back!" instructed Bradford.

Hamlyn needed no second urging. Harding followed him. "Call in here later, when the bank's closed for the night," he instructed and made sure the gate was locked after Hamlyn had passed through it.

Neither man noticed Robert Andrew patrolling nearby. He would submit a report about having seen both men together, before he went off duty.

On returning to the office, Harding was startled to find a policeman and another man talking to Bradford. However, his partner did not seem too worried, by the policeman. The other man looked ill, and he was sitting on a chair.

"Ah, Jacob," announced Bradford, looking up from his writing. "Let me introduce you to Dr Thomas Waldren and Superintendent Mayfield. The good doctor wishes to take out some policies with us, and the superintendent has just come along as his friend."

Introductions were made, and John left Thomas to talk insurance business, after arranging to call back. When he returned, nearly half an hour later, Thomas had signed up for two specific life policies and now owed *Bradford & Harding* £38.10s.6d. Not having that amount of money on him, he and John went next door to *Jersey's Bank*, where Thomas kept his money.

John's appearance in the bank caused a stir amongst the staff. Hamlyn saw him, but decided to keep out of his way. He knew of John's reputation, and was only too aware the policeman was not entirely convinced about Quinn's death being an accident. Having retired to his office, he buried his head in some ledgers and waited for John to go away. His hopes were soon dashed when there was a knock at the door. Moments later, a clerk entered.

"Dr Waldren wants to go down to his safe deposit box. He wants some money out of it!"

Hamlyn felt himself go cold as he heard the clerk's words. For a moment he considered trying to tell the doctor he would have to come back on another day, but he knew he could not do that. Dear God, why did someone need to go to their deposit box today?

As if the anonymous letter was not bad enough, now this had happened. It was all coming apart and, as yet, he had not been given his share of the money. The sooner he could get out now, the better. Reluctantly, he stood up, collected the keys to the vaults and left the office. Thomas and John were waiting for him.

"Good afternoon, Mr Hamlyn," said John. "How's the throat today?"

Hamlyn's hands went to his throat, realizing he was no longer wearing his scarf. "Much... much...ah ... better, thank you."

"My word," continued John. "That looks like bruising round your throat. Wouldn't you think so Thomas?"

John's instincts were now fully alert. There was definite bruising round the man's throat which, although fading, had clearly been the reason for the scarf, and not an infection as Hamlyn had claimed. Obviously the man had been in a fight, but when? And with whom? Could it have been with Quinn? The more John thought about it, the more it seemed to make sense.

Thomas only grunted, in reply, which reminded John why they were at the bank. He waited whilst Thomas and Hamlyn went down the stairs to the vaults. John was concerned at just how ill his friend looked. Quite clearly there was something seriously wrong with him, and his thoughts kept coming back to Julius Hopper's suggestion he was being poisoned. If so, then by whom? Surely not by Sarah? His thoughts were interrupted by Thomas's return.

"John, there's a problem. My key doesn't fit my deposit box. Will you come down and have a try?"

"I can't allow that," interrupted Hamlyn. "Only bank staff and clients are allowed down there."

"I am a client, and I want Superintendent Mayfield, to come down to this vault with me," snapped Thomas.

"I apologize, Mr Waldren...."

"It's Doctor Waldren," corrected Thomas. He was beginning to sway and had broken out in a sweat.

John took his arm. "Quickly man!" he instructed. "Get a chair."

Hamlyn needed no excuse to escape from this confrontation, and he quickly fetched a chair. Once Thomas was sat on it, Hamlyn made to go back to his office.

"Just a moment!" John's voice had an icy tone to it. "Not so fast. We haven't finished yet."

"It's no use. You can't go down to vaults unless you are on the staff or a client. It's Mr Jersey's instructions."

"Then get him."

"It won't make any difference."

"I said get him!"

"I can't. He's gone to Birmingham for the day."

"Very well, but you can tell him, we will be back tomorrow morning, and we will be going down into those vaults, with or without his permission. Understand?"

Hamlyn nodded.

"A final word Mr Hamlyn, I need to ask you some more questions about Mr Quinn's death. We've found some new evidence, and need to discuss it."

"What evidence? What evidence?" pleaded Hamlyn shrilly, and he suddenly started to sweat.

"It can wait, until we've sorted out Dr Waldren's safe box."

Ignoring Hamlyn's pleading look, John helped Thomas to his feet and escorted him outside to his carriage. Once he was settled, John stood back, but Thomas grabbed his arm. "What's going on John?"

"I don't know, but I've got a feeling something's horribly wrong. It's not just coincidence your key won't work. As you know, I don't believe in coincidences."

Back in the bank, Hamlyn watched them leave, with a silent sigh of relief. It could all become Mr Jersey's problem in the morning. Hopefully, Quinn would get the blame. He turned away from the window, and saw the staff all looking him.

"Get on with your work!" he ordered.

* * *

Once the bank closed, Hamlyn waited until the last staff had left, before following and locking up for the night. Only when the last clerk was out of sight, did he go into the *Bradford & Harding* offices, where he was relieved to find only Harding waiting for him. Of the two men, he preferred dealing with this one. Quickly he reported what had happened with the safe deposit boxes. Harding said nothing, just nodded his head from time to time.

"It happens," he said at last. "It's just bad luck to have happened so soon. If your Henry Jersey's anything like the other bank owners, he'll keep delaying the issue. Even if the police become involved, he won't give away details of the owners of the boxes for a few days, which will give us a bit more time. The main thing is not to panic. And, in this case," he indicated the bank. "It should be quite a simple matter to blame Quinn."

"Oh yes. I can prove he was embezzling from the bank. But, since old Jersey's giving the job to his nephew, I've said nothing. He can find out the hard way."

"I understand. But, it might help if you were to give him a clue or two."

Harding then explained how Bradford was already hidden in St Mary's churchyard, where he could watch the spot where the money was to be dropped. It would be an easy matter to catch the person as he came to collect the money, or so he thought.

"In fact," said Harding. "This parcel doesn't contain any money at all. It's full of paper."

"What'll happen to him?" asked Hamlyn.

Harding gave a mirthless chuckle. "Don't you worry about him. Now this is what you have to do."

* * *

St Mary's church clock was striking 11pm, as Hamlyn left *Bradford & Harding* by the back gate, headed through the Old Square and into Northgate Street, passing by the great arches of the church tower. For a moment he hesitated before going through the old iron gates, and into the churchyard. He resisted the temptation to look for Bradford, and Harding, although he wondered exactly where they were.

For a few moments he panicked, wondering if it was all a clever trap to catch him out, and he was tempted to run. Had the package he carried contained money that is probably what he would have done. But, as it only contained cut up paper, he knew there was no point in running. As the other two men had all his money, he had no alternative to go through with their plan.

At last, he arrived at the gate to the college and counted out the paces and stones, until he found the right one. Carefully he pulled out the loose stone, and put the package into the recess. As he did so, a small door on the other side of the recess swung open, and a lantern shone in his face.

"Thanks," said a voice and a hand snatched up the package.

"Hey!" cried Hamlyn, but there was nobody there.

Moments later, he was joined by Bradford and Harding, who ran back to the college gate, but it was locked. Next they ran though the churchyard, into the part known as the *tink-a-tank*, which led to the Butts, only to find the iron gates there were locked. There was no chance of catching their blackmailer.

Hamlyn had hoped tonight would, at least, have solved one of his problems. But this was clearly not now the case. They would have to wait for the blackmailer's next demand, which would almost certainly increase the amount of money he wanted.

Why had he tried to blackmail Quinn? If only he hadn't, there would have been no fight and no death. His world was coming apart. He could only hope to keep his nerve tomorrow, when Dr Waldren and that policeman returned.

The policeman had the reputation of being frightened by nobody, and, when necessary, making up the law as he went along. On reflection, Hamlyn feared John more than Bradford and Harding, although he realized any one of them could be the cause of his death.

CHAPTER NINE

Tuesday

Hamlyn was not at all surprised to find the letter, soon after he had arrived in his office. It was a foregone conclusion, and Bradford had told him to expect it. This time, he was not to make any attempt to come to *Bradford & Harding*, one of them would come to him, as if on a business call. What would happen then very much depended on what was in the letter.

He read:

> *that wer silly u carnt get away from me cos i no wat u dun so same time **TOONITE** u will put £500 by the flat grave behind st nicklus church were theres an ole put it in there if u try n trick me again i go to the crushers*

It was almost a relief when Harding came into the bank and asked to see him. Hamlyn invited him into his office, where he handed over the letter, which the other man quickly read.

"Just do as he says," was Harding's only comment, and he gave a parcel to Hamlyn. Moments later he was gone.

Soon afterwards, Henry Jersey came in, but he was far too busy to see Hamlyn, who wanted to tell him about the proposed visit from Dr Waldren. Several minutes later, Thomas Waldren arrived. For a moment Hamlyn thought the superintendent was not with him, but his hopes were short lived as he came in moments later, with another man who carried a canvas bag.

"You know why we're here," announced John, without any preamble. "Kindly get Mr Jersey for us. I know he's here."

"He's a very busy man," protested Hamlyn.

John said nothing else, but just glared at Hamlyn, who wilted under the icy gaze. Gulping loudly, he went to fetch Jersey, who was not pleased at being interrupted.

"What is it now?" he snapped, as Thomas and John were shown into his office. The other man remained outside. "Whatever it is, it has nothing to do with you, Mayfield, so you can get out."

"Mr Mayfield is here at my request," explained Thomas. "And he will stay." Briefly he explained about the problems with his safe deposit box.

"I repeat," snapped Jersey. "This has nothing to do with Mayfield."

"On the contrary," said John quietly. "I believe there is something not quite right here, and Dr Waldren has asked me to accompany him. If the box does not open, I have a man outside who will force it."

"Like hell you will! Just because you hounded James Cooper to his death, you'll not browbeat me."

John sighed. "That has nothing to do with the matter in hand. As you are well aware, James Cooper was a major criminal who was murdered by one of his associates, in front of several witnesses, some of whom were from both the Bank of England and the Royal Mint. I'm sure they will not be very impressed to hear you suggest they too hounded James Cooper to his death. Now, will you take us down to the vaults, please?"

"You are not coming down to my vaults, and that's final. You'll have to get a warrant first," he added smugly.

He had hardly finished speaking, before John reached inside his tunic, and brought out a folded piece of paper, which he opened. "Here it is," he said simply, and offered the document to Jersey. "If you do not allow me access to the vaults, then I shall return with my constables, and we will force an entry, as I am empowered to do, by this warrant."

Jersey looked at the warrant, before his shoulders sagged. He said nothing but merely selected a key from his desk drawer and handed it to Hamlyn. "Take them down!" he instructed.

"I would prefer you to be with us, Mr Jersey," said John quietly.

Moments later, the four men were in the vaults. Thomas led them over to his safe deposit box and tried to insert his key into the padlock. But his hand was shaking so much, he dropped the key.

"That's why he can't open it," sneered Jersey. "Is he drunk or something?"

"No," replied John icily. "Dr Waldren is ill and that's why he needs access to his safe deposit box. He has just taken out an insurance policy, with the people next door, and now he needs to pay the first premiums."

As he spoke, his gaze went from Jersey to Hamlyn. He was surprised to see Hamlyn's face had gone ashen.

Hamlyn could not believe what he was hearing. *Mr I-know-what-I'm-doing* Bradford, was the cause of all this. It would now only be a matter of time before the robbery was discovered, and he could only hope they would put the blame onto Quinn. He was aware John was now speaking to him.

"Are you alright, Mr Hamlyn? Only you seem to have gone very pale."

"Yes, fine, thank you."

"Excellent, then as Dr Waldren cannot open the box, perhaps you would like to do it for him?"

Hamlyn looked at Jersey for guidance. The banker nodded. Hamlyn took the key and inserted it in the padlock, knowing full well, it would not open. He toyed with the idea of trying to buy more time, by breaking the key in the lock, but it was too strong. After several attempts, he gave up. John took the key and tried it himself, but with the same results. Jersey also tried it, albeit unwillingly, but with the same results.

"Are we agreed," asked John. "There is a problem?"

"Nonsense!" Jersey denied strenuously. "It's obvious the doctor's got this key muddled up with some of his others. I suggest he finds the right one before coming back here causing trouble." He turned to leave.

"Just a minute!" called John. He held out the key to Jersey and pointed to the markings on it. "This key has your bank's name stamped on it. And Dr Waldren only has one box with you. So how can you say it's the wrong key?"

Jersey had no answer. Deep down he began to realize there was a problem here. Something was drastically wrong: and he needed time to prepare for a possible run on the bank, once word got out.

"Mr Hamlyn," instructed John. "Would you please go upstairs and bring the man with the canvas bag down here. He's a locksmith and will open this box."

"**I FORBID THAT!**" shouted Jersey. "It's bank property and Dr Waldren's made a mistake."

"No, I haven't."

Thomas was feeling very queasy, and not just because of his illness. He was also worried about the safe box, where he should have several hundred pounds. If they were lost, it would cause him some considerable problems, which he could well do without in his poor state of health. He turned to Jersey.

"I demand my box is opened. And if you care to read the warrant, you will see we are permitted to use force if necessary."

Jersey sighed, knowing he was defeated.

Hamlyn left. He returned, a few minutes later, with the locksmith. It took him only a few moments to examine the padlock. "What do you want me to do? I can try and make another key, but that will take quite sometime; or I can force the hasp?"

"Force it!" John instructed, before Jersey could protest.

Moments later the hasp had been forced, and they all surged forward. Thomas nodded and John pulled open the drawer. They found the box was empty of any money. Hamlyn stayed at the rear, because he knew the box only contained several pebbles.

After the locksmith had left, Jersey was the first to speak. "Clearly you've already emptied it, and have forgotten you did so." He conveniently forgot about the key not working.

"You might well be right," agreed John. "But if that's the case, why put stones back inside it? There's one easy way to check. I would like the names of all the other box holders and ask them to check on their boxes."

"**NO!**" snapped Jersey. "Their names are absolutely confidential. And if word got out that there was a problem, it would cause a run on the bank."

"Then I'll have to seek a court order," replied John.

"You can try," Jersey smirked. This time he would be prepared. "But I'll oppose it."

He knew he would lose in the end, but such an action would take days, if not weeks to finalize. The financial welfare of his clients did not interest him. Only the survival of Henry Jersey and his bank mattered.

"I'll ask you again, Mr Jersey. I believe there has been a robbery of at least one of your client's safe boxes. It would be very helpful if the other box owners could check if their contents are still there. I'm not remotely interested in their contents, if that's what you are worried about. If the box contents are intact, that's the end of it. If they are not, then you have got a big problem. Surely, it must be in your interests to sort this out?"

"NO! and that's my final answer. Now you can get out of my bank. See you in court."

John helped Thomas out of the vaults and into his carriage. Already he had an idea, and he smiled grimly.

"What are you plotting?" queried Thomas. "I know that look."

Smiling, John touched the side of his nose. "It's best you don't know, old friend, or you might just try and stop me."

He watched the carriage drive away, and worried for his friend. Thomas was not at all well, and it hadn't just been Harriet's death which caused the problem. Julius Hopper had to be right. Somebody was poisoning him. Could it really be Sarah?

Thinking of Harriet made him wince, and he was glad of this problem with the bank, which was helping him take his mind off her. At the same time he wanted to see Laura, but she had not been available. When he called to see her the previous evening, Abbie had taken great delight in telling him how she was out with Dr Gilson. Somehow, he had not expected that.

He returned to the police station, for a conference with Mathew and Caleb.

Firstly they discussed what had happened, and John outlined his plans for the next day. His men grinned in approval.

"That's a bit devious, guv'nor," cautioned Mathew. "No wonder everybody says how you make the law up as you go along. But I'd be surprised if it doesn't bring results. Tomorrow could be a busy day."

"Do you think the bank's been robbed?" asked Caleb.

"Yes, I do, and that makes me even more suspicious about Quinn's death. Have you made any progress yet on your enquiries?"

"Only a little. It seems Quinn and Hamlyn did not get on well together. Quinn always blamed Hamlyn for any problems, whenever he could. Only a short while ago, there was a problem about a bill of exchange which had gone missing. Quinn was quick to put the blame on to Hamlyn, who strenuously denied it. And there's something else, guv'nor. On the morning of Quinn's death, it seems Hamlyn had been at the bank sometime before it opened."

"Had he now? That's interesting. I think the time is coming when we will have to ask Mr Hamlyn some more questions. If you haven't done so, make a note about the muffler and hoarse voice he had. I've already made some about the bruising on his throat."

They discussed the case for a while longer, and Caleb and Mathew stood up to leave. "Just a minute, Mathew there's something I need to mention to you. But, Caleb, will you go round to the *Chronicle Office*, and ask them to make sure this is in the paper tomorrow. I'm sure they will, as there could be a good story in it for them. But, if they breathe one word about it, before tomorrow, they'll never get another job from me. And can you get them to print the usual run of these for me? I will need them later tonight." He handed two letters to Caleb, who left the office chuckling.

"Guv'nor, are you sure this is a good idea?" asked Mathew.

"Perhaps not, but we need to know what has been going on. And as I think time will be important, we must be ready to act as if the robbery has been confirmed."

"And if it's all in order at the bank?"

"You'll probably be looking for a new superintendent. Now, there's something else I must tell you. I don't doubt this will be in the *Chronicle* tomorrow as well." John told him about the report of Harriet's death.

The big man was clearly upset at the news. He had a tremendous respect for Harriet since the *Battle at the White House*, as the affair was still called, when she had saved both his and John's lives. John also considered enlightening him about the possibility of Thomas being poisoned, but decided to wait just a little longer, until he heard more from Julius Hopper. There was always the chance Julius might be wrong.

* * *

As soon as it started getting dark, Billy Beech carefully climbed up a drainpipe, on the side of Eastgate House, and settled alongside the chimney breast. He had just come by the offices of *Bradford & Harding* and seen both partners were still working. Likewise, he knew Hamlyn was still in the bank. He knew he was in for a long wait, but at least from up here he could see the illuminated entrance into St Nicholas churchyard, and ensure no trap was being laid for him.

By the time the church struck 10pm, he had only seen a drunk, in the street lights, shuffling down Castle Hill before going into the churchyard. He did not come out, so Billy happily assumed the man had collapsed in there somewhere. Being late September, the weather was turning colder, just as it was tonight. The money would come in useful, and he could buy himself a new coat, to replace the one he had ripped. At least the heavy rain had stopped.

Just after 11pm he saw Hamlyn hurrying towards the churchyard, clutching a small parcel in his hand. He watched him go into the churchyard and re-emerge a few minutes later, but without the parcel. After waiting for Hamlyn to pass, Billy climbed back down the drainpipe, and made his way to the churchyard. Pausing for a few seconds at the gateway, he looked around before entering the churchyard. Checking all was clear, he slipped inside.

But, he failed to see Harding, hiding in the shadows of Gerrard Street, and who now followed him.

Billy quickly went into the churchyard and turned towards the far end of St Nicholas church. On reaching the gravestone he sought, Billy knelt by a corner, felt underneath until his fingers touched a package. Pulling it out, he held it to his chest and stood up. "That's well done, Billy," he said aloud to himself.

His self-congratulating stopped suddenly, as something pointed and very sharp bored into his left ear. At the same time a hand was clamped over his mouth from behind. Before he realized what was happening, Harding appeared in front of him, took the package from his hands, and stepped to one side.

"It wasn't well done at all, Billy," he said. "You've been very silly. Quite a silly Billy, in fact," he chortled.

Before Billy realized what was happening, Bradford moved his hand from his mouth and transferred it to his hair, which he pulled hard back. Moments later Bradford cut Billy's throat with a single slash of his knife. As the blood gushed forth, Billy sank to his knees and was dead within a few seconds.

"I don't think he'll cause us any more problems," muttered Bradford, as he wiped his knife on Billy's jacket. Next they placed the body behind a nearby tombstone, where, with a bit of luck, it would remain hidden for a while, at least until the morning.

Taking a rag from his pocket, Bradford dipped it in Billy's blood and took it several yards away from the church, in the general direction of the river, where he dropped it. With even more luck, when the body was found, the police would think the murderer had gone towards the river, probably to throw the knife away.

Several minutes later, they entered the *Bull's Head,* where an anxious Hamlyn awaited them. Bradford tossed the package to him. Hamlyn was concerned to see spots of blood on it. "What...what's happened?" he stammered.

"The problem's over. That's all you need to know," chuckled Bradford.

"You've killed him, haven't you?" Hamlyn knew the answer even as he asked the question.

"What do you think?" replied Harding. "Now leave it."

"That problem might be over, but we now have another. A client has discovered his safe deposit box is empty!"

"Damn it to hell!" snarled Bradford. "How did that happen?"

"It seems you sold some insurance to a Dr Waldren and he came round to the bank to collect the premium from his safe deposit box in the vaults."

Harding glowered at Bradford. "It looks like you've been just a bit too clever this time."

Hamlyn went on to explain what had happened that day, and how the police were now involved, and would be seeking to have the other boxes opened. The others listened in horror.

"I always knew your greed would be our downfall," said Harding. "You just had to con the professional classes."

"It doesn't matter. We've got the money, and our friend here," he indicated Hamlyn. "Is going to tell everybody how Mr Quinn was fiddling the books, and robbing the bank's clients. Aren't you? After all, he was the person who had most access to the vault." It was more of an order, than a request.

"When am I going to get my share?" Hamlyn ignored the instruction. "I want to get out now."

"He's got a point," added Harding. "This job is going from bad to worse, and I've had enough now. It really is time to get out."

"No, not just yet. If we pull out now, they'll suspect us. We've got to sit tight and wait this one out," snapped Bradford. Pointing a finger at Hamlyn, he continued. "You've got to make them think Quinn was responsible."

"For all the boxes?"

"You've already said Jersey will fight Mayfield, all the way, so it should be several days before the full extent of the losses are discovered."

"I'm worried about Mayfield. He's got a hard reputation, and he's not convinced Quinn's death was an accident. He keeps asking about it and wants to interview me again," whined Hamlyn.

"Well that's your problem," smirked Bradford. "After all, you were the one who killed him. It wasn't us."

"I still think Mayfield is plotting something. He gave in far too easily this afternoon."

"He may have a point, Giles. Perhaps we should split up now, whilst we're ahead."

"No. We wait, at least until the week-end. It should be possible to stall Mayfield until then."

"Don't forget, I finish on Friday. After then you'll have no inside information. I'd rather go now."

"The answer is still no," stressed Bradford.

Soon afterwards Hamlyn left. The two men sat in silence for a while. "I'm getting worried about him," Harding broke the silence. "I doubt he'll stand up to Mayfield for very long."

"You're probably right, but I have a feeling Mayfield may just have a somewhat more important matter to deal with. So we pull out at the end of the week, and take Hamlyn with us."

"And then what?"

"Half shares go further than thirds," chuckled Bradford.

Harding did not return the chuckle. The more he thought about it, one share would go even further than two. He was under no illusions, and knew Bradford would have no hesitation in murdering him, if the man felt so minded. And the more he thought about it, he knew that would be the case. Get rid of Hamlyn first, and then himself.

But he had no intention of letting that happen. For the time being, at least, he would go along with Bradford's idea and help get rid of the other man. Then, he would strike Bradford when he least expected it. His partner had been right, when they arranged this robbery. This would be their last job together, in more ways than one.

CHAPTER TEN

Wednesday (1)

Edith Spencer was not having a good night. The sudden outbreak of colder weather, and the earlier heavy rain, had sent most of her clients scuttling indoors. Now in her mid-forties, and having lost most of her good looks and sex appeal, she was mocked by her fellow whores. They forgot their time would come. Always short of money, Edith would take any customer and had, over the years, especially of late, suffered for it. Without a pimp to watch over her, she was an easy target, as had just happened.

St Nicholas church clock had just struck 11.45pm, when she had taken a client into the churchyard. She aimed for the flat tombstone at the back of the church, laid down on it and pulled her skirts up. Her client did not take long, and as she stood up, he started to run away, without having paid first. Normally she demanded cash in advance, but had been scared to on this occasion, in case she lost the business.

"Come back here, you thieving bastard!" she cried: but it was no use.

The man had gone, and she knew there was no chance of catching up with him. Edith sat on the tombstone and cursed her fate. In the pale moonlight, she made out what looked like a figure, lying nearby. Looking closer, she saw it was a man, and assumed he was drunk.

Unable to believe her luck, she quickly searched his pockets, but only found a few pence. It was then Edith discovered her hands were sticky. Lifting them to her face, she saw they were covered in a dark wet substance, which seemed to be drying.

She brought her hands closer to her nose, and taking care not to come too close, she sniffed. The smell confirmed her worst fears. It was fresh blood: a smell she knew only too well. Another look at the man convinced her he was dead. In the moonlight, she saw a gaping wound in his throat. Edith ran towards the gate into the churchyard and began to scream.

Constable Sam Perkins was patrolling down Castle Hill, when he heard the screams and went to investigate. He soon found a very hysterical Edith, and it took him several minutes to discover what had brought on her screaming.

Unwillingly she led him to the rear of the church, where a quick look by his lantern light, confirmed Edith's story. Although late, a small crowd of people had gathered, many wearing dressing gowns, and he sent one of them up to the police station to inform John, and another to fetch Dr Waldren or Dr Gilson.

John and Richard Gilson arrived almost together, and were joined soon afterwards by Mathew. Once they had arrived, Sam took Edith back to the police station to interview her.

Richard took one look at Billy, and agreed the man was dead. Next he made arrangements for the body to be removed to the surgery, once John gave his permission. Because of the dark, John could not make a proper search of the scene. He arranged to have a closer look at the body, after it had been removed.

However, before the body was removed, he managed to stake out some string around its outline. In an ideal world, he thought grimly, he would have detailed a constable to protect the scene until daylight. Such were the joys of having several more men under his command, as he used to have in London. He watched dispassionately as Billy's body was moved.

"Just a minute!" instructed Mathew as the body was moved away from behind the tombstone. He knelt, raised his lantern and took a closer look at the dead man's coat.

"Good God. It looks like Billy Beech. I'd know his green coat anywhere, even if I couldn't see his face." He paused then turned the dead man's head. A quick look confirmed his identification. "As I thought, it's Billy Beech. Whoever's he upset?" In a few words, he explained to John about the victim's criminal record and his recent release from gaol.

As Billy's body was being put onto a wooden hurdle, Mathew took the opportunity to search his clothing, not that he expected to find anything. As he did so, Mathew saw there was a piece of material missing from the back of his coat.

"That's interesting: It wasn't torn when I saw him only a few days ago. Knowing Billy, he's probably been burgling and caught it on a nail or something."

"But we haven't had any burglaries reported recently," replied John.

"I know and that makes it even more interesting. I wonder if this is someone taking the law into his own hands?"

The two policemen watched as Billy's body was removed, before they began questioning the onlookers. Nobody had seen or heard anything, although someone remembered having seen a drunk lurch into the churchyard, earlier that evening. When asked further, the onlooker was not able to give any useful description, other than it was a man.

After they had all gone, Mathew searched further round the churchyard where he found the bloodstained cloth. He called John over. "Guv'nor. It looks like the murderer or murderers went this way, towards the river."

"Or that's what they wanted us to think?" queried John, and he took a closer look at the cloth.

"You don't seem very sure?"

"I don't know. If you've just stabbed a man and wanted to throw the weapon in the river, would you bother to wipe it on some cloth first?"

"If you wiped it on anything, you would do so on the body, wouldn't you?"

"Exactly. Certainly not on a piece of cloth like this, which is then conveniently found in the general direction of the river. Let's go and take another look at Billy Beech."

As John had expected, there were lights showing from the Waldren's house, and Redman was clearly expecting them. Knowing the butler's dislike of bodies, John led the way into the laboratory, where Richard was measuring Billy's body, paying special attention to his injuries.

"I'd say his throat was cut by a single slash, probably by someone standing behind him. But, this is the interesting wound." Richard pointed to a small superficial injury to the man's left ear. "It looks as if a knife, or something sharp, has first been pushed into his ear. Do you have any thoughts, gentlemen?"

John took a closer look, and was followed by Mathew. "I'd say someone wanted to attract his attention, and he would certainly have succeeded in doing so. Agreed Mathew?"

"Agreed. And look at his coat. You were right guv'nor. The river was a blind."

Richard and John looked closer. Amongst the heavy blood stains, already starting to dry, they saw other marks, which looked like a knife or something had been wiped on the coat. These bloodstains were of a far different character, and nowhere near so heavy, as the others.

"There are two questions we need to answer," said John. "What was Beech doing in the churchyard? And who killed him?"

"And why?" added Mathew.

"And why?" repeated John. "I'm also intrigued about this wound to his ear. Why his left one?"

"A suggestion, if I may?" said Richard. "If he was grabbed from behind, where would you put the knife or whatever instrument was used? And I'd say it was a knife? Let me show you."

Richard stood behind Mathew. He put his left arm round Mathew's neck and poked his ear with his finger. "Which ear have I just pricked?"

Mathew said "My right."

"Yes, and where's the injury on the body's head?"

"The left ear," replied John. "So, if our assailant attacked Beech from behind, he must have been left-handed." He paused and screwed his face up in concentration. "I've seen a left-handed person only recently. He may not be involved, but I can't remember where it was. It'll come to me in time."

"Correct. I would say he was left-handed," smiled Richard.

"Were there one or two of them?" asked John.

"I can't answer that one. I've looked at the throat wound, but I can't say if it was administered as a forehand or a backhand slash. But it has gone from right to left, which makes me think he was cut from behind, by a left-handed man."

They spent more time examining the body, before returning to the police station.

Richard watched them go, grinning to himself. He had spent a pleasant evening with Laura Grant, and almost felt sorry for John, whom he actually liked. But, his philosophy was all's fair in love and war: and that definitely included the delectable Miss Grant.

He was well aware, that thanks to Redman, Sarah knew what was happening and wanted to warn John. But just for the moment, at least, her problem was Thomas. Once that was sorted, she could help John, if she wished, but by then it would be too late.

* * *

By the time John had written up his notes, and sketched the body, as much as he remembered, and read Edith's statement, most of the night had gone. In three hours time, *Jersey's Bank* would open, and he anticipated plenty of activity when it did. Aware of all this, Sam offered to continue with the murder enquiries on his own, for which John was grateful. Ben Underwood would have to work the night shift, as John needed Caleb and Robert Andrew, for what he had planned later that morning.

Murder or no murder, he had set the wheels in motion to discover whether or not *Jersey's Bank* had been robbed, and that was his number one priority. It was much too late now to go back on his plan. Whatever his doubts, he was certain of one thing: Henry Jersey would not be a happy man before many more hours had passed.

In fact, he would be a very angry man.

* * *

When Henry Jersey first heard about Billy's murder, he burst out laughing. That should delay Mr *busybody* Mayfield for a few days, at the very least, and it would give him time to bring in a locksmith to open the other boxes. Then he would be able to check out their contents himself, and in his own time. He had already instructed his solicitors to oppose any move, by the police, to gain access to the safe boxes, knowing such procedures would all take time. And time was what he needed at the moment.

Much against his better judgment, he actually agreed with Mayfield's suspicions. No doubt Quinn was to blame, and he had been suspicious of the man for some time. Likewise, he did not completely trust Hamlyn, but he would soon be gone. Once he had an idea of the value of the losses, he could bring in some of his own money, to help mitigate any probable run on the bank. He knew it would cost him dear, but he had no alternative if he was going to survive.

Jersey moved into his dining-room where his wife already sat. She knew better than to interrupt him whilst he was enjoying his breakfast. Having started with porridge, he was now eating his second boiled egg and reading the *Warwick Chronicle*. As usual, he had skimmed over the first few pages, which only contained advertisements, and in doing so nearly missed a public notice. Turning back to it, he read.

PUBLIC NOTICE - JERSEY'S BANK

ALL *Persons having a safe deposit box, at* **Jersey's Bank, Market Place, Warwick,** *are summoned to a very important Meeting, at the* **POLICE STATION,** *The Holloway, Warwick, starting at 9.0 o'clock this morning.*

Signed: *John Mayfield, Superintendent of Police.*

Jersey could not believe what he had just read. But, even after reading it several times, he realized what it said. That jumped up bastard, Mayfield, had beaten him: outflanked him. How dare he? By God, he would live to regret having done this.

Suddenly, he was no longer hungry. Pushing his chair backwards, he ran out of the dining-room, calling for his carriage, totally ignoring his wife who had already read the paper, and seen the notice. Yet, even as he did so, Henry Jersey knew he was too late. It would take him at least fifteen minutes to get to the police station, and the meeting would have started by then.

* * *

Long before 9.0 o'clock, there were some thirty or more people waiting outside the police station, including a reporter from the *Warwick Chronicle.* These were far more than John had expected, and too many for his office. Caleb ran across to the *Woolpack,* where a room was hurriedly made available for them, and the meeting started. He and Mathew stood either side of John, but they took no part in the proceedings.

Once the room was quiet, John explained why he had called everyone together. Even as he spoke, several other men came into the room. By the time John had finished, there was an angry murmur of voices in the room. Then the door was flung open, and Jersey stormed in, accompanied by a man, wearing black, whom John rightly assumed was his solicitor. A sudden silence fell on everyone.

"I demand you stop this meeting, at once!" commanded Jersey.

"We have just finished," replied John calmly. "I have explained about Dr Waldren's safe deposit box, and have advised these gentlemen to check their own boxes. So, now it's up to them."

"These allegations are absolute nonsense," continued Jersey. "Clearly Waldren is all muddled up and has lost his key and, says he couldn't remember emptying his box. I hope none of you are his patients!" His feeble attempt at humour was greeted by a hostile silence, which was soon broken.

"I want to check my box!" called an angry voice.

"And so do I!" came several other angry shouts.

"It's not really convenient, at the moment," objected Jersey, but he was met with a chorus of angry voices. John held up his hands for silence.

"Correct me if I'm wrong, Mr Jersey. But I believe safe deposit box owners are allowed access to their boxes, at any time when the bank is open. Is that not correct?"

"Yes! Yes!" came calls from the audience.

Jersey was flustered, but before he could answer, John waved a printed piece of paper at him.

"I'm sure you recognize this," he said, still in the same calm voice. "This contains the policy and instructions, for safe deposit box users, as issued by your bank. Do you want me to read it out? I'm sure that you, and all these good people here, and your attorney, know you must allow clients access to their boxes whenever they wish, once your bank is open for business, as it is now."

For a moment John thought the man would still object, but then Jersey's shoulders sagged, knowing he was defeated, and he led the way across to the bank. Here a noisy crowd had already gathered, including Robert Andrew. John, Mathew and Caleb followed.

Robert Andrew was a thin man of medium height, and was the last of John's original recruits. Apart from having a keen sense of humour, Robert had a photographic memory, and was totally trustworthy and reliable. He was a thinking policeman, who was happier doing office duty than being in a rough house.

His filing system was second to none, and it provided all manner of information, not just from the Warwick area, but also from other parts of the country. This system had the added advantage of Robert's neat handwriting, which his colleagues took advantage of, when they needed important letters to be sent. But he was not a coward, and always played his part in whatever task was required of him

"I hope you're right, guv'nor," mouthed the sergeant, as they approached the bank.

"Not half as much as I do."

Once they arrived at the bank, John took control again. "We can only allow one client, at a time, down into the vaults, and I suggest you go down in numerical order of your boxes. I appreciate this may take some time, so I must ask you please to be patient."

There was some muttering, which soon abated.

"Lastly, neither I nor my men can come down into the vault with you, unless you specifically ask for us. If you agree, then Constable Andrew will make a full record of what happens."

Rupert Wolfe had key number 3, and in the absence of keyholders 1 and 2, he went down into the vaults first. Before doing so, he requested John and Robert went with him. Mathew and Caleb remained upstairs in the bank, to control the ever swelling crowd of people who flocked there. Many were olionto, and having heard numerous rumours, came to withdraw their money from the bank.

Jersey and his attorney led the way downstairs. Having entered the vaults, Robert sat down at the small desk that was there, opened the case he had with him, and took out a selection of pens, ink and paper. Once he had written down the names of all persons present and the time, John instructed Rupert to open his box.

He inserted his key.

Inside the vault the atmosphere was electric. Jersey worried over what Rupert would find. John was worried about what he might not find. Robert was concerned for his guv'nor and just hoped he had got it right. Rupert was worried as all of his life savings were in that box. Their loss would cause him considerable hardship. The only person not affected was the attorney. It was just part of his day's work.

The key did not work.

Feeling considerably relieved, John looked at Jersey, whose face had gone ashen. "Would you like to give it a try?" he invited.

Jersey shook his head, but his attorney came across and tried to open the box. The padlock would not budge. "It would appear to be the wrong key," he announced to the people in the vault.

"Is this another one of your clients, Mr Jersey, who has lost his key?" asked John.

The banker shook his head, totally lost for words. Already his world was starting to fall apart. "Damn you Mayfield!" he spat. "Damn you! Damn you! Damn you! Why did have to do this to me? You could have waited."

"And you could have been more helpful. But arguing amongst ourselves isn't going to solve anything."

"What do you propose to do next?" asked the attorney. "It seems to me we need to get into this box, and probably the others as well. And I fear this could take a long time."

"Guv'nor, a suggestion," interrupted Robert.

"Go ahead."

"As I see it, we may have to break open all these boxes, but before we do that, can we not see if Mr Wolfe's key works on any of the other boxes?"

His idea was accepted, and John tried the key in all the other boxes. It fitted box number 32, whose owner was quickly brought down to oversee the opening of his box. He was horrified to find it did not contain his money: only a collection of stones.

John felt vastly relieved. His gamble had paid off. But discovering there had been a robbery was only part of the problem. Now he had to find out when it had been done, and who was responsible.

Caleb was called down to assist and the key checking process was begun all over again, always with the same result. Once the appropriate key had been found, the box was opened, and discovered to contain stones and nothing else. It was late afternoon before the last box had been opened. Each transaction had been methodically recorded by Robert.

Once he had finished, Robert left the bank, returned to the police station, and started mailing the notices that had been printed the night before. Being well aware of the mail coach times, he had already addressed the envelopes to the police chiefs around the country, in strict order of departure of those coaches. The notice only gave the briefest details of the raid on *Jersey's Bank*, and asked for details of any similar crimes in their areas, to be forwarded, urgently, to Warwick.

He knew the guv'nor had taken a chance on pre-empting their visit today, but it had saved at least a day's work, and speed was very important. With luck, they should start to get the first replies early on Friday afternoon.

Meanwhile, the run on the bank continued, with rumours now spreading of Jersey's impending bankruptcy. Whilst Jersey had sufficient money to cover such withdrawals, replacing the contents of the safe boxes was not going to be so easy, and he began to doubt if it could be done. Jersey just had to hope he could weather this storm, and prayed the missing items were found, although nobody could say when they had been taken.

He reasoned if Quinn had taken them, then he probably had help, but who? And he knew by now, how Quinn had massive debt problems, although it was most unlikely his creditors would ever come forward. So, if they were involved, then he would probably never know.

If only he had been more reasonable with Mayfield, perhaps most of this could have been avoided. But, he had underestimated the policeman, just as his friend James Cooper, and others had done. "Oh damn you, Mayfield!" He lowered his head into his hands.

Hamlyn had watched the day's events unfold, with a mixture of feelings. In some ways he almost felt sorry for Jersey, but the old fool had brought it upon himself. If only he had kept his promise about the promotion, then Hamlyn would have put his trust in the owner: told him about Quinn's death, and warned him about what was going to happen to the safe boxes. He reasoned Jersey had nobody to blame but himself.

Then he thought about Bradford and Harding and the murder of Billy Beech, and shuddered. It would be a good time to tell his employer about Quinn's embezzlement.

Going to Jersey's office, he knocked on the door and went in without waiting. At first Jersey did not want to speak to him, until Hamlyn produced one of the Bank's ledgers, which clearly showed how the late manager had been fiddling the books. Without thanking Hamlyn, Jersey called for his carriage and quickly returned home, where he gave his butler several instructions.

When it was dark, several of his servants appeared, along with a horse and cart. The servants climbed on board and followed Jersey back into town. They passed through Warwick and onto the Emscote Road, where Jersey stopped them, in front of a small house.

"This is Quinn's house," Jersey told them. "Take a room apiece and search it for my money. If necessary take up the floorboards and leave no part of it untouched. Understood?"

They all murmured their assent. "And if we find it," came a voice. "Do we tell the crushers?"

"Never!" hissed Jersey.

CHAPTER ELEVEN

Wednesday (2)

B ack in the vaults, the long afternoon continued. Caleb had been walking around, sniffing for several minutes, and he was getting on John's nerves.

"Whatever are you doing?" snapped John.

He was tired and trying to work out how the robbery had happened. By now they had been joined by Mathew, and they thought the only way it could have happened was by someone from the bank: someone who had access to the vault. And the most likely suspect was Albert Quinn. John made a mental note to arrange a thorough search of the man's house. And he was not impressed by Caleb's prowling and sniffing.

"I was a bricklayer, before being a policeman," replied Caleb. "And you never forget the smell of new mortar."

"So what?" John tried to hide his impatience.

"There's a smell of it down here, and I think I've traced it to these shelves."

Suddenly John was very interested, and his tiredness left him. It did not take long for the three policemen to empty the shelves. Next they unscrewed them and moved them to one side. As they did so, several freshly mortared bricks were uncovered. Using his pocket knife, Caleb removed one of them. They came away quite easily. Next he put his hand into the cavity, formed by the double thickness of the wall, and felt around. The others watched him.

"Guv'nor, put your hand in here," said Caleb.

John did so.

"What can you feel?"

John poked and prodded, then stopped. Moments later, he brought out a small piece of still damp crumbling mortar. Mathew followed with his hand and drew out some more.

Whilst they were doing this, Caleb had taken a candle, which he held into the cavity. They all saw how the mortar was fresh and uneven. No attempt had been made to smooth it over.

"This puts a whole different aspect on matters," smiled John. "Perhaps it not an inside job after all, but has been carried out via next door. Well done, Caleb."

"Just a minute, guv'nor," cautioned Mathew. "If that's the case, who put these shelves back against this new brickwork? This couldn't have been done from next door. There still has to be someone from the bank involved. Unless........" his voice trailed off.

"Are you thinking of Billy Beech and a possible unreported burglary? Is Beech, or rather, was Beech capable of burgling somewhere like this bank, and getting down into the vaults, emptying those boxes and re-bricking up, without it being noticed?" asked John.

"I don't think so. But it might just be an idea to have a look round the back of the bank before it gets dark."

John watched Mathew and Caleb leave. He would need measurements taken of the vaults and the hole, but for the moment he just made rough drawings. When he had finished, John left the vaults, locked the door, and put the key in his pocket. Nobody was going down there unless they had his permission to do so.

There was still a small queue of unhappy clients, waiting in the bank. He ignored them, and went back to the police station, suddenly realizing he was ravenously hungry and tired. Also, he needed to see how Sam was getting on.

* * *

Mathew led the way out of the bank, and round into New Street. Just as he remembered, there were narrowly spaced bars on all of the windows, at the rear of the bank. Satisfied that not even Billy Beech could have squeezed through them, he was about to walk away, when Caleb caught him on the shoulder.

"Sergeant, what's that?" He pointed to a small dark shape, hanging on a nail, at the rear of the offices of *Bradford & Harding.*

Mathew squinted through the gathering gloom. "It looks like a piece of material."

"Shall I go up and get it?" suggested Caleb.

Mathew started to protest, but he saw the sense in Caleb's suggestion. He was not as heavy as the sergeant. Moments later, Mathew had given him a hand up onto the wall. Caleb quickly crossed it, climbed up part of the drainpipe and took hold of the cloth.

Pulling it gently, the cloth came away, and Caleb was soon back on the ground. Both men peered at the material, but all they could see, in the gloom, was a piece of dark cloth, so they took it across to the police station, for a closer inspection in the light.

As Mathew had both hoped and suspected, it was a piece of green cloth that seemed to have been torn from a coat. Unable to tell John, who appeared to have gone off duty, Mathew and Caleb went to see Richard, who was out. However, Redman led them through to the laboratory, and waited outside, whilst the policemen inspected Billy's clothes.

Mathew located the coat, turned it over, and tried the piece of cloth in the tear. It was almost a perfect fit. His discovery put a whole new perspective on both the robbery and the murder.

* * *

Sam had experienced a very mixed day. The statement he had taken from Edith, the previous night, was of little or no use. Firstly he had gone to Billy's lodgings and spoken to the woman who lived with him. All Eliza Callow could confirm was Billy had only been released from prison, on the Saturday morning. With a small degree of persuasion from Sam, she agreed there had been no food in their lodgings, and no money to buy any. Their four children were hungry and Billy had gone out to find some food.

She told Sam, in between her forced tears, how his Saturday night foray had been successful, but not so on the Sunday. However, she added, in spite of that, he was in a good humour when he came home, early on the Monday morning. He would not give her any details, except to say he had solved their money problems for a long time to come. But, he would not elaborate any further. But he had insisted on writing a letter and going out to deliver it, before going to bed.

"How well could he write?" Sam asked.

"Not very well."

"Who was he writing to at that hour of the morning?"

" 'E wouldn't tell, but just said 'e 'ad seen somefink that would make our fortunes."

"Who did he write to? Do you know?" Sam persisted.

She shook her head.

"Did he go out again, after he came back?"

"Not till the early evening."

"Do you know where he went?"

"Nah, but 'e were in a high good mood, when 'e left....." Eliza paused.

"And when he came back?"

"'E were in a foul mood. 'E said they'd cheated 'im. And............."

"Go on," prompted Sam gently.

"'E said if they didn't pay 'im, 'ed go to the crushers. Is this why 'e were killed?"

"Possibly," answered Sam truthfully. "But what happened last night?"

"'E went out just as it were getting dark, and never came back." She sniffed.

"Did he say where he was going?"

"Nah."

Much as Sam questioned her, she could not or would not add anything else. He explained how he would need to write down her story, but not today. Sam was not surprised to discover she was unable to read or write, so would need somebody else with her when he took the statement. As he went to leave, she sidled up close to him.

"'Ave you got a few pence you could let me 'ave?" She started to undo the buttons on her dirty blouse. "I'd make it worth yer while."

"No thank you!" Sam replied curtly and left, making a mental note to have somebody else with him, when he came to see her again.

"BASTARD CRUSHER!" she shouted after him.

Sam went back to the scene of the murder in St Nicholas churchyard. His guv'nor's stakes were still in place, so he spent some time taking full measurements and making a sketch of the scene. Lucy was coming up at the week-end, and, with the guv'nor's permission, he might ask her to do a proper sketch and plan of the scene.

Since meeting at the *White House*, the previous year, their romance had grown, in spite of her living in London. Whenever she could, Lucy visited Warwick, as she appreciated it was difficult for Sam to get to her. It had not taken long for Margaret Harrison, Mathew's wife, to see what was happening. She was more than happy for Lucy to stay with them, on her visits. Margaret knew her husband almost certainly owed his life to Sam, and that was good enough for her.

Sam examined where the body had been found, and saw several sets of footprints in the soft ground. He was easily able to identify those belonging to Edith and her running customer, but two other sets particularly interested him. They went from where the body had been found, through the churchyard in the general direction of the river. Then they stopped, turned round and made their way to the path where their direction could not be followed. The place where they stopped and turned was where the bloodstained rag had been found.

The first set of footprints were obviously from a pair of boots, with a tread similar to Sam's own. Clearly they belonged to his guv'nor. However, the other set were made by shoes and not boots, and they probably belonged to the murderer. He would need to get a plaster cast of them, but, in the meantime, he traced their outline, as best as he could, in his notebook.

On leaving the churchyard, Sam made enquiries at the nearby houses in St Nicholas Church Street, but nobody had seen, or was prepared to admit to having seen anything, other than a drunk, just as it was getting dark. Although the man had been seen entering the churchyard, nobody had seen him leave. This information made Sam think Billy's death was a premeditated murder, and not just a robbery gone wrong. As yet, he did not know what had happened at the bank.

During the late morning and throughout the afternoon, he had heard snatches of conversation, from people talking about *Jersey's Bank*, and there being a run on it. He was relieved if that was the case, because it meant the guv'nor had been right. At last, he decided he could do no more, and went back up Castle Hill, to return to the police station, and go off duty.

Walking up the Hill, he saw a carriage pass him, and recognized Dr Gilson. Sam went to raise his hand in greeting, but stopped when he recognized the passenger in the carriage, laughing and touching the doctor.

It was Laura Grant.

Sam was not pleased to see them together. Like many other people in Warwick, he had been devastated by the report of Harriet's sudden departure and her later death. Having seen just how badly John had taken the news, he was glad to see him making some progress with Laura. But now, it seemed he was about to lose her as well, if he had not already done so. The knowledge made him feel guilty about his growing love for Lucy. Mentally, he decided to do whatever it took, to break up Laura and the new doctor.

"Constable! Constable!" The words interrupted his thoughts, and he turned to find an elderly lady speaking to him.

"Good evening madam," he replied with a smile. "How can I help you?"

"I'd like you to take a look at these."

Mrs Mary Agatha Palmer led him into the nearby garden of Eastgate House, where she lived with just one maid and a cook, and showed him a flowerbed near a drainpipe. "What do you think of these?" She pointed at some footprints in the soil.

"Obviously they're footprints," he replied as politely as he could. He was tired and not in a mood for playing games.

"Yes, but they shouldn't be here. Somebody's been trespassing in my garden. They weren't here yesterday afternoon."

Now Sam was alert, and he studied the footprints in the fading light. One set had the toes facing the drainpipe and one footprint was on its own, and much deeper than the others. Likewise, there was another similar set, which turned and walked out of the flower bed. The inference was someone had climbed up and down the drainpipe.

"Have you checked to see if anyone has broken into your house?" he asked as casually as he could. Already he was starting to get an idea about what might have happened, and he needed to get into Eastgate House.

"Oh no! Surely nobody's broken into my house?" came her anguished reply.

"Would you like me to check for you?" Sam beamed his most boyish and charming smile. The woman happily agreed.

Sam went through the motions of checking every room and insisted on going up into the attic. One of those windows gave him a reasonable view of the gateway into St Nicholas churchyard. He would get an even better one from the roof.

What if, he reasoned, Billy Beech had climbed the drainpipe to watch the churchyard? If that was so, who was he meeting there and why? And was it the same person who had killed him?

He had no idea what the weather would do overnight, but having checked the house for the woman, she happily lent him a wooden box, which he put over some of the footprints to protect them. They would need to be examined properly in daylight, and checked against Billy's shoes. The case was not now looking quite so hopeless, but even if the footprints were Billy's, how would they help in finding his murderer?

Sam returned to the police station only to find neither John nor Mathew were there. He knew the bank was now closed, but as yet he had no knowledge of what had happened there: only what he had overheard during the day. And he had no guarantee that was true.

Although tired, he faithfully sat down to write up his notes. Before he had finished, Mathew and Caleb returned and they shared notes with him. It certainly seemed as if the murder and the robbery were connected. But where was the guv'nor, because he was not in his quarters in the police station?

* * *

On his return to the police station, John had found a note waiting for him, from Julius Hopper, summoning his attendance at the earliest possible moment. With two violent deaths having happened, in less than a week, John knew he was out of order for not having reported earlier to the coroner, but he had just been too busy. So, it was with some trepidation when he arrived at Hopper's house. John still remembered their first stormy meeting, soon after he had first arrived in Warwick.

As he was shown into the coroner's study, Julius stood up. "Come on in, Mayfield: a glass of Madeira?"

John politely declined, as he was still in uniform, but gladly accepted the offer of some tea. He started to apologize for not having been to see him, but Julius quickly brushed his apologies aside.

"I know you have been rather busy," he chuckled. "But, can you tell me, unofficially if you like, or in my capacity of magistrate, how you got on today at *Jersey's Bank*?"

John told him, having every confidence in the man's integrity.

"How much do you think is missing?"

"Bearing in mind, we still have to make contact with some of the box owners, I should say, somewhere in the region of more than £5000."

Julius whistled. "And that doesn't include the run there's been on the bank today. I'd be surprised if Jersey can survive all this."

"It was never my intention to ruin him, but he brought it upon himself."

"Don't lose any sleep over him. He's a pompous arrogant bastard, and all this lot serves him right. Did you know he was a friend of the late unlamented James Cooper?"

"He lost no time in telling me."

"Anyway, what's the latest on these two bodies, only I'll have to convene an inquest fairly soon."

John explained what had happened so far, but he was unaware of how Sam's enquiries had progressed. Julius listened intently, nodding his agreement from time to time. When John had finished, he agreed to open and adjourn the inquest on Billy Beech.

However John agreed the inquest on Albert Quinn should also begin the next day, with special attention being paid to the evidence given by Hamlyn. John agreed to have him warned as soon as possible about having to attend, and he would instruct Ben Underwood to do that tonight. With luck, it would give Hamlyn a sleepless night and make him more prone to making mistakes.

"Now, the real reason why I've asked you here tonight, is I've had those samples analyzed, that I took from Thomas Waldren. My contact cannot identify the poison, but I'm afraid he's in no doubt at all. Thomas is being slowly poisoned by something and someone."

"Dear God. Can it really be Sarah who's doing it?"

"We don't know, but it has to be a very real possibility."

"Can you save him?"

"Possibly, but I need to know what the poison is. Until I know that, I cannot begin to consider what antidote to use."

"What else can we do? Saving Thomas's life is our main priority. Finding the guilty party has to come second."

"I agree entirely, but I wonder if there is a way of doing both. Let's keep you out of it for a moment. If it is Sarah, then the less she knows about our suspicions, the better. We're lucky in having young Gilson on hand. It'll be quite normal for him to take over Thomas's care. He can play down the poison side of things, but arrange for only a few people to handle his food and drink."

"That sounds a good idea. But what is the risk if we don't act fast?" queried John.

"It seems to be a slow acting poison. Anything fast would result in too many questions being asked. This way it will look like a wasting disease, which has got us doctors fooled. So, there will be little or no chance of an autopsy happening. His death would look like natural causes and that will be the end of the matter. And to be honest, even with an autopsy, we may not be able to identify the poison."

They discussed the case for some while, and then John took his leave. His mind was in turmoil at the news someone was poisoning Thomas: and that someone quite possibly might be Sarah. At the same time, he refused to believe it, but he still had a nagging doubt, that it might be her.

Wives murdering their husbands had gone on for hundreds, if not for thousands of years. From his own experience he knew of several such cases, although they tended to have been where the wives had been ill-treated. Somehow that did not seem to be the case with Thomas and Sarah. For the moment he would keep the news to himself, but he knew he would soon have to take Mathew into his confidence.

His mood was lightened, when he arrived back at the police station and heard about the rest of the day's events.

CHAPTER TWELVE

Thursday

When Sam came on duty next morning, his first task was to visit Richard and borrow Billy's shoes. He was intrigued to know more about the new doctor, especially after seeing him with Laura Grant. Previously he had only seen him fleetingly on the night of Billy's murder. As it happened, Richard was holding a surgery, but he came out to see Sam. In spite of his preconceived ideas about the man, Sam found himself liking him, and he explained what he wanted.

"If you can wait for about fifteen minutes," said Richard. "I'll have finished surgery, and I'll be with you. I'll bring some medical plaster, and we can make some casts of the victim's shoe prints, as well as the ones in the flower bed: then see if they match up. After which, I'll give you some plaster so you can do the other footprints yourself, in the churchyard."

Sam was quite happy to wait, especially as Sarah gave him a mug of tea, and asked how his romance with Lucy was progressing. Almost embarrassed, Sam told her how everything was going well. He added how sorry he was to hear about Harriet, and he knew Lucy would be upset. The two women had become good friends in the aftermath of the James Cooper affair.

Sarah liked Sam. She knew his mother had been one of Thomas's very first patients, just after he had came to Warwick, before she had married him, nearly two years later. She had watched the young Sam grow, and now he was one of John's men. "How's John?" she asked suddenly.

"Devastated. He was sad enough after Mrs Foxton left, but then he seemed to be getting over it, especially when Miss Grant appeared. Now it looks like he's losing her as well."

"To Dr Gilson?"

"You know?"

"Oh yes. I very much have the feeling he's a lady's man. I knew someone just like him once, back in Gloucester. It was before I married Thomas. He promised me the world, and I believed him," she mused. "I think I'd fallen in love and would have done anything for him. But I discovered, only just in time, that I was about to become another notch on his bedpost." Sarah paused "And yet, I still thought I loved him, and I was prepared to forget about the other women in his life. But then I met Thomas."

"What happened to the other man?"

"He died in rather strange circumstances. It was always believed some wronged husband was responsible."

Further conversation was curtailed as Richard appeared, carrying Billy's shoes. Sarah watched them go, and wished Richard would find himself another woman. She also wished John would be more positive with the women in his life, and not let them go quite so easily.

Harriet's death had hit him very hard, and she feared Laura would become a casualty because of it. Looking at the clock, she sighed and saw it was time to give Thomas his next dose of medicine.

* * *

Sam led the way to Eastgate House, and introduced Richard to Mrs Palmer. At once, Richard was all charm, and full of re-assurance. He explained what they wanted to do, and politely asked for her permission. Totally charmed by him, she agreed, and they set to work, whilst she watched.

Removing the wooden box, Sam tried Billy's shoes in the footprints, and was not surprised to see they matched. Richard made up some of the plaster, whilst Sam, as instructed, erected a small paper boundary around the most pronounced footprints. Once it was secure, Richard poured in the liquid plaster. Next they used Billy's shoes to make further imprints in the soil, and took casts of those.

Whilst waiting for the plaster to set, Sam took measurements of the flowerbed, footprints and drainpipe. Hopefully Lucy would draw this scene for him as well. Once the plaster had set, Sam wrote on the casts to identify them. His pencil only left faint marks, but it would suffice until he could ink them in.

When they had finished, Sam asked Mrs Palmer if he could leave the plaster casts at Eastgate House, until he returned for them in a short while. She happily agreed. Richard had already given Sam some more plaster, and the two men made their farewells to Mrs Palmer.

She watched them leave. The new doctor was such a nice man, and she wondered how Dr Hopper would feel if she left his practice, and went to Dr Gilson? At the same time, she also found the young looking policeman quite friendly. If only I was younger, she wished!

Richard parted from Sam as he had the inquests to attend. They arranged to meet later that afternoon for Richard to make a statement. Somehow, Richard's charm with Mrs Palmer, coupled with Sarah's observations, only served to strengthen Sam's resolve to save Laura from him. But then he queried, was it really his business?

* * *

Henry Jersey remained an unhappy man. Although his servants had totally ransacked Quinn's house, they had found none of the missing property. So where was the money that had been taken from the safe boxes? Possibly Quinn might have taken it, but now Jersey was having serious doubts. Obviously the man was heavily in debt, but he doubted it had been to such an extent, to lead him to rob the bank. Gradually another thought struck him.

It would have taken some considerable time to pick all those locks. They were top of the range and would need an expert to do it. Somehow he doubted Quinn had the necessary expertise, or likewise, did he really have the intelligence to do that, and then muddle up the padlocks? Not that it let him off the hook. With no obvious signs of any apparent breaking into the bank, the thieves must have had inside help, and that could well have come from Quinn. But had it?

The more he thought about it, Quinn was too obvious. It had to have been somebody else. And that now made Hamlyn the most likely suspect. None of the other clerks know the lay-out of the vaults, or had access to the keys. Also, it was Hamlyn who had given him the information about Quinn fiddling the books. Had that been said to put him off the scent?

If so, it had almost succeeded, but these new suspicions did little to improve Jersey's temper. Whilst he had suffered a long, frustrating and sleepless night, it had not been entirely unprofitable. He now knew what he was going to so. The time was fast approaching when he would have to have words with Bernard Hamlyn. He realized the man would be unlikely to volunteer information willingly, so he would probably need to be persuaded.

Jersey chuckled, but it was not a pleasant sound, because he knew just the men to help him: Jesse and Isaac Morgan. They did the occasional little jobs for him, usually in persuading late payers to settle their overdrafts, with the minimum of delay. He would arrange for them to kidnap Hamlyn as he left the bank, and take him to a quiet outhouse he knew. There he would ask several questions and invite Hamlyn to reply.

Although Jersey was not a killer, he had no qualms about using violence, especially where his financial empire was concerned. Hopefully Hamlyn would see sense and admit his part in the robbery. He would be promised his freedom once the money was recovered. However, once that had happened, Jersey would have great delight in handing him over to Mayfield. If nothing else, it would show Mayfield up as being totally incompetent. At the very least, it would cause him a lot of trouble, and it might even cost him his job.

For the first time since the robbery, Henry Jersey smiled. But, it was not a pleasant smile.

* * *

Hamlyn had not enjoyed a good night's sleep.

Acting on John's instructions, Ben Underwood had called the previous evening, and advised him about the inquest, the next day. He also emphasized just how important Hamlyn was as a witness.

"It's important you get your evidence right," stressed Ben.

Along with Caleb, he had joined the police as John's first replacement officers. A big man, he towered over Hamlyn, which made him seem all the more menacing.

"But why? It wasn't me what found him."

"Ah, that may be so. But, you see, the coroner will want to know just how well you got on with him. You see, with this robbery just having happened, it's just possible Mr Quinn's death may be connected with it."

Ben paused and was gratified to see the other man go very pale. The guv'nor was right. This man knew more than he was saying about the death or the robbery: or even both.

"But you don't know when the robbery happened, do you?" The question came quickly: too quickly.

"We've got a good idea," Ben tapped his nose. "You see, the guv'nor has been around quite a lot. He's come across these jobs before. And usually they're an inside job: you know, involving someone from the bank." He paused and looked straight at Hamlyn. "The guv'nor usually knows too, when people are telling him lies. Is there anything wrong, Mr Hamlyn?"

The chief cashier was now sweating profusely, but he nodded. "It's nothing, just the cold I had last week."

"Oh yes. That's when you had a sore throat or something, wasn't it?"

It seemed such an innocent enough question, yet it reminded Hamlyn of all the events of the past week, and not just the robbery. What really concerned him was he had never spoken to this constable before, yet the man seemed to know all about him. That could only mean the police had discussed him amongst themselves: and they were clearly suspicious about his supposed cold.

"I'll leave you be now, Mr Hamlyn. Just you get a good night's sleep and be ready for whatever the coroner asks you tomorrow. Good night!"

Hamlyn had barely slept. For a while he contemplated running away, but having very little money, it was not an option. He'd have to bluff his way through the inquest, get his share of the robbery proceeds, and leave Warwick. Better still, he would leave the country. Damn Albert Quinn! Damn Henry Jersey! Damn Jacob Harding! Damn Giles Bradford! And damn Mayfield!

As the first grey light of dawn began to creep across the sky, he got out of bed and made himself some tea. When it had cooled sufficiently, Hamlyn took a swallow, but almost immediately vomited it back up again. Abandoning that idea, he selected his clothes with care, not that he had a wide choice, but he needed a shirt with the highest collar available, to help cover the bruises on his throat. They had faded quite considerably, but were still visible, and the last thing he wanted now was to be asked questions about them.

* * *

At noon he made his way from the bank to the *Woolpack*, where the inquest was being held. To make matters worse, when he arrived, Hamlyn was told he would have to wait for a while, as there was another inquest to be heard first.

"Good morning, Mr Hamlyn, or should I say good afternoon: my apologies for the delay."

He spun round and came face to face with a smiling John Mayfield.

"How's the throat, this morning? Much better I hope? You know, you never did tell me how you came by those bruises. Did somebody try to strangle you? It wasn't Albert Quinn was it?" John grinned and walked away.

But not before he had seen the other man go deathly white and sit down shakily. He now had no doubt at all, that Hamlyn and Quinn had been in a fight, which had probably resulted in the manager's death. His problem was how to prove it: and that would be easier said than done.

Hamlyn sat in a daze whilst the inquest was opened into the murder of Billy Beech. As he sat listening, Hamlyn realized he was involved, however unwittingly, in that crime as well. If only he'd bolted that damn gate as he had been instructed. God, what a mess he was in. He sat holding his head, very conscious of how John was watching him closely.

The Billy Beech case was adjourned for one week and then it was time for Quinn's inquest to begin. During the slight interval, before it began, he was aware of Henry Jersey coming into the room. The banker nodded at him, with what appeared to be a friendly smile, but Hamlyn knew Jersey only too well. Whilst there might be a smile on the man's lips, his eye were as cold as ice.

Once the proceedings started, Richard was called to give his evidence. Hamlyn felt a surge of relief when the doctor confirmed Quinn had died from a heart attack. If that was so, then he had not killed him. And he had not been involved in Beech's murder, only the robbery. Suddenly the idea occurred to him to tell Mayfield everything, including where the money was. With luck, he would be permitted to *Turn Queen's Evidence* at the trial, testify against Bradford and Harding, and escape being punished. He brightened up considerably.

"Was the heart attack caused naturally or had something brought it on?" asked the coroner

"It's hard to say sir. But, to be honest, I am not entirely convinced the injury, to Mr Quinn's eye, was caused when he fell."

"Why's that?"

"I feel it's in the wrong place, when compared to the other injuries. In my opinion, it is not consistent with having been caused by the ink well."

"What do you think caused it?"

Richard hesitated. "If I'm honest, sir, I don't know for certain. But, it looks to me like a blunt object was poked in his eye."

"Could it have been a finger or a thumb?"

"Yes."

"Could it have been Mr Quinn's finger or thumb which caused the injury?"

"Possibly, but I doubt it. I feel the injury was probably caused by somebody else."

Immediately there was uproar in the room, and the clerk had difficulty in restoring order. Hamlyn felt his heart begin to race, as his recently grown confidence now quickly evaporated. He knew Mayfield was studying him intently, and so was Jersey. There was little doubt in his mind that they both knew, or at the very least suspected the truth. Bradford had to give him his money and let him go.

But what would he do if they refused?

Then he remembered. He knew where the money was hidden. It would not be impossible to wait until Bradford and Harding had left for the night, break into their offices, dig up his share, and run. They could hardly go to the police and report him, could they? Suddenly things felt a lot better once more, but it was only to be very temporary relief.

"Mr Hamlyn!" came the coroner's petulant voice. "For the third time, will you come and take the oath. We can't wait all day for you."

It was not a request.

Hamlyn had been so wrapped up in his own misery he had not heard the coroner calling his name. Reluctantly he stood and took his place, where the witnesses stood, at the large table in front of the coroner. He was duly sworn in and gave his evidence, explaining how Quinn's body had been found. After what seemed a lifetime, he finished and went to go back to his seat.

"Just a moment," came the coroner's voice. "You haven't finished yet." Reluctantly Hamlyn returned to the table.

"Now Mr Hamlyn, would you please tell me what your relations were like with the deceased?" asked the coroner.

"Quite cordial."

"I would remind you that you are under oath, and lying to me constitutes perjury. Do you understand?" The coroner's piercing eyes bored into Hamlyn's face.

"Yes." Hamlyn's voice was very quiet, and barely audible.

"Good: then I'll ask you again. What were your relations with Mr Quinn? Do bear in mind I live in this town and I hear things. Also I can call other members of the bank's staff if necessary. So, what were your relations like with Mr Quinn?"

"I believed he was embezzling money from the bank. In fact, I know he was."

A buzz of excited chatter ran round the room and Julius had to wait for silence before continuing. "And what did you do about it?"

"I was going to tell Mr Jersey, but then....then....Mr Quinn....died, and it didn't seem so important any more."

"Did you challenge Mr Quinn about it?"

"No."

"Are you sure you didn't accuse Mr Quinn of this embezzlement and then had a fight with him, which resulted in his death?"

"No." Hamlyn felt himself blush and he was aware he was sweating profusely.

"Are you sure? Is that how you got those bruises on your throat? Is there something wrong, Mr Hamlyn? Only I see you've gone very red and are sweating. I didn't think it was that hot in here."

Hamlyn's hands went to his throat. "Bruises? Bruises? Oh yes, I...I... was attacked on the way home, the night before."

"Did you report the attack to the police?"

"No."

"Why not?"

"I...I...er....don't know."

All eyes were on him now, and he was particularly conscious of Jersey's and John's intensive stares. Both men were satisfied Hamlyn was not telling the truth, and knew he was much more involved in this business than he would like them to believe.

"Very well," continued the coroner. "That will do for the moment, although I'm sure Superintendent Mayfield will be interviewing you at some length in the very near future. Meanwhile, I am adjourning this inquest until next Thursday."

As Hamlyn hurriedly left the *Woolpack*, he did not see Jersey point him out to two thickset, rough looking men, who stood just outside. They nodded slightly in acknowledgment and moved away. Now they knew what their prey looked like, they would make plans to abduct him later that evening.

* * *

Meanwhile Sam had returned to High Street to await Richard's return. Sarah was upstairs with Thomas, so Redman showed him into Richard's surgery, where he waited. When Sam passed the *Woolpack,* he had learned when the inquest should soon finish, yet he still had to wait for a while before Richard appeared. They talked generally for a few minutes, before Sam took out his pens, ink and paper and began to go through Richard's report in some detail, knowing it would take some time.

"Why are you writing all this down?" asked Richard.

"It's what my guv'nor wants. He's always bothered in case something happens to a witness and we'd lose all the evidence. Between you and me, I think he's being excessively cautious, but he's the guv'nor."

In fact Sam completely agreed with John, and he was meticulous in everything he wrote down. Lucy had similar views. And, it was she who had suggested that professional witnesses, such as Richard, should always have their qualifications and experience recorded, in their statements, which is what Sam now did.

He began by asking Richard where he had previously been in practice. Richard told him in Deal, Bury St Edmunds, Oakham and finally for the shipping company, and he produced copies of his references to support his claims.

It was nearly an hour and a half later, when Richard signed his statement, and Sam stood up and gathered his papers together. Richard was helping him gather his inks and pens, when he accidentally knocked a small wooden box off the desk. On hitting the floor, it opened, spilling a selection of small arrow heads and containers in every direction. Sam bent to pick them up for him.

"STOP! Don't touch any of them!" instructed Richard.

Sam recoiled and looked up at him. Richard's face softened, but still had a serious look on it. "The arrow heads are all poisoned: and the small earthenware containers all hold poison," he explained. Picking up one of the containers, he carefully shook it. Sam could hear the slight sound of liquid coming from inside it.

"I was given them in South America by a local witchdoctor," continued Richard. "He respected what I did, and gave them to me with his blessing. But they carry a curse if they're thrown away. So, I'm stuck with the damned things," he grimaced, and began to pick them up, very carefully, using a pair of forceps.

"That's strange. There's some missing." He pointed to some empty spaces in the box.

Sam offered to help look for them, but Richard declined his offer. They shook hands, and Sam left. He left Richard on his hands and knees on the floor, looking under the desk.

* * *

Sam returned to the police station, where Robert Andrew was finishing the last of the series of letters that had been printed for sending off to other police forces, seeking information about similar bank robberies.

Robert put down his pen and flexed his aching fingers. Being the guv'nor's chief clerk had its disadvantages, although generally speaking, he enjoyed the quieter way of life. All the same, he sometimes missed being out in the thick of it. He looked up as Sam came in, carrying a mug of tea, which he gave to him.

"Robert," he wheedled. "My old friend: I'm sure you will appreciate this tea. And you do write so much better than me."

"What do you want?" Robert asked resignedly. "I assume you want a favour doing, right? You want me to write a love letter to Lucy for you? Eh? But, thanks for the tea, nevertheless."

Sam told his friend what he wanted. Robert drank a mouthful of tea, took out some more paper and began to write at Sam's dictation.

* * *

After the inquests, John had been summoned by the coroner to a meeting, and he was not surprised to find Richard was there already. Without any preamble, Julius Hopper reverted to his medical role, and told Richard of his suspicions about Thomas being poisoned.

"I'm relieved to hear you say that because it echoes my own suspicions," said Richard. "I've looked at every symptom Thomas is showing, but nothing is obvious. If we accept he hasn't contracted some rare or hitherto unknown disease, then someone is poisoning him. I take it we can rule out him taking his own life?"

John and Julius nodded.

"At present Thomas does not know of our suspicions and I think it's best to keep it that way. The problem is, though, if he's being poisoned, then who's doing it?" Julius continued.

"Suspicion has to fall on Sarah," said Richard sadly. "But it could just as easily be somebody else in the household." He looked pointedly at John.

"I'm inclined to doubt that," said John. "Most of the servants have been with him for years ..... but ... I realize people do change. Just for the moment, I would still prefer to keep an open mind."

"What I'm going to suggest," said Julius. "Is to put Thomas entirely into your care, Gilson. Just have Sarah to assist you. Between you, you must tend to all his needs, including preparing his food etc. If he improves, good: But if he doesn't, then I think Sarah must become our number one suspect. And be treated as such."

He paused for his words to sink in. "And I think, the sooner you start the better. We must try and save Thomas at all costs."

CHAPTER THIRTEEN

Later on Thursday

C aleb came on duty in the early afternoon, but he had been briefed, already by John, as what needed doing. John had insisted that all of them, who knew about the brickwork, in the bank vaults, had to keep it secret. He stressed how important it was that nobody else, particularly the bank staff should know about it.

"This is what I want you to do," John had instructed. "Visit all premises in the vicinity of the bank, and go down to each of their cellars. Tell the owners you are trying to get an up-to-date plan of the bank's vaults, in relation to the other premises in the Market Place."

"But you want me to concentrate on *Bradford & Harding's* cellars?"

"Yes, but not to the exclusion of the others. I know it will be, for the most part, a waste of time, but Bradford and Harding must not suspect they're being treated any differently to the others. Measure their cellar, but above all, pay particular attention to any new brickwork. You know what to look for."

"Leave it to me guv'nor."

By late afternoon, Caleb found himself at the *Bradford & Harding* offices. He opened the door, went in and was met by Jacob Harding.

"Yes? Can I help you?" The greeting was not warm, and Caleb felt there was a slight edge to it: not exactly hostile, but wary.

Caleb explained what he wanted and showed Harding the measurements and sketches he had done of the other properties. Although he noticed Harding relax slightly, he could see the man was not entirely at ease. He explained how their premises was nearly the last cellar to be measured. As he finished speaking, Bradford appeared and asked what was going on.

133

"He wants to look in our cellar," answered Harding. "It seems the police have nothing better to do than measure up everyone's cellars: something about a plan of them all."

"Don't tell me," sniggered Bradford. "You think Guy Fawkes has hidden some gunpowder down there?"

Caleb joined in their laughter. "That's a good joke," he chortled. "I'll have to tell that one to my guv'nor. No, on second thoughts, perhaps I won't. He doesn't exactly have a sense of humour. I think he's just making sure no one's burrowing into the bank next door. If they are, then I fear they have left it too late."

"So I heard," replied Harding. "I'm glad we hadn't had time to put too much in our box down there."

Bradford gave him a warning glance, which Caleb affected not to have seen. Whilst not having been a policeman all that long, he had developed the feeling that something was very wrong here. At the same time, he was glad the guv'nor knew where he was. Somehow he did not feel easy with these two men. Harding took him down into the cellar.

The first thing Caleb noticed was the cellar had been painted very recently. His nose told him the paint was still very fresh, but he made no comment. Whilst he measured the walls, Caleb noticed some of the flagstones, on the floor, were loose. Affecting an air of total boredom, he completed the measurements, thanked the men and left the office. From there he moved to the top end of the Market Place, adjoining the Old Square. Going into the first shop, he began his measuring all over again.

Bradford watched him go. "What do you think?"

"Nothing to worry about. He was totally bored with the measuring and just could not wait to get it finished."

"I don't know. I'm not so sure. He gave the impression of not being very intelligent, but..." He shrugged his shoulders. "I suppose you're right. But it's a bit too coincidental. Wanting to look in our cellar so soon after the discovery of the robbery: it's possible, I suppose....but....." Bradford was thoughtful.

"True, but there's been no mention of anyone digging into the bank. So they must think it's an inside job. And, if Hamlyn's done his job properly, the blame will all go onto the late Albert Quinn." Harding sounded still not completely convinced. "But what if Hamlyn's failed? I hear he was something of a disaster at the inquest this afternoon. I'm starting to think he's losing his nerve and that could be a problem."

"I think you may have a point, there, Jacob. He's got two more days at the bank after today, and then he'll be gone."

"When's he going to get his share?"

"What share?"

Both men laughed.

* * *

Sarah listened as Richard outlined his plans for looking after Thomas, who had now taken to his bed permanently, as his condition was getting worse. He was failing to hold down much food, and he was only eating a thin gruel and drinking some water.

"Is he being poisoned?" asked Sarah. "Please don't try to fool me. I've been a doctor's wife for too long. I just don't believe you are talking about his own water supply, away from the rest of the house, and only you and me to nurse him, without there being a very good reason for not trusting our servants."

"I think you may be right, Sarah. Neither Dr Hopper, nor myself, can find any reason for him being so ill. His symptoms just do not tally with any known diseases. And in this respect, having spent a few months in South America, I've probably got more experience in this field, than Dr Hopper."

"If he is being poisoned, then it has to be by someone in this house?"

Richard nodded. "Sadly, it looks like it."

Even as they were talking, John came to visit Thomas, and he was appalled to see how ill his friend looked. For a few minutes he was able to talk to Thomas, and break the news about the robbery at the bank.

Thomas chuckled wryly, which sent him off into a fit of coughing. "Serves that old bastard Jersey right," he coughed. "Never could stand the man. But his father was a gentleman, and my father knew him. It's the only reason I went to his bank. I meant to change banks years ago, but I never got round to it."

For a while they talked about other matters, and John went to leave. As he stood up, Thomas grasped his arm. "I'm being poisoned, aren't I?" John hesitated. "No, don't deny it. I can see it on your face. I'm right aren't I?"

"We think so," replied John sadly.

"Do you know who by?"

"No," John shook his head. "That's why we're going to keep all your food and water separate, with only have Sarah and Richard attend you."

"It'll be too much for Sarah. You'd do better to find me a nurse. Someone you can trust. Will you do that for me?"

"Of course." John did not know of any nurses, but he made a mental note to ask Mathew.

* * *

By the time he returned to the police station, Sam had gone off duty, but Mathew was able to confirm Billy Beech had climbed up onto the roof of Eastgate House, some time prior to his murder. When Mathew finished, John told him about Thomas's suspected poisoning, and the need for a nurse who could be trusted.

Once Mathew recovered from the shock, he suggested Margaret, his wife, might be able to act as a nurse. "She's done it before," he added. "And, she could act as our eyes and ears at the same time."

Mathew went off to ask Margaret, whilst John sat down to catch up on his paperwork. He was very much aware he had not spoken to Laura for a few days, and knew he really must make the effort to go and see her. Ironically, thinking of Laura made him think of Harriet. She would not have let him ignore her. She would have been round to see him and offer advice on his cases.

But Harriet was dead.

He thought fleetingly, and longingly, about Kate Whiting, but that could never have worked, certainly not back here in Warwick. Here she was still too well known, and had too many enemies. And it would not have been right to take her away from Silas.

Caleb's arrival provided him with a welcome break from his thoughts.

"Excellent," said John after Caleb had finished.

"And there's another thing, guv'nor. I checked with the letting agent. Their cellar hadn't been painted in years, but it's been done in the past few days."

"Excellent. And what's the rest of the building like, as far as being painted?"

"As you would expect, the offices were painted just prior to their opening. The agent says upstairs hasn't been done for a while, and whilst he arranged for the offices to be painted, there were no instructions for anywhere else. And the cellar was not included anywhere."

"I feel we have a definite connection between the bank, Messrs Bradford & Harding and Billy Beech. It is just too much of a coincidence that part of Billy's coat was found on their premises."

"And we don't believe in coincidences," smiled Caleb.

"Correct. I also feel our Mr Hamlyn knows much more then he's letting on. He's the weak link, so we'll bring him in tomorrow and see what we can learn."

"There's another thing, guv'nor: I spoke to the ironmonger in the Market Place, whilst I was measuring his cellar. He hasn't sold any paint to either Bradford or Harding in the past two weeks. So they didn't buy it locally, which is odd. Why didn't they want to buy it from a local supplier? Was it because they did not want anyone, locally, to know what they were doing?"

"I think so," added John. "It's too much of a coincidence and......."

"We don't believe in coincidences," finished Caleb with a smile.

For a while they discussed the case until Mathew joined them. Finally, they decided the best plan of action would be to obtain a warrant, the next day, and make a thorough search of *Bradford & Harding's* offices.

After Caleb left, Mathew remained and confirmed Margaret was only too happy to act as a nurse for Thomas Waldren. Just as they finished making the arrangements, Sam appeared.

"I'm sorry, guv'nor, but I couldn't help hearing what you were saying about Dr Waldren. I'll do anything I can to help. He saved my mam's life and we will be forever in his debt."

"Thank you," said John, and returned to his paperwork. Sam went to leave, but stopped suddenly, returned and told John about Dr Gilson's missing poisons.

* * *

At last, Hamlyn was able to close the bank for the day. Then, unusually for him, he left with several other clerks and offered to buy them a farewell drink. They were totally surprised and accepted his offer. In truth, he felt the need of company, and he did not relish the thoughts of having to go home on his own. And he had plans for later on that night, which called for something to drink, just to steady his nerves.

Jesse and Isaac Morgan kept to the shadows and watched him go into the *Green Dragon.* It would not have been difficult to have dragged him out of there, but Mr Jersey had wanted them to be discreet, and there was no telling how Mickey Cassidy would react. He did not like the Morgan brothers, or any members of their family, which was a mutual feeling. They decided to wait outside.

It had gone 11 pm, when Hamlyn finally staggered out of the *Green Dragon.* As he stood out in the Market Place, struggling to adapt to the dark, he pulled his coat round himself more tightly, and shivered in the cold night air. He started to cross the Market Place, but then he saw Sam walking his beat, and changed his direction towards the Corn Market. The Morgan brothers followed.

Suddenly Hamlyn caught sight of them, and fearing he was about to be robbed, started running up New Street. As he did so, he put his hand in his coat pocket, and gripped the small crowbar he had there. He had not brought it with him as a weapon, but he would use it as such if he had to. For a moment he thought about calling for help, which would have alerted Sam. But the last thing Hamlyn wanted was any further involvement with the police.

The brothers followed him into New Street, where they grabbed his coat. Terrified beyond belief, Hamlyn screamed and started to struggle. In his panic, he forgot about hitting out with the crowbar. The two men tried to hold him, but Hamlyn's panicking caused his adrenalin to flow and he twisted away, still screaming. But his freedom was short lived as they grabbed him tightly once more.

"What's going on here?" Sam called out, having come to investigate the cause of the screaming.

"Piss off, crusher!" spat Isaac.

"You 'eard, 'im. Piss off!" echoed his brother.

"Let him go!" commanded Sam.

"Piss off or get 'urt!" Jesse hissed at Sam, thrusting his face towards the policeman, and swinging his cudgel towards the policeman's head.

It never landed, as Jesse found his arm blocked: his legs were kicked away from under him and he landed heavily in the road. Isaac released Hamlyn and went to help his brother. Sam sidestepped his charge and tripped the man, who also fell heavily onto the road. Jesse was quickly on his feet again, and swinging his cudgel. But Sam now had his own staff out.

Ducking under the cudgel, he rammed his staff, bayonet fashion, into Jesse's stomach. The man grunted and doubled up, gasping for breath. Sam punched him hard on the back of his exposed neck, and Jesse sank to the ground, where he stayed.

Isaac carefully got to his feet, and was now much more wary of the young looking policeman. He had heard about this man's fearsome reputation, but still felt he could beat him. For several moments the two men circled each other, before Isaac charged. Sam waited until the last moment, before he stepped to one side.

Letting his staff go, so it swung on its lanyard on his wrist, Sam caught hold of Isaac's coat collar. Then using the man's momentum, he thrust Isaac's head hard against a nearby shop wall. Isaac collapsed without a sound.

Sam went to find the intended victim, but found he had gone. In spite of the dim light, he had little doubt the victim was Bernard Hamlyn, but why was he being attacked? Perhaps it was just coincidence they had picked on him.

But, like his guv'nor, Sam distrusted coincidences.

* * *

The moment the brothers had released him, Hamlyn had sprinted up New Street. On reaching the rear of the *Bradford & Harding* offices, he glanced backwards but saw nobody was behind him. Quickly he pulled the crowbar out of his pocket, and put it by the gate's lock. It did not take him long to lever it open. Moments later he had slipped inside, closed the gate, leaned heavily against it and waited.

His heart was pounding, and not just from the physical exertions. How ironic, one of the crushers had saved him! He chuckled quietly to himself. If he only knew? Then he heard Sam's boots coming up New Street, and he leaned against the gate with all his strength, but nobody tried to open it. Minutes later, he heard Sam returning down New Street.

* * *

As he had expected, Sam found the two attackers had gone. He was fairly certain they were Jesse and Isaac Morgan, but he could not be sure. And without any complaint, there was little point in pursuing them. By rights they should have been arrested for trying to assault him, but Sam knew he had hurt them more, than they had hurt him, and he was prepared to leave matters there. It was doubtful if they would make any complaint against him. All the same, he would let Mathew know what had happened.

* * *

Once Sam's footsteps had died away, Hamlyn waited for several minutes. Only when he was satisfied all was quiet, did he walk up the small path to the back door of the *Bradford & Harding* premises. Tentatively he tried the door handle, but as he expected, it was locked. Taking up his crowbar again,

Hamlyn inserted it between the door and the jamb and levered. At first nothing happened, but on his second attempt, the door opened. He waited for only a few moments, before he went into the premises, and closed the door behind him.

* * *

John had sat for a while, in his office, but his mind was not on his paperwork. Suddenly he sprang out of his chair, picked up his greatcoat, and put it on. Gathering up his kepi, he left the police station and made his way down Mill Street. He really wanted to see Laura. But, it was not to be.

"She's out," Abbie told him gleefully. "She's gone with that new doctor. He's such a nice man," she added maliciously. If she was honest, Abbie thought the doctor was a far better catch for Laura, than a policeman.

John's shoulders slumped and his face fell. Thanking Abbie, he turned and walked, dejectedly, back up the Street. Abbie watched him go. "Good riddance!" she hissed.

For a while John thought about calling on Sarah, but it was late, and she had enough to worry about with Thomas. Anyway, he was not quite sure he wanted to run the risk of meeting Richard, just at this moment. And there was always that possibility. At least, that was what he told himself. With nothing else to do, he returned to the police station. He was there when Sam returned and told him about his encounter in New Street. John made a note and told him not to worry. At about midnight he went to bed.

* * *

Once he was inside the offices, Hamlyn felt his way along to the kitchen, where he knew there were some candles. Minutes later, he had found and lit one, and used it to light his way to the cellar door. It was then he remembered he had not brought anything to dig with, other than the crowbar. Cursing, he went back into the kitchen, where he found a large knife and fork. A further search revealed an old ladle, which he added to his collection. Although not ideal, they were better than nothing.

Entering the cellar, he went to where the loose flagstones were. Having levered one up with his crowbar, he pulled up several more. Once they were out of the way, he began to dig down into the earth underneath, with the carving knife and ladle. Soon he had unearthed the first bag, which now gave him a problem.

He had not really decided whether to take all the money or just some of it. In the end, he decided to take an approximate third of the money. That meant about £1800, which caused another problem. Not having brought a case with him, he did not know how he could he carry it all? It would have to be in the bank's bags, and he just hoped nobody would recognize them. That question made him think about the attack on him earlier.

It could have been arranged by his new partners, but somehow he thought they would have done their own dirty work. The crushers would have taken him officially, and it was a crusher who had rescued him. No, that could only mean Jersey had arranged it. Now he remembered the mirthless smile Jersey had given him at the inquest.

Whilst he suspected Jersey's bully boys would be in no state to take him right now, the man might have some others he could use. If that was so, then going home was no longer a good idea. He had to get out of Warwick fast. One of the new trains left at about 3.0am, and he should be able to make it, and just hope the staff did not pay too much attention to his lack of luggage, or the bags he was carrying.

The first bag he opened contained some coins and a small bag of pearls. Quickly he put the pearls into his pocket and began opening other bags. During the next fifteen minutes, he opened several and tipped out their contents.

Next he counted out approximately £1800, and transferred the money into some of the other bags. Counting money quickly was one of his banking skills, and the whole job did not take him too long to complete. For the most part, the money was made up of sovereigns. There were some banknotes, but as they all had serial numbers and bank names printed on them, he knew they could be traced, so he discarded them.

Soon he had another problem. The pile of sovereigns he was taking, weighed nearly 30lbs, and would need to be carried in the bank's coin bags.

Without wasting any further time, he quickly filled up several bags with the sovereigns, spilling some on the floor as he did so.

When the bags were full, but still able to be carried by their necks, he put the spilled coins into his coat pocket. Conscious of the time, he decided to call it a day. Scooping up the bags and the candle, he climbed back upstairs. On arriving in the hallway, he blew out his candle.

As the light went out, Hamlyn suddenly felt something cold and hard press against the back of his neck.

"Well! Well! Well!" The voice was ominously familiar. "And just what have you been up to?"

* * *

When Hamlyn had been drinking in the *Green Dragon*, earlier that evening, he had forgotten it was where Bradford and Harding were staying. They had come back to the inn, and been intrigued to see their unwilling partner sitting there. Moving to a more secluded part of the tap room, they had watched him. After his colleagues had all gone, Hamlyn had sat on his own for a while, and his watchers had noted how little he actually drank. It seemed to them he was waiting for something or someone.

When he finally left, they started to follow him, but saw the Morgan brothers going first, clearly with him as their target. They had noticed the men standing around outside the inn earlier. From the way the brothers quickly followed Hamlyn, it was obvious they had been waiting for him. Intrigued, they followed to see what happened, and were just in time to see Hamlyn attacked.

Whilst they remained undecided whether or not to intervene, Sam had come to the rescue, and they had made themselves scarce, and waited until he had gone. But, by then, Hamlyn was nowhere in sight.

Clearly Hamlyn had upset somebody. Could it have been an upset client from the bank? If not, who else could it have been? A little chat with Hamlyn was now necessary. Knowing where he lived, down the Saltisford, by the canal basin, they went to see him there. However, there was no sign of him.

"Perhaps he's gone with a woman?" suggested Harding.

"I doubt it. But he's up to something. We'll wait a while."

When Hamlyn did not appear, they lost interest, and growing cold, they decided to return to the *Green Dragon.*

"Giles," said Harding suddenly. "I've just had a thought. You don't think he could have gone to the office, do you? I mean, why else was he walking up New Street."

"You could be right. We'll go there now."

When they arrived at the rear of their offices, it did not take them long to find the back gate forced open. "You little bastard!" hissed Bradford, as he led the way up the path. They soon found the back door forced open. Both men drew their revolvers, and quietly entered the hallway. Sounds coming from the cellar steps confirmed their worst thoughts, as a heavily laden Hamlyn came into the hall and blew out his candle.

It was at that moment when Bradford pushed the muzzle of his revolver into Hamlyn's neck. "Well! Well! Well! And just what have you been up to?"

Hamlyn moved so suddenly he caught both of them off guard. Swinging round with a handful of several money bags, he knocked Bradford's revolver away. He lost two of the bags in the process, but they hit Harding in the face. Pushing by them, Hamlyn threw open the door, and ran into the small yard. Moments later, he was through the gate, and into New Street, where he ran into the Old Square. Crossing by St Mary's church, he went into the churchyard. For the moment, at least, he was safe.

Harding followed him into the churchyard, but quickly lost sight of him, as he disappeared into the dark.

"Bernard! Bernard!" he called. "We didn't know it was you. We can talk this through."

Hamlyn kept quiet, hoping if he waited long enough, Harding would pass by him, and he could escape back out into Northgate Street. And he still had most of the money. He assumed Bradford had gone down Church Street and was working his way through the churchyard from there.

Ever so quietly he took some of the guineas from one of the bags and put them in his pocket. He reasoned they would only be interested in the money, and that was their weakness. If he threw some of it away, where they could find it, he should get the chance to escape with the rest. In the dark, he failed to notice some coins fall out of one of the bags.

At last Harding went by still calling his name. Crouching and moving from gravestone to gravestone, Hamlyn made his way back into Northgate Street. Feeling more confident, he stood upright and started walking towards Church Street. With luck both men should be somewhere in the churchyard.

Suddenly Bradford appeared from behind one of the arches of St Mary's tower, with his revolver pointed at Hamlyn. "You didn't think we were that stupid, did you? Put the bags down!"

Thinking his plan was working, Hamlyn laughed and went to throw the bags back towards Northgate Street. He was still laughing when Bradford shot him twice in the chest. Hamlyn was thrown backwards by the shots, and slumped to the ground.

Almost at once a window was thrown open. It was soon followed by others.

"Who's that?"

"What's happening?" came various shouts.

Bradford ignored them and bent to pick up the bags. But then he hesitated as he heard running footsteps. Quickly he slipped behind one the church arches again, as Sam ran up to the scene.

Seeing Hamlyn lying on the ground, bleeding, Sam quickly assessed the situation as being serious. After waving his rattle, to sound the alarm, he knelt beside the dying man, and immediately recognized him. Clearly Hamlyn was trying to say something, and Sam leaned closer.

Bradford saw what was happening and he could not afford to run the risk of Hamlyn telling the crusher what had happened. The crusher would have to be killed.

Carefully he aimed his revolver at Sam and began to squeeze the trigger.

CHAPTER FOURTEEN

Early on Friday Morning

A hand reached out and pulled Bradford's revolver down. He turned sharply, ready to fight, but relaxed when he saw Harding standing there. Harding shook his head and pointed up Old Square and Northgate Street. The area was full of people. "You'd never get away with it."

"But he might have told that crusher something."

"I doubt it, but it's a chance we'll have take. He wasn't there long enough. And if you shoot the crusher now, we'll both hang. Let's go."

"What about the money?" Bradford pointed to the bags, and the sovereigns which had fallen out of them.

"We'll have to leave it. If we go and claim it as ours, how are we going to explain it's all in *Jersey's Bank* bags?"

"We tell the truth. We were robbed."

"Then how do we explain the cellar floor being dug up? And how do we explain all the other bags? And why should Hamlyn have robbed us, just after the bank was done? Your greed will ruin everything."

Bradford said no more, but he allowed himself to be led away by Harding. He cast a last, longing look at the money lying beside Hamlyn's body.

It was all going very, very wrong.

* * *

Sam never knew just how close he had been to death that night. As it happened, Hamlyn had not been able to say anything clearly before he died. Now Sam was back in charge. Firstly he sent for a doctor and his

146

superintendent. Before he had finished giving his instructions, Mathew had arrived on the scene. Someone else appeared with a horse blanket, which he draped over the dead man. Sam saw the money and bags lying nearby, for the first time.

Picking up one of the bags, he was not surprised to find the *Jersey's Bank* logo on it. The big question was what was Hamlyn doing with them? Had he been on bank business? That seemed most unlikely at this hour of the morning.

John arrived next and was also very intrigued about the bank's money bags, and he began to wonder about their real origin. Out of habit, he searched Hamlyn's pockets, where he found the pearls and some other gems. Mathew and Sam watched him. When the pearls were found, all three men looked at each other.

"I think," said John. "These are some of the items stolen from the bank."

"Does that mean our late friend here, was involved in the robbery?" queried Mathew, nodding towards Hamlyn's body.

"It looks like it. But, if Caleb is right, and there's no reason to doubt it, then the bank's next-door neighbours are also involved."

"But, guv'nor, if that's so, and we think they're involved in Billy Beech's murder, could they be responsible for this one as well?" asked Sam.

"It looks like it, but let's keep an open mind for a little while longer. Ah, here's Doctor Gilson."

Richard arrived. "Morning gentlemen."

"Morning doctor."

They each acknowledged him, although Sam was interested to notice how John's greeting did not seem quite so cordial. Perhaps he already knew about Laura?

"We're fairly certain it's Bernard Hamlyn, late of Jersey's Bank," said John, as he pulled back the horse blanket and uncovered the body. "It looks like he's been shot: possibly twice, if what people are telling us is true, about hearing two shots."

"I certainly heard two," confirmed Sam.

"I remember him now. Wasn't he present when Albert Quinn was found?" Richard looked at John, who nodded in reply.

He too had noticed the sudden coldness between them, and assumed it was all to do with Laura. Not that it mattered very much to him. Laura did not really figure in his long term plans. Once she had been conquered, he would leave her to Mayfield, should he still want her. If he didn't want any soiled goods, then that was too bad. It would not be his problem.

Richard knelt beside Hamlyn's body, and peeled back the man's bloodstained coat and his shirt. "Can you bring your lantern a bit nearer?" he asked Mathew. "Ah yes," he continued, as the lantern shone onto Hamlyn's chest. "You're quite right. He was shot twice, either of which would have killed him. I'll have a closer look at him in daylight. This is a dangerous town, isn't it?" They all chuckled, and he pulled Hamlyn's shirt and coat back around his body.

Meanwhile, John had produced a stick of chalk, and he drew round the outline of Hamlyn's body. When he had finished, John stood up and looked down towards Church Street, which appeared to be the direction from where the murderer had fired. He knew it was too far away for an accurate shot from a revolver. Whilst it was possible the murderer had used a rifle, he thought it was most unlikely. Therefore, he reasoned, Hamlyn's killer must have been much nearer: almost certainly underneath St Mary's tower.

So, he mused, had Hamlyn known his murderer, or was it a random robbery, which had gone wrong? Had it not been for the earlier attack on him, that Sam had foiled, then John could have believed it was a robbery. But, it was too coincidental, and his murder now made such a theory unlikely to be true.

"Sam, where were you when you heard the shots?" It was the first time John had called him by his shortened name, and Sam preferred it.

"Almost at the bottom end of New Street, I'd just come from the Old Square and was going towards the station."

"Had you seen anybody by the church?"

"No, guv'nor. If I had, I'd have wanted to know who they were, and what they were doing."

"Sure."

Some men now arrived to take Hamlyn's body to Thomas's laboratory. They lifted him onto a makeshift stretcher of planks, covered him with a blanket, and went to put it onto the back of a cart. As they did so, the body's right leg slipped over the edge.

"Just a minute," called Mathew, and he put the leg back under the blanket. In doing so, he saw Hamlyn's shoe was covered in mud and grass. Quickly he looked at the other shoe and found it in a similar state. "Guv'nor," he called. "Look at this. I think our friend has come from the churchyard."

"What was he doing in there at this hour? After all he lives in the Saltisford," queried Sam.

"Being paid for his part in the robbery?" suggested Mathew.

"Then why kill him?" continued Sam.

They looked at John.

"I wonder," he said after a moment. "What if he had just robbed his fellow thieves?" John paused. "Just say for a moment: the men who attacked him earlier, were not opportunist thieves, but had been specifically tasked with the attack. Then when their first attack failed, they waited for him."

"Who employed them?" asked Sam.

"Forget that for a minute," continued John. "I've made it quite clear that I didn't believe Hamlyn's story about Quinn's death. Neither does the coroner, and our Mr Hamlyn was a very frightened man. He knew I was going to be interviewing him very soon. So, who else has he upset?"

"Albert Quinn, possibly by having found out about his gambling problems and embezzlement," suggested Mathew.

"Yes," replied John. "But Quinn has no known friends or family: and he's dead."

"What about Quinn's creditors? Believing Hamlyn was responsible for them not getting their money?" suggested Sam.

"Possibly, but it seems unlikely, unless they were putting pressure on Hamlyn to repay Quinn's debts. Say they knew he was responsible for Quinn's death. Would that make him rob the bank just to pay them off?" queried Mathew.

"It's a possibility," agreed John.

"Say they suspected Hamlyn had killed Quinn: Might they have threatened to expose him to a murder charge?" suggested Sam. "That would almost certainly mean a hanging. Robbing a bank might be the less dangerous way out of his problems?"

"Good thinking Sam. But somehow Bradford and Harding are involved with that robbery, and almost certainly with the death of the late Billy Beech. Although just how much they were involved is unclear."

Everyone nodded in agreement with John's observation.

"What about Henry Jersey?" Sam asked. "Nobody seems to like him, and wasn't there some suggestion made about our friend here," he pointed to Hamlyn's chalked body outline. "Expecting to become the new manager, only to find Jersey has given the job to his nephew?"

"And Hamlyn was due to finish at the bank tomorrow," added Mathew. "With no prospects: nobody round here would employ him, certainly not so soon after the robbery, which has not yet been cleared."

"Let's assume for a moment, that Hamlyn was involved in the robbery, but he had to have help, say with the next-door neighbours," John took up the argument again. "Only now, with all the pressure on him, he wants his share to get out."

"But the others, possibly Bradford and Harding, won't agree." Sam paused.

"Go on," prompted John. He liked to develop his officers' powers of logic and deduction, and he always encouraged them to do so.

"So, he didn't wait, but took his share now," Sam continued.

"And they found out about it and killed him," added Mathew. "But by shooting him, and disturbing the local residents, they did not have time to get their money back."

"Quite possibly," said John. "In fact I am sure that is almost certainly what happened. But if that was so, did they act on their own, or did they employ those two coves tonight to do it for them? I think we shall have to go and find the Morgan brothers, and bring them in now for questioning."

"Our pleasure, guv'nor: but we need to go in mob handed," cautioned Mathew. "There are four brothers all told. Then there's Ma and Pa Morgan. He's a former prizefighter and was very good in his day. Ma Morgan's even harder, if that's possible. We need to hit them first and ask questions later. If we give them too much time, we'll have a real hard scrap on our hands. And we'll have to get all of the men in on this. We'll need them!" stressed Mathew.

"But let us not forget Bradford and Harding," cautioned John. "We need their premises watching. Sam, you take the rear and I'll take the front. Mathew, go and get Caleb and Ben out of bed to take over from us. After that, can you make one of your special arrangements for watching the premises, when it gets light? I'll pay them, not you."

John eyed Mathew intently, knowing full well he would have his two sons do the job. They were both keen to follow their father, and become policemen. From to time to time, Mathew used them for watching people and premises. But they could only do it when Margaret was not around.

"Willingly, guv'nor," grinned Mathew.

"And warn Robert he will have to be on duty earlier than he expected."

* * *

Dawn was just breaking when John, and his officers, neared the area of town known as the Pigwells, where the Morgan family lived. Robert drove a carriage, and the others all crowded on board. Sam carried two sets of manacles. Acting on John's instructions, they had all left their uniform coats and hats back at the station. They stopped just before they arrived at the Pigwells.

"Remember," instructed John. "We only want Jesse and Isaac, and nobody else. If Sam's right, and I've no reason to doubt him, they will be rather bruised and battered. That should make them easy to recognize." A quiet nervous chuckle greeted his remarks. Sam's fighting ability was well known. "Once we've got them, we get out quickly. Good luck!"

John drew his staff and the others followed his example, except for Mathew, who carried a large, two-handed heavy hammer. Robert remained behind with the horse and carriage which he turned round, so that it faced back towards town, ready for a quick exit.

The policemen crept quietly, down the Pigwells, to where the Morgan family lived. Following their earlier briefing, Caleb and Ben went to the rear of the building, in case the brothers tried to escape that way. Mathew waited until they were out of sight. Having counted to ten to give them time to get into position, he looked at John, who nodded.

Mathew swung the hammer with all his might, and smashed the lock. The door flew open with a loud crash, and the three of them charged into the singled storied hovel, which served as a home for the Morgan family.

* * *

When Jesse and Isaac had arrived back home, after their encounter with Sam, the family had expected an immediate visit from the police. Consequently, they had prepared for battle, whilst Ma Morgan treated her sons' injuries. After a while, when the raid did not happen, they began to relax, firmly believing they had not been recognized. Ma Morgan was not so sure. She had insisted that Luke, her youngest son, spent the night on a stool leaning against the front door, keeping watch just to be on the safe side.

Although he was only fifteen, Luke was quite capable of wielding a cudgel, and he had been most disappointed when the police did not arrive. Luke had wanted to be in a fight with them, and he had already rehearsed the tale he would tell his mates. He would have sent the crushers packing single-handed.

After struggling to keep awake and dozing fitfully, he had finally fallen deeply asleep, only to be woken by Mathew shattering the door. He had barely woken, before he was hurled from his stool, and slammed hard against the wall, by the violently opened door. Luke's head hit the wall hard, and he took no further part in the fight.

His brother Jethro, aged nineteen, was the first to react, only because he happened to be awake. By the time the door was flung open, he was already on his feet, wielding a cudgel.

His first strike only caught Mathew a glancing blow on the shoulder, as he had seen it just in time. Mathew dropped the hammer and drew his own staff. Before Jethro could strike again, Mathew caught his arm. But, their wrestling slowed down John and Sam's advance, giving Ma and Pa Morgan time to wake up.

Sam went for Ma Morgan, who was coming towards him with a meat cleaver in her hand. Clearly she meant business. He dodged her first swing and put out his staff, partly to distract her and deflect the cleaver. Her second swing, with the cleaver, sliced his staff into two pieces, but now he was closer to the woman.

He hit her hard, in her quite substantial stomach, but she merely grunted and charged at Sam again. This time, she had the cleaver over her head, and brought it down with all her strength towards Sam's unprotected head.

Sam waited for the last second before moving to one side. It was a gamble, but it paid dividends. Ma Morgan had used so much force, that the cleaver missed Sam's head and embedded itself in the wall, where it stuck fast. Whilst she struggled to release it, he kicked her hard on her right kneecap, and was gratified to hear her cry in pain. Releasing the cleaver, she bent down to hold her knee, and exposed the back of her thick neck.

Luckily for Sam, her hair was thinning and gave her neck no protection. Clasping his fists together, he brought them down hard on her neck. Ma Morgan fell to the floor and stayed there.

Meanwhile Pa Morgan had punched John hard on the side of his head, and knocked him to the floor. With a gloat of triumph, he brought his right foot back, intending to kick John's head.

Freed from Ma Morgan, Sam caught the swinging foot and pulled it backwards, knocking the other man off balance. Pa Morgan reacted surprisingly quickly and he hopped away, freeing his foot. In one movement, he turned and charged at Sam, with his huge arms spread wide. In his hurry, he failed to see John thrust his foot out, and he stumbled over it.

For such a big man, Pa Morgan's reactions were very quick. Clearly the skills he had acquired, over the years as a prizefighter, still remained with him, and he soon regained his balance. Then he was at Sam, and wrapped his huge arms tightly round the slimly built policeman.

Sam was aware of John hitting the other man with his staff, but the grip only tightened. In desperation, Sam raked the metal plate, on his boot's heel, down Pa Morgan's shin and onto his instep. He felt the grip slacken a little, and he raked the man's shin again and again. Then John managed to get his knuckles just under Pa Morgan's ears, and pressed hard into the points of his jaw. The pain was excruciating. Pa Morgan roared, released Sam, and went for John's hands. However, anticipating such a move, John had removed them.

Mad with pain, Pa Morgan turned on him, but he was too late. As he turned, John raised his staff, and aimed for the man's head. But at the last moment, he kicked Pa Morgan in the testicles. He sank to his knees and Sam brought his fists down onto the back of his neck.

Pa Morgan joined his wife and Luke on the floor.

John and Sam then turned their attention to Jethro Morgan, and were just in time to see him floored, by a tremendous punch from Mathew. For a moment the three officers stood panting, but then they heard noises coming from the rear yard.

* * *

Awoken by the fight in the other room, Jesse and Isaac quickly realized it was the police. They climbed out of the window, into the yard, only to find Ben and Caleb waiting for them. Neither brother had picked up a cudgel before they left their room. It had not occurred to them there might be more constables waiting in the yard. Still hurting from their earlier encounter with Sam, neither brother was in a state to put up much resistance.

But they were still fighting when the back door opened. Hoping to see the rest of the family coming to their rescue, they were dismayed to see more police. When they recognized Sam, the fight went out of them, and they surrendered.

"Quickly," instructed John. "Get the manacles on them and let's get out of here."

"**ROBERT!**" shouted Mathew and blew a whistle. It was the prearranged signal for Robert to be ready to get them away.

Already a hostile crowd had started to gather around the house, having heard the fracas. With their prisoners in the middle, John and his men formed an escort round them, and they all ran to where Robert waited.

They were just in time, as the crowd had become increasingly hostile and started throwing stones at them. The prisoners were unceremoniously bundled into the carriage, and the policemen followed, or else hung on as best as they could. Moving off at a fast trot, the carriage quickly outdistanced the pursuers.

Only when they were all safely back in the police station, and the prisoners locked up, did their adrenalin stop, and reaction set in. Minutes later, they all sat drinking hot sweet tea, whilst John praised them and insisted they all be looked at by Dr Gilson, whom he had sent a boy to fetch.

"Sam," John added. "I owe you a big thank you for getting Pa Morgan off me."

"No, guv'nor. I should be thanking you. He's the hardest bastard I've ever fought. And as for Ma Morgan? If she's a sample of what women can turn into, I think I'll leave the police and go into a monastery. It'll be a damn sight safer."

"Are you going to tell Lucy that?" said Mathew, trying to keep a straight face, but failing miserably.

They all laughed, and it helped to relieve the tension.

* * *

When the crowd began to gather around Hamlyn's body, Bradford and Harding slipped quietly away. Bradford now appreciated his partner's wisdom, in recommending he did not shoot Sam. Had he done so, there was little doubt he, or both of them, would soon have been under arrest.

They slowly walked into New Street, trying to be inconspicuous, and not drawing attention to themselves. Moments later they passed through the rear gate, and went into their premises. After wedging the rear door shut, and putting a stool up against it, Bradford went into the kitchen and came back with two saucepan lids. He put them on the stool, close to its edge. Anybody trying to force open the door would knock them off. It was a temporary but effective alarm. Once he was satisfied, he followed his partner into the cellar.

They saw how Hamlyn had clearly done a thorough job, and there were bags and banknotes strewn all over the flagstones, intermingled with soil. The whole lot would have to be filled up again.

"Wouldn't it make more sense, to cut our losses and get out now, while we can?" suggested Harding.

"You're probably right, but if we leave it till tomorrow, we'll have the week-end in which to vanish. And don't forget, I've three good customers coming in today. Their money will be a nice extra bonus, and make up for some of what Hamlyn took. At the moment we're not suspected, but if we run now, we soon will be."

"We can't go on like this. Mayfield's no fool. I've heard a lot about him, and he's got quite a reputation. As I've told you before, just watch out your greed doesn't ruin everything."

"Mayfield's not a problem. He's going to have his hands full, investigating Hamlyn's death as well as this.....what's his name? Beech?"

"It won't be long before he makes the connection between us and the bank: that is if he hasn't done so already," warned Harding.

"But you've forgotten one or two important things. Firstly: he will find Jersey's money either on or near Hamlyn. There were enough money bags lying in the street. With luck, that'll put him right off the track for a while. Then, why was Hamlyn killed outside the church? The crushers will think it was a robbery gone wrong." He paused. "Plus the fact, he already has two suspects, doesn't he?"

"Us?"

"No. What about the two men who attacked Hamlyn out the back here? You know: the ones the crusher floored?"

Harding smiled and visibly relaxed. "Of course." He became serious again. "I still think we should divide the loot into two, so we're ready to go as soon as we can tomorrow."

"A good idea. You go and make a start while I go and get some more candles. And how about some tea?"

"A brandy would be better." Harding held his hands up in mock surrender. "No, I know you're always right: no alcohol until the job's been done."

Harding took his coat off and began to lever up some more flagstones. He was so engrossed in his work, he never heard Bradford return quietly into the cellar. It was more of a sixth sense which alerted him to the presence of the other man. "That was quick. Did you make the tea?" he asked, as he continued digging.

"No, but I've got something else for you."

"What's that?" Harding began to stand up and looked towards his partner over his left shoulder. Too late, he saw the long knife in Bradford's left hand.

"Sorry Giles," was all Bradford said as he stabbed his partner.

The knife entered Harding in the left side of his back. There was a momentary hitch when it struck a rib, before it entered his heart, and the blood-stained tip protruded from his chest. Death was instantaneous. Bradford let go of the knife and watched his former partner fall forward onto the pile of earth he had just dug.

Harding had not even had time to cry out, before he died. And Bradford knew there was little or no chance he had been heard. Stooping over him, he gave the knife a slight twist, and pulled it out of the body, gazing dispassionately at his dead partner.

Suddenly he had an idea, and already a possible defence was occurring to him, in the unlikely event he might be charged with Harding's murder. Rolling Harding's body over onto its back, he took hold of the knife again, and carefully studied both the entry and exit wounds in the body.

He spent some time, checking out the angle until he was satisfied he had it right. Then, he put the knife's point into the exit wound and pushed it back into the body. This time it passed straight through his ribs, and exited from Harding's back. He reasoned, if the body was found it would look as if the man had been stabbed from the front, and not the back. In the event of his being questioned, he had already prepared an answer, as to what had happened.

Meanwhile, he now had plenty of work to do.

For a moment he thought about taking the money and going, until he remembered the three clients due to see him today: and they were going to part with hefty sums of money. They were just too good to miss. In fact, they would be the icing on the cake. He picked up the spade, and whistling tunelessly, began to dig.

Just to be on the safe side, he decided to rebury all the bags, and their contents. When he had finished, Bradford started to dig another hole for

Harding's body. It took him much longer than he had first anticipated. However, after he had buried his partner, Bradford discovered another problem. He had a considerable amount of soil left over.

As there was no soil in the rear yard, he could not put it there. After a few moments he came up with a solution. Gathering up the soil he made several trips to the privy. Here he tipped the earth down into it. No doubt it would cause some problems, but by then he would be well away.

* * *

When Richard arrived at the police station, he could not help smiling at the sorry state of John's men. They were all bruised, and John's face looked well battered, complete with a black eye. Mathew and Sam were not looking much better.

"What a sorry looking lot," he laughed. "What was it? An argument over who made the tea?"

"Just get on with it!" snapped John. "It's not a laughing matter, and I don't have time for fun and games. If it's beyond you, I'll find another doctor."

"A word, Mayfield! Please! Now! In your office!"

John led the way into his office, leaving a stunned group of men behind. "Yes, what is it?"

"I assume this sudden hostility is about my seeing Miss Grant?"

"You don't deny you're seeing her?"

"No, of course I don't. I could say it's none of your business, but since the matter has arisen: yes, I am seeing her. Perhaps, just perhaps, if you'd made more of an effort, then she would have refused my first invitation. But, I doubt you can even remember when you last saw her, eh?"

The barb struck home. "It's been rather busy of late," John replied lamely.

"Do you think you're the only one who's busy, right now? I am on my own, and having to learn about new patients. As you know, Dr Waldren is in no condition to discuss cases with me." He paused. "Yet I drop what I'm doing to help you investigate, what is it ...two murders and an unexplained death, all within a few days. And," Richard stressed. "I dropped everything just now to come and look at you and your men. But, in spite of my work demands, I still find time to visit Miss Grant. If I can do it, then so could you."

John said nothing, but he felt his ears redden. He knew all Richard had said was absolutely true.

"You must realize, and now I'm talking to you as a doctor, and I still hope as a colleague, if not a friend, but Harriet has gone." He continued relentlessly. "She can't come back, John. Stop living in the past and stop blaming yourself for her death. What is done is done."

Richard waited for John to absorb his words.

"I appreciate she meant a lot to you, but you've lost her," he continued. "But, you haven't lost Laura yet, but you might. It's up to you. Remember: all's fair in love and war."

"My apologies, Richard. That was very churlish of me and my remark about your ability was uncalled for. Please accept my apologies. Can we forget what I said just now?"

"Of course."

They shook hands.

Any further conversation was stopped by Mathew knocking on the office door, and entering without waiting to be invited.

"Guv'nor. We may have a problem. Pa Morgan is here and wants to see you?"

CHAPTER FIFTEEN

Later on Friday

Leaving Richard to check over his men, John went to the front counter where Pa Morgan waited. Acting on instructions, Mathew and Sam waited just out of sight, but within hearing.

"Ah, Mr Mayfield," started Pa Morgan, but then he burst out laughing at the sight of John's battered face. "Your face gladdens me 'eart. But, it were a damned good fight, weren't it? I must say you lot fight hard, not exactly cleanly, but then neither do I. And it took a lot of guts to come and raid our home like you did." He continued laughing.

John found himself warming to the man, and he began to relax. "What can I do for you, Mr Morgan?"

"I want to know what me lads 'ave done? Surely you didn't come down, just like that, for the run in they 'ad with Mr Perkins?"

"You're quite right. At the moment, they're in here on suspicion of committing murder."

"Murder? You got to be joking?" Pa Morgan looked visibly shocked.

"Sadly no. I'm not."

"But we ain't a murdering family. Hard? Yes: Felons? Yes....but not murderers!"

"That wasn't exactly the case with your good wife, and her meat cleaver, was it?" said Sam, who had now joined John behind the counter.

"That were naughty of her and we're both glad, she missed."

"Not half as glad as I am."

"How are the ribs, lad?"

"How are your balls?"

160

They all laughed and the remaining tension dissipated.

"Seriously. 'Ave you really got 'em in for suspected murder?" Pa Morgan sounded surprised and concerned. He was either genuine, thought John, or else a very good liar. In spite of himself, he believed the man, when he denied they were a murdering family.

"I'm afraid so," confirmed John.

"'Oo are they supposed to 'ave killed?"

"The man they attacked last night, before Constable Perkins here rescued him. Bernard Hamlyn from *Jersey's Bank*. He was found dead later."

"What do me lads say? They came straight home after their scrap with Mr Perkins. They weren't really in much of a state to go out again."

"They're saying nothing, at the moment. That's the problem."

"'Ow long are you going to keep 'em here?"

"That very much depends on them. We need to know why they attacked Mr Hamlyn?"

"I suspect they were paid to do it. You say the dead man worked for that old bastard Jersey?"

John nodded.

"They do little jobs like that for 'im. Look: let me speak to 'em. In front of you, if you like."

"What do you think?" John asked Mathew, who had now joined them.

"We've nothing to lose."

"I agree," added Sam. "I'll go and get them."

"Bring them into my office," instructed John.

Minutes later, he brought a sorry looking Jesse and Isaac Morgan into John's office. They were surprised to see how their father seemed to be on very good terms, with the two crushers who had laid him out, only a few hours ago: but that was their Pa. Totally unsure, they looked at each other in bewilderment. John looked at Pa Morgan and nodded.

"Listen lads," Pa Morgan said, seriously. "The crushers 'ave got you in 'ere for murder."

"What?" they asked together. "We never killed no one. 'Oo are we supposed to 'ave killed?"

"The man you attacked last night in New Street," said Sam. "The one I rescued from you. He was murdered later."

"Pa!" pleaded Jesse. "We never killed 'im. 'E ran off when the crusher arrived. Didn't 'e?" His question was addressed to Sam, who nodded in agreement. "Anyway, we don't do murder: you know that Pa!"

"The policemen 'ere want to know why you attacked 'im?"

The brothers looked at each other, and Isaac licked his lips. "We ain't saying nothing," he said.

Pa Morgan stood up. "Very well, you'll go to the Assizes and swing for 'is murder."

"But we didn't go out again. You can vouch for us," whined Jesse.

"And what jury will believe us? I'm sorry lads: I can't help you any more." Pa Morgan turned to go.

"If we tell 'em what 'appened, what'll 'appen to us, Pa?" asked Isaac.

Pa Morgan stopped. Slowly he turned to face his sons. "That'll depend on what you say, won't it?" He looked at John, who nodded.

"We was paid to take 'im somewhere so 'e could be asked a few questions," said Jesse.

"Who paid you?" asked John.

"Mr Jersey. You know: 'im from the bank."

"Thank you: and where were you going to take him?"

"There's an empty building on 'is land," added Isaac. "'E was going to meet us there when we'd got 'im."

"How long would he wait?" John asked, as he had an idea.

"'E'd stay at home until we sent a message to 'im," continued Jesse.

"Now, lads, do you want to earn your freedom?" asked John.

They nodded, and John outlined his plan. They listened, but were obviously unhappy about what John was proposing. When he finished, they both shook their heads.

"Then it's back to the cells for you both. I'll have you charged with the attempted abduction of Bernard Hamlyn. You'll go to the Assizes and can look forward to going to Australia. Then we'll charge your ma with the attempted murder of Constable Perkins. With luck, provided we say a few words on her behalf, she'll go to Australia with you. It's up to you. Lock them up Sam!"

"'Ang on a minute!" pleaded Isaac.

Sam looked at John, who nodded.

"Pa, what do we do?"

"Do as the man says."

"We'll do it."

Whilst John put the rest of his plan together, he had the two Morgan brothers and their father treated by Richard. When he had finished, Richard looked at Sam with a new found respect. He would not relish the prospect of ever having to cross him. The officer's baby-faced looks and slender body totally belied his strength and fighting ability.

Back at the front counter, Pa Morgan stopped, as he went to leave. "When can I have me lads back?"

"By late afternoon hopefully," replied John.

"Look Mr Mayfield, you and me will always be on opposite sides. That's the way we are. I dare say some of us will fight again. But, I want you to know one thing. You're a hard man and so are your men. That's the nature of life. I've never been beaten before, although it took two of you to do it." He paused and grinned. "Seriously though: We don't bear grudges. It were a good fight and we'll all talk about it for years to come. The better side won, this time. But it might be different next time." He held out his right hand.

John took it willingly. "Thank you. Good luck to you and your family. I'll let the lads go just as soon as they have helped me in this little job."

* * *

Henry Jersey was growing more and more impatient, as he waited to hear from the Morgan brothers. Even allowing for Hamlyn being difficult, he could have stood no chance against the brothers. Hopefully nothing had gone wrong: but if it had, it could not be traced back to him. After another sleepless night, he had arisen early and was waiting for his breakfast to be served. His thoughts were interrupted by the arrival of a footman.

"Excuse me, sir," he announced respectfully. "But there's a man to see you." The footman struggled to keep his composure. His master's visitor had not impressed him. "He says it's about the job last night. I've instructed him to wait in the kitchen."

"About time too," snapped Jersey, as he stormed out into the kitchen. "Where the hell have you been....?" His voice tailed off as he saw Isaac Morgan's bruised face. "Did...did he do that?" Jersey asked incredulously.

"No, sir," grimaced Isaac. It hurt him to speak. "That were a private matter, later this morning."

"Have you..?"

Isaac nodded. "'E's where you wanted 'im, all neatly trussed up, waiting for you. Me bruvver's with 'im and e's got a sack over 'is 'ead, like we agreed."

Both men left the kitchen and made their way to the isolated building. Jersey rode on horseback, while Isaac hurried alongside him. At the old cottage Jersey was gratified to find Jesse standing guard over the figure of a slightly built man, lying tied up, on the floor, and with a sack over his head. Jersey saw the front of the man's trousers were wet and he pointed at them.

"'E's pissed 'imself," answered Jesse to the unspoken question.

"You dirty little bastard," sneered Jersey and gave the prisoner a kick in his chest area. He was gratified to hear the prisoner grunt. "Lift him up!"

Moments later the brothers had pulled the captive to his feet. Jersey grabbed the man's coat lapels. "Now, listen to me, Hamlyn," he hissed. "I need to know exactly just what is going on. That's why I've had you brought here. Do you understand?"

The prisoner nodded.

"And you're going to tell me, aren't you?"

The prisoner nodded again.

"Listen to me carefully, before you answer. You'll only get one chance. If you tell me the truth, and I get my money back, then you can go free. I want to find this money before that stupid crusher Mayfield does. Now, did you take my money?"

The prisoner made no reply.

"Refresh his memory!" instructed Jersey.

But neither brother moved.

"Hit him!"

Almost reluctantly, Isaac gave the prisoner a half-hearted punch. Jersey was not impressed. "This is how you refresh his memory," he snapped and punched the captive hard. Once more he was gratified to hear a muffled grunt of pain. "Now Hamlyn, let's try again. I've had you brought here to answer my questions. Do you understand?"

The figure grunted and nodded its head.

"Whether or not you live is my decision. Do you understand?"

The figure nodded again.

"So, for the very last time: what have you done with my money? Where is it?" He looked at the brothers. "Give him some encouragement to answer my questions."

But neither brother moved, which was most unlike them. Normally they needed little or no persuasion to use violence on someone. It seemed to Jersey that their behaviour was all wrong. There was something not right about this little meeting. He refused to believe the brothers had changed their attitudes towards his prisoner.

All of a sudden, he realized whoever their prisoner was, it was not Bernard Hamlyn.

"Take his hood off!" he instructed.

Jesse removed the hood and Jersey was aghast to find John Mayfield's bruised face looking at him. "My dear chap," he blustered. "I'm afraid there's been a terrible mistake. They weren't meant to......"

"What weren't they meant to do, Mr Jersey?"

The banker turned to flee, but he ran straight into the arms of Mathew Harrison. Frantically he turned, only to find Sam standing in front of him. Jersey's face went a deathly white, and he was vaguely aware of John being released and rubbing his shoulder, where he had been kicked.

Quickly Sam slipped a pair of manacles on Jersey's wrists, whilst Mathew whistled shrilly for Robert Andrew to bring up the carriage. It was a solemn group which made its way back to the police station, with a particularly subdued Henry Jersey.

Back at the station, Robert and Sam began to take written statements from the Morgan brothers, whilst John and Mathew interviewed Jersey. The interview seemed almost friendly, as all three men sat with mugs of tea to hand. Jersey felt his confidence growing, but not for long.

"Let me start, Mr Jersey," announced John. "You have been arrested, on suspicion of having had Bernard Hamlyn murdered, some time during the night." He was gratified to see the other man nearly fall off his chair in shock.

"**NO! NO! NO!**" Jersey shouted. "What do you mean murdered? If he's dead, then its nothing to do with me! That's not what I wanted. Please, you must believe me!"

"Then, perhaps you might care to tell us exactly what it was that you wanted, and planned with the Morgans? Remember, we have their stories, so I hope, for your sake, they agree with your version of what happened: don't you sergeant?"

"Indeed, I do sir. Indeed I do."

Tears had formed in Jersey's eyes, and they were now flowing freely down his cheeks. In a few sobbing breaths, he confirmed what the Morgan brothers had said. Unasked, he told John and Mathew about searching Quinn's house, and finding nothing. The more he spoke, the more the tears flowed.

By the time he had finished, his nose was running, and Henry Jersey was a gibbering wreck. Nobody who knew the prosperous banker would have recognised Henry Jersey in his current state.

"Thank you, Mr Jersey," said John, when he had finished. "We do believe you, but had to make absolutely sure. You see, someone did murder Bernard Hamlyn last night, and the Morgan brothers were seen attacking him. We had quite a scrap bringing them in this morning, hence all their bruises and ours. However, I am fairly convinced that whilst you and they tried to abduct him, none of you killed him."

Henry Jersey gave tremendous sigh of relief, and stood up. "Then I'm free to go?"

"Not just yet. There's remains the matter of conspiring to abduct him. And for that, you could still go to the Assizes, and enjoy a long sea voyage, followed by an even longer stay in Australia. You would be there for several years."

Jersey sat down again.

"However, that's not what I want. Like you, I want to solve the mystery of the robbery, and I'm getting a good idea now, about who's responsible. So rather than fighting each other, I would prefer it if you gave us more co-operation and stopped working against me."

John's steely blue eyes bored hard into Jersey's, who found he was unable to return the policeman's look.

"Or, if you rather," continued John slowly and deliberately. "We will press ahead with the conspiracy to abduct charges, plus assaulting me. It is your choice."

John knew this was the moment of truth. He was not entirely sure, just how a court would view his ruse, to get Jersey to admit his part in the abduction. But, he had lived up to his reputation of being unconventional, and making up the Law, as he went along, when necessary.

Also, with the intended victim now dead, from an unrelated incident, it was unlikely any charge would even get as far the Grand Jury stage, let alone be heard at the Assizes. And, any charge would involve the Morgan brothers, which after the help they had given him that morning, would not really be fair.

"You win, Mr Mayfield. What do you want from me?"

"All the background information you have on Bernard Hamlyn and Albert Quinn, plus a proper audit of your ledgers. You see, we believe Hamlyn was involved in Quinn's death. As you know, he died of a heart attack, but we think it was brought on by a fight, almost certainly with Hamlyn. It would be helpful to know why, because we think it has some bearing on the robbery. And, why he was murdered."

"I'll help you all I can. I fear I owe you an apology: in fact several apologies, not least for hitting you. I think, no I'm certain Quinn had personal debts and that was why he was stealing from the bank. Hamlyn told me, but I fear I treated him rather badly. Perhaps if I had been more reasonable, he might still be alive."

He paused as he realized the significance of what he had just said. "Oh God. If only I had given him Quinn's job, then all this might not have happened. You know, I really thought you had pissed yourself, and that's why I kicked you. Please, will you accept my sincerest apologies?"

"It was only water, but whilst I am happy to accept your apologies, I must remind you, both the brothers are making written statements about you, and what you paid them to do. I will keep those statements. Please be advised, if anything happens to either brother, their statements will be produced and I will definitely commence criminal proceedings against you, or I will let their family know about you. Do you understand?"

"I don't want any more trouble, Mr Mayfield."

John smiled, inwardly, at the sudden respect which had crept into Jersey's attitude. Now he was being called *Mr Mayfield,* instead of just *Mayfield.*

"Good. Now come with me, because I want to show you something."

John led Jersey over to his safe. Having selected the correct key, from his watch chain, he opened the door, and invited Jersey to look. The banker gasped in surprise, as he saw several of his bank's money bags, piled inside.

"Are ...are they?" he asked, unable to finish his question.

"Almost certainly," smiled John. "We found them on or near Hamlyn's body. There are 1,683 sovereigns, some pearls and other jewels. Obviously we can't identify the sovereigns as belonging to your clients, but we should be able to have the gems and pearls identified."

"I agree about the sovereigns," acknowledged Jersey, unable to believe his luck, in having some of the stolen property recovered. "What can I do to help?"

"It would help," answered John. "If you would carry out an audit of the bank's coins, when you leave here. That will ensure these sovereigns aren't missing out of your general fund. If that's intact, and the jewels are identified, then I believe it's about a third of the missing property. And that makes me think, even more so, that Hamlyn did not act alone."

Jersey stammered his thanks, and on leaving the police station, went straight across to his bank. He had made a big mistake in underestimating Mayfield. Reluctantly, he had to agree the man knew what he was doing. With luck, if the other missing money was found, Henry Jersey would survive this crisis.

And, if he did so, it would be thanks to John Mayfield.

CHAPTER SIXTEEN

Friday afternoon

John and Mathew watched him go, but before they could speak, Sam knocked and came into the office. He placed a partly filled bank bag on John's desk.

"Some more sovereigns, guv'nor. They were found in the churchyard. It really does look like Hamlyn was trying to hide from someone, only to be ambushed by St Mary's tower. Caleb's still in the churchyard, seeing if there's anymore money to be found, but I doubt it."

"I think you're right, Sam. Don't you Mathew?"

"Yes, and bearing in mind what Caleb has told us, then we should be looking at bringing in Bradford and his partner Harding."

Further conversation was halted by a knocking at the front counter. Sam went to see who it was. A few minutes later, he returned.

"Guv'nor, I think you'd better come. It's a gent who's come in response to one of Robert's notices, about the bank robbery."

"Bring him in here."

Moments later, he showed not one, but three men into John's office.

The first one, an elderly, fussy man introduced himself. "I'm Francis Westwood, from York: I'm a banker whose safe deposit boxes were robbed, some three years ago." He paused and waved one of the notices that Robert had sent out on the night coach on Wednesday. "I've come down straightaway after I was told about this by my local police. We've only just arrived on the train."

Francis Westwood introduced his two companions. "This is Constable Duckworth, from York."

Cedric Duckworth, a middle aged, thickset man, acknowledged them.

"And this is Mr Smith," concluded Francis.

He gave no further information about the large man, who seemed to be too big for his coat. The man had a broken nose, and a cauliflower ear. Sam looked at his huge hands, complete with scarred knuckles, and he recognized them, as belonging to a prizefighter. Clearly Mr Smith, if that was his name, was Mr Westwood's bodyguard.

John let the banker explain the purpose of his visit.

Westwood's Bank had been entered via the next door cellar, which belonged to an Insurance Agency, called *Barton & Howard*. All three Warwick officers looked at each other, when Westwood gave that information.

"I see I've struck a chord, gentlemen," Francis commented, on seeing their looks.

John explained about *Bradford & Harding,* and how it just seemed to be just too coincidental. "And we don't believe in coincidences," he added.

Constable Duckworth grinned and nodded his head in agreement.

"People using false identities often keep the same set of initials. *Barton & Howard* is very close to *Bradford & Harding."* John went on to explain about Quinn's sudden death and Hamlyn's murder.

"That's interesting, because my chief clerk went missing at the same time and has never been seen since."

"We were just on the point of paying Messrs Bradford and Harding a visit when you arrived. I wonder, would you recognize either of them?"

"Certainly I would. The one who called himself Barton was left-handed."

Now John remembered. He had noticed how Bradford was left-handed, but had not been able to remember when looking at Beech's body. "And so is Mr Bradford, which gives us the excuse to arrest them and get the premises searched. Mathew, will you get some warrants organized, please? Then let Robert know I shall need him the moment he's finished with the Morgans. Sam, can you go and organize some refreshments for us please, to include you, Robert, Mathew and his watchers, whom I assume are still there. I think they will be able to go home soon."

* * *

St Mary's church clock was just striking 3.0pm, when John, Mathew, Francis Westwood, and Mr Smith, left the police station and went in the general direction of *Bradford & Harding's* offices. Robert and Cedric Duckworth had left earlier and were now waiting at the rear of the premises in New Street. Sam had left soon afterwards and he was waiting in Old Square. They had left Mathew's sons eating, back at the police station.

Bradford was in his office quickly packing up anything of value, having decided not to wait until tomorrow before leaving. He was going tonight. Whatever he had left at the *Green Dragon* could stay there. After all, he now had more than enough money to keep him in luxury for some time, if not for the rest of his life. And, as an added bonus, he had collected another £162 that morning, in newly sold policies.

It was silly really, he thought. Having buried the money again, after murdering his partner, his change of plans meant he had now dug it up again. The problem was it was very heavy, and he would need a cab to take him and the money to the railway station.

He was interrupted by the sound of the bell on his front door, and he went to investigate.

"Good afternoon, gentlemen," he greeted his three visitors. "I'm Giles Bradford, and how can I be of assistance to you?" In spite of his cheerful greeting, Bradford was a little disconcerted to see one of them was John Mayfield. He looked at the policeman.

"Please don't worry about me, Mr Bradford," John smiled. "Please do attend to these gentlemen first. I'm considering taking out an insurance policy for myself, so I'm not here on duty."

Bradford relaxed. He had quickly worked out the thickset man was the elderly individual's bodyguard. Taking a closer look at the elderly man, he clearly had money. Otherwise, why should he bother with a bodyguard?

Francis looked hard at Bradford, who returned the look with a smile, which slowly faded. His eyes narrowed, as the stranger suddenly seemed vaguely familiar to him. This man spelt danger.

"Ah, Mr Barton. How are you? I haven't seen you for a while!" Francis spoke quietly.

"I think you are mistaken. My name is Bradford, Giles Bradford. Not Barton," corrected Bradford. "And you are?"

"Francis Westwood, of *Westwood's Bank*, in York. I'm sure you haven't forgotten me. Don't you remember? You had the next door offices, to me, where you traded, selling insurance, under the name of *Barton & Howard*. And how is Mr Howard?"

"I'm sorry, Mr Westwood. But I really don't know what you are talking about."

"Then let me remind you," Westwood's voice had become cold. "You and your partner robbed my bank!"

Whilst the exchange had been going on, Bradford had been aware of John paying particular attention to it. Then to his horror, through the smoked glass of his front door, he saw the silhouette of the big police sergeant, Mathew Harrison, standing just outside. He was also aware of the thickset man moving to the back door of the office, effectively blocking any escape through there.

Bradford did not need to be told why they were here. Just at the very last minute this had to happen. Of course he remembered Francis Westwood and York only too well. In spite of all their hard work, there had not been that much money at the end of the job. Why, oh why, had he not left that morning? How the late Jacob Harding must be laughing, as he proved himself right. Bradford's greed had caught him out.

There was only one chance left.

Without hesitating, Bradford suddenly ran straight at the office window. Wrapping his arms round his face, and crouching, he hurled himself at the glass. It shattered and he was though it, before all the falling glass had landed. Quickly regaining his balance, he pushed two screaming women to one side and ran round the corner into Old Square, heading towards St Mary's church.

Too late he saw a policeman moving from out of a doorway.

Sam put his foot out, and Bradford tripped over it, pitching full length onto the road. As he struggled to his feet, he felt a cold metal manacle fasten onto his right wrist. Before he had time to register what had happened, both his arms were pulled behind his back, and another manacle was fastened onto his other wrist. Then he was hauled, unceremoniously to his feet, and he started to struggle.

"I shouldn't, if I were you," said Sam quietly, as he thrust Bradford's right arm higher up his back and marched him back to *Bradford & Harding*. On the way, he passed the two still screaming women and smiled sweetly at them. It did the trick, and they stopped screaming. Clearly they had only been frightened and not hurt.

Pushing his way through the small crowd of people who had already gathered outside the office, he went inside, where John waited. As he entered, Mr Smith and Constable Duckworth came down into the office.

"It's all empty, upstairs sir," said Cedric, who had come into the building via the yard.

"So's the cellar, guv'nor. But there has been some digging, and it will need further examination," added Matthew, who reappeared from below.

"Thank you, gentlemen. Would you please be good enough to call Robert in from round the back. There's no need for him to stay there any longer, as I fear Harding has flown. Mathew, when Robert's here, will you and Cedric search the property thoroughly, and have Robert make the necessary record of what you find."

Francis was now sitting in Bradford's chair, looking at some documents. "There's no doubt, Mr Mayfield. But even if there was, will you look at these?" He held some pages of writing towards John, who saw they were application forms for an insurance policy.

"Now, will you look at this, please?" He took a similar form from his pocket and gave it to John.

He saw the writing was identical to the other form. John saw the name at the top of the form, and he looked at Francis.

"Yes, it's me. This...this person," he indicated Bradford. "Sold me some insurance. The only problem was he pocketed the premiums."

"What do you have to say about this?" asked John.

Bradford looked out of the shattered window and said nothing for a moment. Shrugging his shoulders he turned back into the office. "I don't have the faintest idea what you are talking about."

"Then why did you jump out of the window?"

"Because I thought these people were going to rob me, and I was frightened."

"But I was here. How could they have been going to rob you?"

"For all I knew, you could have been in league with them."

"Where's Mr Harding?" asked John.

"Who?"

"Your partner: Jacob Harding.?"

Bradford shrugged. "I haven't seen him for a while. He went out this morning to see a client, and hasn't come back yet."

"Which client?"

"He did tell me, but I've forgotten his name."

"Excuse me, guv'nor," interrupted Mathew, who appeared carrying a large carpet bag, with difficulty. "I think you'd better have a look in here."

He opened the bag, and they all looked inside. They saw the bag contained several bags of gold coins, in smaller bags, each inscribed with the *Jersey's Bank logo.*

"I've never seen that before, in my life," stressed Bradford, before anyone had a chance to question him. "You've planted it upstairs, to incriminate me."

"You can deny it as much as you like, Mr Bradford, but I know for a fact that *Jersey's Bank* was entered from your cellar." John paused. "I can prove where you purchased the paint, to redecorate it after the robbery. I've also got a very good idea you or your partner, or probably both of you, murdered Billy Beech and Bernard Hamlyn. So where is your partner?"

"I told you, he went out sometime this morning. You'll have ask him about all these fanciful stories of yours."

"Tell me, Mr Bradford, when did your partner leave the office?" John did not disclose how the premises had been watched, front and rear, since the previous night.

"About half past eleven I think, but I can't be sure. I was with a client at the time. I went out myself an hour or so later."

"Would your client have seen Mr Harding leave?"

"I doubt it. Look, the robbery was Jacob's idea. I would have nothing to do with it. As for Hamlyn, I've never even met him or the other person, what's his name? Bush?"

"Sam! Go next door for me please. Will you ask Mr Jersey if any of his staff can recall Mr Bradford here, or his partner, going into the bank and talking to Bernard Hamlyn? And while you are there, ask the same questions regarding our friend here meeting with Albert Quinn."

"On the way, guv'nor."

"Don't bother. I remember now, it was the manager I saw about setting up an account. Would that have been Bernard Hamlyn?"

Robert Andrew had appeared during the latter part of the questioning and scribbled a note, which he handed to John.

The privy's full of earth - far too much from where the money might have been buried in the cellar. It's possible Harding's down there. Shall I start digging?

After reading it, he nodded his thanks to Robert. "Go ahead," he instructed. "Take Sam with you."

Then he returned his attention to Bradford again. "You know full well the manager was Albert Quinn. He took you into the vaults where you arranged for a safe deposit box."

"Just like you did with me, before you robbed my bank," added Francis, who had been listening to the exchange, with interest.

"I don't know what you are talking about."

"We'll not waste any more time," said John. "I accept your initial dealings were with Albert Quinn, who came to your opening night here. Soon after his death, Bernard Hamlyn was also seen by one of my officers coming in here." John paused. Then he turned and issued some orders.

"It seems Harding's gone, but we've got most of the money back. Constable Duckworth, would you please begin to pack up these documents in here, for me please?"

"It will be a pleasure, sir."

A few minutes later, Robert re-appeared. "I think you'd better come down into the cellar, guv'nor," he announced in a serious tone. "But, with all due respect, Mr Westwood, sir, you might prefer to stay up here."

Franois shook his head and all of them, including Bradford followed Robert down into the cellar.

In the flickering candlelight, they saw some of the flagstones had been removed, and several holes dug in the earth underneath. From one of these, a pair of legs, enclosed in boots protruded.

They had found the missing Jacob Harding.

CHAPTER SEVENTEEN

Friday evening

Whilst the others watched, Robert and Sam carefully uncovered the remainder of the grave, taking great care to avoid the knife still protruding from the body. Once his face was uncovered, they looked at John.

"I take it this is Jacob Harding?" he asked Bradford.

"Well, yes. But what's he doing down here?" replied Bradford.

"I had hoped you could enlighten us."

"As I said, he left here this morning, so this must have happened whilst I was out, myself."

"And that's all you have to say about this death?" asked John.

"Yes: it's as big a mystery to me as it is to you."

"Sam, go and fetch Dr Gilson. If he's not available, then any other doctor will do. Robert, will you and Cedric take Mr Bradford back to the police station, and lock him up."

"But why? I haven't done anything wrong."

"Suspicion of fraud, robbery and murder will suffice for the moment. Mathew, will you wait here with me. Mr Westwood, would you and Mr Smith please go across to the police station, as we shall need statements from all of you. I fear it could be some time, so may I suggest you arrange accommodation for the night? I can recommend the *Woolpack* or the *Warwick Arms*."

When they had all gone, John and Mathew sat down. It had been a very long day which was nowhere near finished yet.

"I think we may have a problem with friend Bradford," Mathew broke the silence. "He's admitting nothing, and our evidence is only circumstantial. I don't doubt he's our killer, but it will be difficult to prove and, I suspect he'll put all the blame onto the late unlamented Jacob Harding."

"True, but Harding's body is quite stiff, and rigor mortis is well advanced. If what Bradford says is true, and we know it isn't, Harding can't have been dead for much more than four hours. At which time rigor mortis should just be starting, not be completed."

"So he's been dead for what....at least ten hours, which means 6 o'clock, this morning, at the very latest. The doctor's evidence will be crucial."

Half an hour later, Richard arrived. "Not another body?" he asked, raising his eyes to the ceiling and smiling.

"I'm afraid so," John returned the smile, then he led the way into the cellar. "By my reckoning, he has not been dead that long, but at least ten or twelve hours."

Richard examined the body, and turned it one to one side. He pulled out Harding's shirt and exposed the postmortem staining. "It would need at least four hours for the staining to start. And, as you say, rigor mortis is complete. So, I would estimate his time of death as being somewhere between midnight and 6 o'clock this morning."

"Thank you, Richard. That's what we hoped you'd say."

"If you can get his body back to the laboratory, I'll take a closer look at that wound. It looks like a straightforward stabbing, but you never know. And I suppose you'll want to know about it by yesterday?"

They all chuckled.

After Richard had left, John carefully staked out the outline of Harding's body, as they had found it. Quickly he made a rough sketch and added some measurements.

"Guv'nor," interrupted Mathew. "Sam's Lucy is arriving tonight for a few days. Do you think, if we asked her nicely that she'd do these plans for us?"

"What a damned good idea. Now let's get our friend here, removed to High Street, then it's back to the station for us. But, will you do a quick job for me first?"

Mathew agreed and he called in on Mickey Cassidy at the *Green Dragon.* As they thought, Mickey confirmed neither Bradford nor Harding had slept there the previous night.

* * *

Some time later, John and Sam interviewed Bradford again, back in the police station.

"Do you still say you last saw Mr Harding at 11.30 this morning?" asked Sam.

"I keep telling you, yes."

"Then perhaps, you can explain why his body has been dead for well over twelve hours?"

"You can't prove that."

"Oh yes we can. Rigor mortis, or the post death stiffening of limbs, was far too advanced for him only to have been dead three or four hours," said John. "And, I have had your premises watched, front and rear, since last night, so I know neither you nor Harding left there all day."

Bradford said nothing for a moment, but just sat examining his finger nails, whilst John and Sam sat patiently waiting. At last he spoke.

"You're quite right, he has been dead for a long time. Let me tell you what happened."

Both John and Sam felt their pulses race.

"It was an accident," continued Bradford. "You see, I came back late to the office, and found Jacob in the cellar. He had been digging and he was surrounded by Jersey's money bags. I startled him and he drew a knife on me. I ran up the stairs and he followed. But..but...but..." his voice faltered. "But he tripped and fell onto his own knife. I...I couldn't do anything to help him."

"Why didn't you tell us?" asked John.

"I'm afraid I panicked. I realized what he had done. With all that money, he had to have been part of the robbery. So I buried his body."

"And what about the money, in the bag? What were you going to with that?" asked Sam

"I was going to go away tomorrow. But, before I went, I'd have sent the bank a note of where to find it. I think Jacob must have put in there."

Bradford resisted all their attempts to make him change his story, and they returned him to his cell.

"Damn!" snapped John. "And I was so certain we'd have him there. I know he's as guilty as hell. But just how can we prove it?"

"He's not going anywhere for the moment," replied Sam. "If all else fails, Cedric Duckworth can take him back to York, on their fraud charges. And, look on the bright side, he'll go to Australia, for at least seven years. But, it would be nice to clear the murders."

Sam paused. "Guv'nor. Let us forget Harding's death for a moment. When I was in St Nicholas Churchyard, I took various plaster casts of footprints. One set led to where you found that bloodied rag. Let's check them against Bradford's shoes."

They were interrupted by Mathew. "Sorry to bother you guv'nor, but can we go and see my Margaret at Dr Waldren's. She says it's urgent."

"Can I leave you to do that Sam?" John felt a major twinge of conscience. With all that had been happening, he had completely forgotten about how his friend was being poisoned.

* * *

Redman showed them into the drawing-room, where Sarah sat. After passing the time of day with her, Mathew went off to find Margaret, leaving John with Sarah.

"Oh John," she said, standing up, and kissing him on the cheek. "Whatever's happened to your face?"

He told her about the fight in the Pigwells, and Bradford's arrest.

"I'm so glad you've come," she continued. "Thomas isn't getting any better. In fact, I think he's getting worse. Neither Richard nor Dr Hopper can find out what's wrong with him."

John made sympathetic noises, but, at the same time, he was appalled by how drawn and ill she looked. Surely she could not be the person poisoning Thomas? Of all the people he knew, she was the least likely for him to have suspected. But, as he knew only too well, appearances could be deceiving. And, as he kept reminding himself, it would not be the first time a supposed loving wife, had murdered her husband. Yet, he still found the idea of Sarah poisoning Thomas hard to believe.

"How are you progressing with Laura?" Sarah changed the subject.

"I'm not. She's going out with Richard, and is clearly no longer interested in me. I suppose it's my fault, but life has been a bit hectic just lately."

"Don't give up on her just yet," Sarah cautioned. "She's not stupid and she'll soon see Richard for what he is. Yes, he's a charmer where the ladies are concerned, but I suspect he wants just one thing from her. And when he's got it, she'll just be another one of his conquests, and he'll quickly start looking to find another."

"Do you really think so?"

"Yes I do."

She forbore to tell him, at least for the moment, about her recent meeting with Laura. Although she had made it seem accidental, Sarah had been waiting for the chance to see her. When she did, Sarah had taken the opportunity to voice her concerns about Richard, but Laura had said nothing, preferring to make up her own mind. However, she had agreed to come and join Sarah for a quiet supper on Monday.

"I ought to go and see Thomas now. It'll give Mathew a little bit of time with his wife."

"Of course. You know the way. And, Margaret's been wonderful. One last thing, John: I would like you to come and join me for supper on Monday night. And I won't take no for an answer." She made no mention of also having invited Laura.

John agreed, and after leaving Sarah, he made his way to see Thomas, who was now in one of the guest rooms. He found Margaret waiting on the landing, and she took him into the small room she had been given. Mathew was already there.

"I'm really worried," she said, without any preamble. "Even if you hadn't warned me about what was going on, I would soon have realized. I don't think there's any doubt at all, but Dr Waldren is being poisoned. And it has to be by someone in this house."

"Margaret, I have to ask," said John. "Do you think it could be Sarah Waldren?"

"I'm not sure, Mr Mayfield: I really am not sure. It could just as easily be Redman, or the cook or any of the kitchen staff. Everybody else has been banned from the kitchen. But someone has to prepare the doctor's food and bring it up to him. Dr Gilson always tests the water, at least once a day. And he drinks it himself, without any ill effects."

John was thoughtful for a few moments. "Who prepares his food and brings it up to him?" he asked finally.

"The cook prepares it and Sarah, or one of the kitchen staff brings it up to him."

"Do you have the same food, love?" asked Mathew in a worried voice.

"Not really. He can only cope with broth or porridge. No meat or anything like that. But, I'm fed as well, and before you ask, I've had no ill effects."

"Then it's only Thomas's food which is being poisoned," said John thoughtfully. "Margaret, how easy would it be for you to purchase and prepare Thomas's food yourself, and use your own water supply for preparing it?"

"No problem, John," she replied, and then realized what she had said. "Oh, Mr Mayfield, please forgive me, for calling you John." Her face reddened and Mathew looked embarrassed.

John touched her on the arm and smiled. "Don't worry, Margaret. After all, my name is John, and Mr Mayfield is so very formal, and should only be used on formal occasions. I call you Margaret, so why shouldn't you call me John?"

But Margaret remained flustered.

"Do you want me to start right away doing the doctor's food for him? My sister's staying for a few days to look after Mathew and the boys. I can tell her what to buy."

"That's a great idea. Now look, take what the servants bring for him, but, on no account must you or he taste it. You must get it to me and I'll have Dr Hopper analyse it. Thomas is to have nothing, and I mean nothing that you have not prepared. And it must not go out of your sight."

"Couldn't I just give it to Dr Gilson?"

"No, I think we'll keep this to just the three of us. In fact I don't want him or Sarah, or even Thomas to know about this arrangement."

They nodded and John left them together, whilst he went to see Thomas. For a while he told him about the developments in the bank robbery case, and reassured Thomas that his money had been recovered. But, Thomas had fallen asleep before he had finished. John left the sleeping man, collected Mathew, and went downstairs, where they were met by Richard, who looked quite excited.

"I was coming to find you," he announced. "But Redman told me you were already here, so I thought I'd wait. Come and see what I've found."

He led the way to the laboratory, and went straight towards the furthest of three covered bodies. When the sheet was pulled back, John and Mathew recognised the features of Jacob Harding.

"You remember when you first showed him to me, he had a knife in his chest." Richard pointed to the wound in the man's chest.

"Yes. Our current lodger, in the cells, now says that our friend here, was chasing him, with the knife when he fell on it," answered John.

"Help me roll him over," instructed Richard. They did so and found Harding's back had now been opened up. He pointed in the vicinity of the knife's exit wound. They saw it was larger than would have been expected, and they looked askance at Richard.

"You're quite right. It is wider than the entry wound. What does that suggest?"

"The knife's been moved whilst it was in the body," replied Mathew.

"And you John; do you agree?"

John said nothing but looked more closely at the wound. "I suppose it could have happened when he fell, but, if that's the case, shouldn't the entry wound also be wider?"

"Yes, it should be, but it isn't."

"So, if he didn't fall on the knife, how do you explain it?" queried Mathew.

"Whether or not he fell is immaterial, for the moment," said John thoughtfully. "That knife, as we found it, never entered his body first from the front. I suspect he was stabbed in the back, and the knife taken out, and then reinserted, via the exit wound, to back up his story of Harding having fallen on it."

"Exactly," triumphed Richard. "And now look at this." He pulled aside some of the flesh on Harding's back and pointed to one of his ribs. "It has been damaged, almost certainly by the knife."

"By being pushed from back to front," added Mathew. "The lying little bastard: he killed his mate."

"There's more yet," continued Richard, as he pointed to small threads of cotton, which were caught on the inside of the ribs, and faced towards the dead man's chest. "These came from his coat. There's no doubt at all, in my mind, he was stabbed from behind, which was a fatal blow. Then he removed the knife, reversed it and pushed it into Harding's chest, to justify his story of the man having fallen on it."

For a few moments, John studied the front of Harding's shirt, which did not show very much blood. However, he soon saw there was a copious amount on the rear of the shirt. Richard and Mathew had watched him intently. Mathew slowly nodded his head as he saw the way John's mind was working. At length he stopped his examination and looked at Richard.

"Yes. You are quite right," Richard grinned. "The blood's in the wrong place for a frontal wound. He's obviously been stabbed from the rear, and was clearly dead when the knife was inserted again."

They spoke for a while longer and then left. Mathew went back home to pay his boys for the work they had done and, in their mother's absence, to ensure they were alright. Meanwhile John went to see Julius Hopper.

Quickly he briefed him on the events of the day, including the discovery of Harding's body. "Do you have enough evidence to charge him with the murder?"

"Certainly Harding's. But I doubt we'll get the necessary evidence to prove the others. Also with Hamlyn now dead, I'm not proposing to spend any more time looking into Quinn's death."

"I agree. Now, what about Tom Waldren?"

John told him of the latest developments and what he had arranged with Margaret.

"I'm surprised you're not telling Gilson. Surely you don't suspect him?"

"Good God, no! He's been an absolute Godsend to me this week. No, I just want to try and get Thomas well first, and I feel the fewer people who know what we're doing the better. Sadly, I'm having to accept that Sarah might well be the one responsible. Have you had any luck finding an antidote yet?"

Julius shook his head in frustration. "I can't even identify the poison let alone find an antidote for it. All I can really hope for is to stop the source of the poison, and then let it work its way out of his body. That's what I'm hoping for. If we can do that, then we can set a trap, hopefully, for our poisoner. But I fear we do not have too much time left

"Sadly I have to agree."

They discussed the various cases for a while longer, then John stood up to leave, but Julius detained him for a few more moments.

"Speaking as a doctor, Mayfield, you look all in. I recommend you go and get some sleep."

* * *

Before returning to the station, John decided to go and see Laura. He was almost at her school, in Mill Street, when the front door opened. John stepped back into the shadows and waited. His heart sank when he saw her emerge, arm-in-arm, and laughing with Richard Gilson.

For a moment he was tempted to challenge them, but thought better of it. Instead, he watched them go up Mill Street, in the general direction of the town centre.

Suddenly a wave of loneliness spread over him. Oh how he missed Harriet. How could he have been so stupid as to let her go just like that? Would it have been different if he had only got to the port in time? Now he would never know. For a moment he wondered what Kate Whiting was doing: but they had agreed not to communicate with each other.

On arriving back at the police station, he realized jut how hungry he was. Somehow, he was not surprised to find Mathew there. "How are the boys?" he asked.

"Fine. Margaret's sister was there, so I left them to it."

"Have you had any supper yet?"

"Since you ask, guv'nor, the answer's no."

"Come on. Get out of your tunic, put a coat on and I'll buy us some supper. We've both earned it today."

"Give me ten minutes. By then young Ben will on duty, and I can leave the station to him. What about our friend in the cells?"

"Let him wait till tomorrow. He's not going anywhere."

Twenty minutes later, they were in the *Woolpack*, but John never bought them any supper. The first person they met was Francis Westwood, who was accompanied by the ever present Mr Smith and Cedric Duckworth. The banker was so pleased with the results of his visit to Warwick, he insisted on paying for everything.

It was long past midnight before the party broke up.

* * *

Laura was not particularly enjoying her evening out with Richard. Although she had not said anything, she had seen John standing in the shadows as they passed him. She was firmly convinced he was not spying on her, as she did not think he was that sort of person. Only that evening had Abbie told her about his earlier visit, and Laura felt more than just a twinge of conscience, especially after she learnt about Harriet being lost at sea. In many ways she was relieved Harriet had gone, and hoped John would come to accept her death, and now look to the future.

True, Laura liked Richard, but she would not want to put it any stronger than that. Also, she was thinking over her accidental meeting with Sarah, or so she thought, earlier that day. At first she had bridled at the older woman's interference, but then found she was agreeing with some of her comments.

She confided to Sarah, how she felt there was something about Richard, that made her just a little bit wary of him. It had not taken long for her to realize he was a charmer, and very much a lady's man. Laura had noticed how he was always looking at other women, especially attractive ones, even when he was with her.

Although she found Richard was good company, Laura found herself missing John, and she was feeling guilty at not having made any attempt to see him.

Sarah had stressed just how busy John was investigating two murders, a suspicious death and a bank robbery. At that time, neither woman knew about the fight in the Pigwells and the third murder. Speaking from her own experience, Sarah told her just how difficult it was being married to a man who worked unsocial hours but, she added, if you really loved your man, then that was the price you had to pay.

Before they parted, Sarah had invited Laura for supper on Monday night, and intimated she would invite John as well. Laura readily agreed, although she wondered how John would react.

Richard took her to an art exhibition at the *Bowling Green*, followed by supper at the *Warwick Arms*. Laura noticed how he kept plying her with drink during the evening, which only served to put her on her guard. Wherever possible, she tipped much of it away, but she still had to go through the motions of enjoying his hospitality, and becoming slightly intoxicated as the evening progressed. At last the moment came for them to leave.

He hired a cab to take them back to Mill Street. Once inside, he put his arm round her shoulders, and gave her a long passionate kiss. Later, she had to admit he was rather good at it. When they stopped outside her school, he got out first and helped her down.

"Aren't you going to invite me in? For a last drink?"

"Well....I....."

"Come on." He helped her to unlock the door and they went inside. Once in the hall, his arms went round her once again, only this time, he started to undo the buttons on her blouse.

"No! Richard! No!" she protested. But he ignored her, and carried on undoing her buttons, and put his hand on her breast. For a few moments, she was tempted to surrender, but found she kept thinking of Sarah's advice. What was it she had said? *"He only wants one thing, and once he's got it, you'll just become one of his conquests and he'll be looking for another."*

Moments later he had picked her up and carried her into the drawing room. Once he had laid her down on the sofa, he began to pull her skirts up.

"No, Richard!" she cried. But he ignored her. "No!" she insisted. "It's the wrong time of the month!"

This time he stopped. "I'm sorry," he said. "I didn't know. I hadn't noticed any signs and, after all, I am a doctor."

"I've only just started. Now please leave." Even as she spoke, Laura did up her blouse buttons, before escorting him to the door. "Good night, Richard," she continued, fairly coldly.

When he went to kiss her, she turned her cheek to his lips. "Are you doing anything tomorrow night?" he asked.

"Yes and for the next few nights. Good night Richard."

After he had left she closed and locked the door behind him, then she leant against it. Had she overreacted? She certainly was not having her period, but as a ruse, it had worked very well.

Possibly, if he had continued, then her resistance might not have lasted very much longer. It had required quite some effort, just to say no, and mean it. Almost regretfully, she had to admit Sarah was right. She could so easily have become just another one of his conquests.

But would John accept that nothing had happened? What was even more worrying, would she be able to resume her relationship with John?

Hopefully yes, with a little bit of help from Sarah.

CHAPTER EIGHTEEN

Saturday through to Monday morning

John did not feel at all well when he was woken up, by Ben Underwood knocking on his bedroom door.

"Sorry to wake you, guv'nor," Ben said after having heard a grunt from John. "But it's half-past five, and you said you wanted calling."

John muttered something, which sound like thank you, and sat up, wincing at his pounding headache. Vaguely he recalled having volunteered to take the early shift, to give Mathew a later start. He felt he owed it to him, and they had all worked long hours during the past few days.

Gently he swung his legs out of bed, and stood up. Forlornly, he had hoped his head would stop pounding if he did so but, if anything, it hurt him even more.

Slowly he remembered the previous night. Francis Westwood had been the perfect host, and provided food and drink for everybody. By the end of the night, they were all on Christian name terms, with the exception of Mr Smith, who never lowered his guard once, and drank nothing alcoholic. John had no recollection of what time they all finished. All he knew, was it did not seem that long ago. It took him several attempts to both find and light a candle, and the sudden glare made his eyes water.

Having shaved after a fashion, he put on his uniform and made his way out into his living quarters, and stopped. On the sofa, he could see the vague shape of a body, lying under various blankets, and snoring loudly. The room smelled of stale alcohol and other bodily odours.

He recalled Mathew had been totally oblivious to what was happening, and in no state to go home. Consequently he had spent the night, or what was left of it, in John's quarters. John let him lie and staggered down into the police station.

"All correct, guv'nor!" grinned Ben quietly, getting to his feet. He had seen his guv'nor and Mathew stagger back late last night, or rather early this morning, and did not begrudge them. It showed a human side to them both. And, he also appreciated when John had let him take some extra time off duty, when his young daughter had been ill. Fortunately she had made a good recovery, and Ben's heavily pregnant wife, had been glad of her husband's help nursing the sick child.

Likewise he knew Sam was having some hours off over the weekend, because Lucy had come up from London on the late train. But, that was how they all worked: as a team, if not as a family, helping each other when necessary.

"Some tea guv'nor?"

John nodded his head, but wished he had kept it still, as waves of pain hit him. Going into his office, he sat down gingerly, and waited until Ben appeared with the tea. After Ben had left, closing the door quietly behind him, he could hear the sounds of the market stalls being erected, and the shouts of the first traders to arrive. Leaning back in his chair, he closed his eyes, hoping to ease the throbbing pain in his head.

When he opened them again, he found his tea was cold and sunlight flooded in through his office windows. Looking at his watch, he was aghast to see it was nearly 9 o'clock. Thankfully his headache had diminished considerably, and he felt much better. Pushing his chair back, John stood up, took the mug of cold tea and went out to the station's small kitchen. There he tipped his cold tea away, put the kettle on to boil, and went to check on Giles Bradford.

The prisoner was still asleep, or appeared to be, so John let him lie, after first checking the man was still breathing. Going back to the kitchen, he made a pot of tea. When it was ready, he took a mug up to Mathew, who was just starting to stir.

"Room service!" John called cheerfully, as he went into his own living quarters. Mathew sat up, bleary eyed and looked around him, in astonishment.

"How did I get here, guv'nor?"

"Can't you remember anything about last night?"

"Oh yes," he winced, as his memory came back. "But, please don't tell Margaret. She would not approve."

John grinned, went back downstairs, and began to plan their next interview with Bradford. Not that it would be much of an interview, but he would have to be told what Richard had found. Thinking about Richard, meant thinking about Laura: and the thought hurt him.

Sarah seemed confident he would win her back, and knowing her, she would undoubtedly help him. But thinking about Sarah reminded him of Thomas, and the very real possibility she was the one who was poisoning him. It was inconceivable, but .....?

He had to admit it was not impossible.

* * *

Lucy Penrose also awoke in a strange bed. For a moment she had forgotten she was in Mathew and Margaret Harrison's house. She really appreciated their kindness. Surprisingly, after the momentous events of the previous evening, she had slept quite well.

Sam had met her off the train, and taken her straight to the Harrisons' house. On the way he explained what he had been doing all the previous week. Immediately she had expected her visit to be cut short, but he quickly reassured her that was not the case. In fact, he had been given some extra time off duty, to be with her.

From there, he managed to steer her towards asking him what he would be doing, when he was next on duty. He told her about the murder sites he had to measure up and sketch.

"Samuel Perkins!" She wagged a finger at him. "I can see right through you. What you and John Mayfield want is for me to help you? Am I not right?"

He had the grace to look abashed. "Well.......if you weren't doing anything........... And I would be there to help you."

"Of course I will. I'd be delighted to help."

"Bless you," he smiled. Then he threw his arms round her and gave her a kiss.

She responded passionately. "Oh Sam, I do love you so much."

"And I love you, too. How I wish you lived nearer."

"So do I!" She hesitated for a moment. "There's something I must tell you, my love. I've just got a new job and it means, I'll have to move from London."

Sam's heart sank for a moment, until he saw the mischievous twinkle in her eyes. "And, where are you moving to, my love?"

"A firm of surveyors and estate agents."

"Yes, but where? Tell me! The suspense is killing me."

"At a little town, about two miles away from here, called Leamington Spa."

"Oh you darling." He picked her up and twirled her round several times. "Does that mean...does that mean........"

"Does what mean Sam?" she teased.

"Does that mean we could get married?"

"Is that a proposal, Samuel Perkins?"

"Yes it is."

"Then ask me properly."

"Miss Lucy Penrose," he began and sank onto one knee. "Would you do me the honour of becoming my wife? Becoming Mrs Samuel Perkins?"

"Oh my darling: of course I will!"

* * *

They spent the morning making plans, but all too soon it was time for Sam to go on duty. After strolling round the market, he bought her a small scarf, which took most of the money he had.

"Will you accept this as my engagement present to you, until we can choose a ring?"

There were tears in her eyes as she took it from him. "Of course I will, my love."

Then she kissed him, to a rousing cheer from the assembled market traders, who had been watching them and listening to their conversation, with interest. Most of them knew and respected the young policeman. Sam went red with embarrassment, and grabbed her hand. Laughing, they ran through the market, and into the police station.

"You're looking remarkably happy," said John, wistfully, as he saw them arrive.

"Can we have a word, please guv'nor?" asked Sam nervously.

John invited them into his office, trying hard to keep a straight face, as he had more than an inkling of why they wanted to see him.

In the days following Charles Pearson's arrest, the previous year, he had come to like Lucy and respect her work. For a woman to have such a job, as an expert plan drawer and artist, in a man's world, said it all. He knew it had been love at first sight for the pair of them.

"Firstly, guv'nor, Lucy's agreed to do those drawings for us. Haven't you Lucy?"

"Well, yes I have. But it comes at a price."

"Tell me," replied John, trying to be stern, but failing miserably. His eyes twinkled as her saw her give Sam a nudge.

"We want to get married, and will you give me your permission for us to do so?" Sam spoke nervously.

"Of course I will." John burst out laughing. "I'd be delighted to, and I'll make sure the Watch Committee agrees."

They all knew the Watch Committee had to agree. Whilst it was usually a formality, Watch Committees elsewhere in the country, had been known, on the odd occasion, to refuse such permission. To be fair, it was usually for a very good reason.

John shook Sam's hand just before Lucy hugged him.

"Oh thank you," they both said together.

"There's one other thing," said Lucy. "You know I haven't got a father. So, would you be the one to give me away please?"

"I'd be delighted to and would consider it an honour."

Lucy hugged him again, and gave him a kiss.

"What's this I hear?" interrupted Mathew, who had just appeared. "Do I believe congratulations are in order?"

They all talked generally for a few minutes, until Sam went to put on his uniform. Whilst he was gone, Lucy asked about the scenes John wanted measuring and drawing. John told her about them and she decided to go out of the station and into the town to wait for Sam.

"Did you check those shoe print casts with Bradford's shoes?" John asked Sam when he reappeared.

"Yes and I left you a note. They're a good match, especially with the nail patterns on the soles"

"Sorry Sam, I missed the note. But that's great news."

He went on to explain about the medical evidence Richard had found on Harding's body. "Caleb's going to get a statement from him this morning."

* * *

Richard was also in town, still feeling frustrated and fairly resentful, at the way Laura had acted towards him the previous night. Whilst he accepted there might have been some truth in her excuse, he actually doubted it. And, he was not very pleased when she refused to say when they could meet again. Perhaps it was time to move on and look for somebody else.

As if in answer to his silent prayer, he saw a good looking woman wandering around the market. She was of medium height, slim with blond hair, and a fresh complexion. The royal blue dress she wore, accentuated her deep blue eyes.

He did not recognize her, but then he had not been in town all that long himself. Carefully he sidled up to her, and began looking at the items for sale on a nearby stall. As if by accident, he stepped backwards and collided with her.

"I am so dreadfully sorry," he smiled, all apologetic. "I was thinking about other things, and I just did not see you behind me. Please, please forgive me."

"That's all right," she smiled. "Accidents do happen."

"Forgive me for asking, but are you from here? Only I don't think I've seen you before."

"No, I'm just up here visiting."

His pulse quickened as he noticed how she made no mention of being accompanied. "If you're doing nothing tonight, I would be delighted to buy you dinner, to make up for my clumsiness."

She studied him closely for a few moments, before replying.

"I work in a man's world, and I can recognize a male predator when I see one. Thank you for your offer, but I do not have the slightest intention of becoming another notch on your bedpost."

Richard was taken off guard by her directness, and caught her arm as she walked away. "That's not what I want....." he flustered.

She tried to shake his hand off, but he persisted.

"That's not what I meant."

"Let go of my arm please." Her voice was cold, and her eyes had lost their friendliness. He smiled but still kept hold of her arm.

"I think, doctor," a voice came from behind him. "That Miss Penrose doesn't want to go with you. So I suggest you let her go."

He spun round and found himself looking into Sam's hard eyes.

"This is nothing to do with you," he snapped. "I'm doing nothing wrong: merely asking this young lady here, who appears to be on her own, if I can buy her dinner tonight. You overreach yourself and I've a good mind to make a complaint about you."

"Please do, doctor. I'm sure Mr Mayfield will be impressed when the facts are reported to him. After all, you have managed to come between him and Miss Grant, so I'm sure he'll be very sympathetic to your case."

Richard stood still, his temper rising. "That's none of your damned business."

"I should add," continued Sam, as if Richard had not spoken. "That Mr Mayfield will be standing in for Miss Penrose's father, when we are married. So I don't think he'll take kindly to your trying to seduce her."

Richard went cold, as the truth of the matter sank in. This woman was engaged to be married to Constable Perkins, and he had seen what damage he could inflict on people. It was time to make a dignified retreat.

"No offence, Perkins," he said. "I did not know she was to be married to you. Had I done so, I would never have ...." his words faded away.

"None taken, doctor, this time," Sam stressed. "What you do with other women, provided you act within the law, is none of my business, but Miss Penrose is my business. As long you understand that, we'll get along fine."

"My apologies, Miss Penrose," Richard said stiffly, raising his hat and walking away.

"Watch that man," warned Lucy. "There's something about him, although I can't exactly say what, but I feel he would make a dangerous enemy."

"I know."

* * *

Later that morning, John and Mathew spoke to Bradford again. Even when he was told about the evidence Richard had found, concerning the stabbing, he refused to change his story.

"Nevertheless," announced John. "You will be charged with Harding's murder, and then it will be up to the jury as to whether or not you hang. I have no feelings one way or the other. You're both felons, and he's no real loss to the community, but it's not up to you to kill him. Now I want to talk about the murder of William Beech."

"Who?"

"The man who was murdered, in St Nicholas churchyard."

"I've never been there in my life. I know nothing about it."

"Then perhaps you can explain how your footprints came to be found at the scene?"

"It must have been Jacob. He often borrowed my shoes."

"No: I don't think so. His feet are much larger than yours."

Bradford folded his arms and looked away.

"Why did you target doctors and solicitors with your fraudulent insurances?" asked Mathew, changing the subject, trying to catch him off guard.

"There's nothing wrong with those policies." Bradford had been ready for such a tactic.

"Oh yes there is. Very much so," added John. "We've spent quite some time speaking to Francis Westwood and Constable Duckworth. They told us how you creamed off a considerable sum of money from the York doctors, solicitors and other businessmen."

"You used the same fictitious companies here, in Warwick. And we can prove they don't exist." Mathew took up the story.

"And both your's and the late Jacob Harding's signatures appear on all sets of documents." added John, showing some of the forms to Bradford, who studied them for a few moments.

"They're nothing like my signature. Let me show you." Bradford laughed.

Taking up a pen he scribbled his signature on a sheet of paper. John and Mathew studied the signatures on the insurance applications, and compared them with the one they had just been given.

The signatures were not the same.

"I think you'll agree they're completely different," smirked Bradford.

Mathew said nothing, but left the room, returning several seconds later with a large ledger. He opened it and pointed out something to John, who smiled and took the book.

"Yes, I have to agree with you these are different signatures. But," John paused and showed the book to Bradford. "This is the register, where you signed, yesterday, for the property we took from you on your arrest. I think you will find, and so will any jury, that this signature is the same as those on the application forms. And not this fake one you've just given us."

Bradford's self-confidence visibly collapsed, and he seemed to shrink into his chair. Too late he realized all the stories, he had heard about Mayfield, were true. He was a formidable opponent. Perhaps if he confessed to the frauds, although it would mean a long stay in Australia, he might still escape with his life. Hopefully it might just convince a jury he was telling the truth.

"You win," he sighed, and pointed to the insurance forms. "Yes, I admit they're my signatures. I hate doctors and solicitors. They've never done me any good, but they've always taken my money. This was my way of getting my own back on them."

He spent some time describing, in detail, how he and Harding had both committed these frauds. Harding had specialized in defrauding anyone, and

Bradford in defrauding doctors and solicitors. But, at the end of his confession, Bradford was adamant he had not murdered anyone.

After he had been returned to his cell, John and Mathew discussed the confession. Although they were both convinced Bradford was guilty of murdering his partner, the only evidence came from Dr Gilson. And they both knew that, without any corroboration, it might not be enough to secure a conviction. It was not the most satisfactory situation to be in, to ensure a victory in Court.

The remainder of the day passed without any difficulties, and John began preparing the paperwork they would need, to take with Bradford to court on Monday. After Mathew had gone off duty, John thought about going to see Laura, but he was unwilling to do so, fearing a rebuff. And, if he was really honest, the thoughts of having an early night very much appealed.

Had he but tried, John would have found Laura at her home, hoping he would visit. However, she waited in vain, but at least Richard had not called. Had he done so, she did not know how she would have reacted.

* * *

The next morning, John went with Francis Westwood and his party to the railway station, and saw them off on the train, back to York. Both Francis and Cedric Duckworth were more than happy to leave the prosecution in John's hands. Francis accepted the murder was the more serious charge, and Cedric was only too happy not to have extra paperwork to do: and he would not have to look after a prisoner on the journey. As ever, Mr Smith remained in the background, not saying anything, but he was always there.

Once John had seen them off, he returned to the police station and began compiling his report, and the case papers for the Bradford case. It would take him some time, so he concentrated on the immediate work needed for court the next day.

It was early afternoon when Mathew knocked on his door and entered.

"My apologies, guv'nor. But I've just heard from Margaret. She wants to see us urgently."

Fortunately Sarah was out when Redman showed them in, and led the way to Margaret's room. John was relieved to see she looked quite excited. She closed her door as they entered.

"I do believe he's a little bit better. He's only had food I've prepared for him, and he's kept it down."

Moments later, John was with Thomas, and he had to agree his friend looked better, although he was clearly still not at all well. "How do you feel, old friend?"

"Just a bit better, I think. I've managed to keep some food down, without the help of any medicine, thanks to you."

"What do you mean?"

"Margaret says you instructed her not to give me anything that she hasn't prepared herself. And she's included my medicine. She says it's on your orders. I don't know what you've done, but it seems to be working."

John was quiet for several moments, and very thoughtful. "Yes, she's very competent," he smiled.

They spoke for a while before Thomas drifted off to sleep, and John went back to Margaret's room. He stood by the door, which he kept ajar, so he could still watch Thomas's room.

"Did I really say Thomas was not to have his medicine?" he asked Margaret.

"Well, not exactly. But when you said he was to have nothing that I hadn't prepared, I assumed it meant the medicine. Have I done something wrong?" she asked nervously.

"On the contrary," he reassured her. "I think you've done the right thing, and probably solved the mystery for us. If he's only had food and water from you and has improved, then quite likely the earlier food might have been contaminated." John paused.

"But," he continued. "That was checked regularly, and there have been no other illnesses reported in the household. So, let's put the food on one side for a moment. What else has Thomas consumed?"

"Only his medicine," replied Margaret. "But I don't see...." Mathew stopped her for a moment, as he found himself thinking along the same lines. John let him continue.

"All along we've assumed he was being poisoned by what he was given to eat or drink. We never considered the possibility that the poison might be in his medicine, did we guv'nor?"

"No, Mathew, we didn't. Who prescribes it?"

"Dr Hopper," replied Margaret. "And he always brought it with him."

"Where is it kept?" John continued.

"In his bedroom: usually on the shelf by the door."

"So anybody coming in could tamper with it?"

"Oh yes. Until I took over, servants, Dr Gilson and Mrs Waldren would all go into the bedroom."

"Just one more question, Margaret. What happens when you go to prepare his food?"

"My sister takes over. Dr Waldren is never left on his own."

John removed the remaining bottles of medicine, and thanked Margaret, leaving her and Mathew together for a while.

On leaving the house, John went straight to see Dr Hopper and asked him to analyse the medicine he had prescribed Thomas. At first Julius was reluctant to do so, feeling his medical ability was being brought into question. Finally he agreed and took John to his laboratory.

Firstly he selected a large bottle from which he had made up the smaller doses. He poured some of its contents into a glass dish and let them settle. Next he poured some the smaller doses, from the bottles John had given him, into similar glass dishes. He went a deathly white.

The second sample he poured out was a different colour.

"Dear God! This isn't what I prescribed. What is it?"

"I was hoping you'd tell me."

John told him about the missing poisons in the Waldren household. He added how Sam's enquiries in the house had not located them. Redman had been alerted, but they had not been found. Neither had Redman the slightest suspicion as to where they might have gone.

For the next two hours, Julius tried various tests, but was unable to identify any specific poison.

"I have to confess, Mayfield, I do not know what it is." He sat down, his face grey with worry. "Yet you say Thomas has managed to keep his food down, since Mrs Harrison stopped giving him this medicine?"

"Yes. It reminded me of when my regiment sailed to India, and many of the troops were seasick, just like they'd been given a purgative or something to make them sick. Then suddenly they stopped."

"What did you say? Something about a purgative?" Julius almost shouted John repeated what he had just said.

"Dear God, I've been looking at this the wrong way," Julius said and slapped his head. "He's not been poisoned, and that's why we can't find any traces," he paused as he gathered his thoughts.

"I've been looking for the wrong thing," he explained. "I prescribed and made up a medicine, that should have stopped his bowel movements, and the sickness. But this medicine," here he pointed at the sample. "Has been replaced by a purgative, with the opposite effect. It made him permanently sick and continually voided his bowels. The idea was to make him die of exhaustion and dehydration. I don't know what this is," he indicated the sample again. "But I'd stake my reputation on it being a powerful purgative. From what you say, it would be but the work of a few seconds to replace his proper medicine with this."

"And the best treatment?"

"Keep off the medicine, and only eat and drink what Mrs Harrison prepares. We should have him back on his feet in next to no time."

"That's excellent news, but it still doesn't tell me who did it. And I have to say it still looks very much like Sarah is responsible, though I'm having great difficulty in believing it."

"I'm afraid, Mayfield, I can't help you there. But, I think we both deserve some tea after all that work."

* * *

By the time John left Julius, his mind was already working on how to set a trap to unmask the culprit, but without much success. Having discussed his ideas with Mathew, they decided the only way would be for Margaret to keep a very close watch on the medicine, after Thomas had received any visitor.

First thing in the morning, Julius would call, and leave some proper medicine for Thomas. He would mark it a special way and only give it to Margaret. Other medicine would be left in the usual place, as bait. After that, it would be a question of watching and waiting.

Even then, it would not necessarily be enough evidence for a prosecution. However, it would identify the culprit, and perhaps give them more time to find the necessary proof. He hoped against hope that it wasn't Sarah, but all the indications were to the contrary. As John expected, he did not sleep well, and was grateful when it was time to get up.

But he had no idea just how the day would end.

CHAPTER NINETEEN

Monday

J ohn and Sam escorted Bradford to the magistrates court, and outlined the
facts of his arrest. He had been charged with murdering Billy Beech and
Jacob Harding, plus other counts of fraud and burglary at *Jersey's Bank.* As
expected, he was remanded in custody, at the County Gaol, until the next
Assizes which were still several weeks away.

After leaving the court, they had spent some time at a special Watch
Committee meeting, discussing the case. Although pleased with the outcome,
the Committee had some reservations on the way John had forced Henry
Jersey's hand, with his public notice. Privately, several of them held safe
deposit boxes at the bank, and they had been overjoyed to get their money
back.

Yet, after having made a formal complaint, Jersey had since withdrawn it.
The Committee also agreed with John's decision not to pursue his enquiries
into Albert Quinn's death.

Likewise, they accepted either Bradford or Harding had murdered
Hamlyn, but in the absence of any firm evidence, a successful prosecution
against Bradford would be unlikely. As Bradford stood a good chance of
being hanged, or at the very least transported, they agreed for John to close
that particular case.

Generally speaking, John was pleased with the way the morning had
gone, and it was just past noon when they returned to the police station. Sam,
had intended going off duty for a few hours, then he would return, for night
duty. Lucy had already returned to London, but not before roughing out the
sketches of the various recent crime scenes. She would have the finished

plans ready in a few days, which would give her an excuse to come to Warwick.

However, when they arrived at the police station, Sam found Robert was waiting for him, with two letters. "It looks like some replies for you," he said mysteriously, and dangled the letters in front of Sam, who made a grab at them.

Robert whisked them away. "Say please!" he teased.

"Please," replied Sam entering into the bantering, and took them a little self-consciously. Ignoring John's questioning look, he went into the charge office, and opened the first letter with some trepidation. Having read it, he gave a tremendous sigh of relief and cried "Yes!" which they all heard. Next he opened the second one, which told a similar story. Moments later, he returned to the others with a large grin spread over his face.

"Are you going to share it with us?" asked John.

"Oh yes! Oh definitely yes."

Sam handed the letters to John, whilst Robert waited. Having written the questions, he had a good idea what the answers were, but he was still impatient to see for himself.

John's face registered total surprise as he read the first one. Without a word he passed it over to Robert, before starting on the second letter. When Robert had finished the second letter, John spoke. "This changes everything I had planned for today. Whatever made you check up on this?"

"Partly you're always telling us to be thorough and partly, I don't know why," replied Sam. "Something just did not feel right, and I acted, or rather we acted on it." He nodded towards Robert. "I didn't want to tell you before, in case it came to nothing."

"I'm afraid Sam, this means you can't have the afternoon off."

"It's what I expected, and I'll be glad to help."

"Sam, go and arrange for everybody to be here for half past four. And get Sergeant Harrison here as soon as possible. Robert, please find Dr Hopper and get him here right away, I don't care how busy he is. Arrest him if need be." John rapidly gave his instructions.

Robert looked aghast.

"No, that's a joke, but I do need his help urgently. And I need to speak to him here, not anywhere else. We're all going to have a busy night."

At the time John spoke, he had no idea just how busy the night would be.

They went to leave the station, but John stopped them. "I know I don't have to tell you, but keep this information to yourselves for the moment. It's vital, for what I'm planning that nobody else, and I mean nobody must know about it."

"Yes guv'nor," they both replied.

* * *

Less than half an hour later, Julius Hopper arrived. "This had better be important, Mayfield. I'm rather busy at the moment," he snapped. Clearly he was not in the best of tempers.

Having sat his visitor down, John showed him the two letters Sam had received earlier that morning. Julius read them, and John was gratified to see him lost for words. "This is incredible: it's utterly unbelievable," he said finally. "But I doubt it will be adequate evidence to get a conviction for what's happening here."

"I agree, and so I have a plan. But it needs your help. I mustn't be seen anywhere near the house until our suspect has gone out."

"What do you want me to do?"

For the next few minutes, John outlined his plan.

"I sincerely hope you know what you're doing," cautioned Julius. "If it goes wrong.......?"

"If it goes wrong, then I've lost a very good friend and Warwick a very good doctor. But, will you help me?"

"Of course I will."

They discussed the final details of John's plan, and Julius left, passing Mathew on the way.

"Guv'nor, I've just heard we've got a breakthrough with the poisoning."

"Yes."

John handed him the letters, explaining why they had been received, and he waited patiently until Mathew had finished reading them. "And this is what I need you do now, but still be back here for half past four."

John passed on his instructions.

* * *

By 4.30pm, all of John's men, including those who should have been off duty, had assembled in his office. It left very little room.

"Thank you all for coming in, especially at such short notice," he began. During the next few minutes, John explained what had been happening to Thomas, and how Julius had discovered he was being slowly murdered. Next he outlined the main suspects, and then gave Sam the floor, to explain what he had discovered. When Sam had finished, John explained his plan and detailed where he wanted his men.

"Please don't be offended if you think you could be better employed. I've had to choose those who are best suited for their particular part in the plan. All of you are important, and it's vital we get this absolutely right."

They all murmured their agreement.

"Those of you, who are watching the house, need to be in position by five-thirty. The arresting party needs to be there for six. Are there any questions?"

There were none.

"Good luck. I can't emphasize enough that we are dealing with a formidable and very dangerous person. Whatever you do, take no chances, and be on your guard at all times." John waited whilst they nodded in agreement.

"And lastly, until this has been resolved, you are not to discuss it with anyone, and I mean anyone, not even amongst yourselves, outside this building. If any word gets out, my plan cannot work. And it must work if we're to save Dr Waldren's life and bring a very dangerous criminal to justice. We will only have the one chance to do it."

* * *

Richard was having an enjoyable afternoon. He had been called out to an attractive young woman, who had injured her ankle. After examining her carefully, he could find nothing obviously wrong with the ankle, although he accepted she might have twisted it.

"Can't you do anything for it?" she asked. "Can't you massage it or something, please? Can't you do anything to help me take my mind off it?" She pleaded, turning her large blue eyes appealingly towards him.

"I feel that is possibly something your husband could do much better than I," he replied, only half in jest, feeling his pulse quicken.

"He's not here at the moment, and he won't be back for several days. Even then......" She shrugged her shoulders.

"Would you really like me to massage it for you?"

"Oh yes please."

Richard began to massage the ankle before he gradually moved his hands, tentatively, further up her leg. He was gratified to find she did not protest, but merely lay further back in her chair. Slowly he moved his hands up to her thighs.

"I have found when doing a massage that sometimes you have to spread it to other parts of the limb, for the best effect. Would you agree?"

"Oh doctor," she moaned in a husky voice. "Can you massage my shoulders, please?"

He needed no urging to stand behind her and massage her shoulders. Slowly his hands crept forwards over her blouse and onto her breasts. Unlike Laura the other night, she did not protest. And, he thought, if her husband was not up to much, then she could provide him with some pleasant interludes. Suddenly she pulled him round to face her, and began to kiss him passionately. Minutes later she had taken him into her bedroom.

When St Mary's clock struck five-thirty, she informed him she had visitors coming. But added how she would love to see him again. Reluctantly he took his leave of Bella Carson, promising to see her again and returned to High Street.

* * *

As he arrived, he found Sarah and Redman in the hall. She had just come back from town. Sarah remembered she was providing a late, and hopefully, a reconciliation supper for John and Laura, and wanted to choose the food herself. Redman had gone with her to carry her purchases. Neither of them paid any particular attention to a cab standing on the other side of the street.

However, as they entered the hall, she was confronted by Dr Hopper, who was pacing up and down in the hall, obviously waiting for her.

"Sarah, thank heavens you have returned. Where on earth have you been?"

She told him. "What's the problem, Julius? I can see you're worried."

"There's no easy way to tell you. But, I fear Thomas will not last out the night."

"**Nooooh!**" screamed Sarah and she ran up the stairs. Richard went to follow her, but Julius grabbed his arm.

"There's nothing either of us can do. Let her spend his last few hours with her husband."

Redman had listened to the exchange, before showing Dr Hopper out. Then he went into the kitchen to pass on the news he had heard.

Upstairs, Margaret Harrison sat on her bed, totally unable to believe what she had just heard. It simply did not make sense: but Dr Hopper was adamant. They had done all they could, but it had not been good enough. He insisted she was not to go back into the sick room, but was to pack her belongings and be ready to leave the house.

Her role here was finished, but still she could not believe what had happened. Thomas had been getting on so well. How could he have declined so quickly? Perhaps Dr Hopper was wrong? Perhaps she ought to get Dr Gilson to come, and get him to give a second opinion. Yes, that's what she would do. Margaret stood up and went towards her bedroom door.

As she did so, there came a loud knocking at the front door, and she went out onto the landing.

* * *

By 5.30pm, Sam and Ben had quietly left the police station and walked to High Street, where they parted company. Ben made his way into Castle Lane, where he found a secluded place, under some trees, but was still be able to see the rear of Dr Waldren's house.

Sam had other plans for watching the front of the house. He called in a favour from one of his old school friends, and met him and his cab in West Street. Here Sam climbed on board, and the cab moved back up High Street and stopped close to the surgery.

Back in the police station, Mathew was finalizing his own plans for the arrest he was soon going to make. He looked at his watch, and saw it was only 5.30pm. As he knew only too well from experience, that the next thirty minutes would take an eternity to pass.

Caleb tried to do some paperwork, but like Mathew, he was too tense and unable to concentrate properly. "Do you think the guv'nor's right about this?" he asked, putting down his pen.

"I hope so. Either way we'll find out soon enough."

They talked about various matters, but were glad when it was time to move. A cab, as arranged, drew up outside the police station. They left the station, climbed into it and gave the driver his instructions. The cab stopped outside the Waldrens' house, where they climbed down and instructed the driver to wait. He regularly helped the police and knew something was afoot.

Now all he had to do was wait, think about the money, and the drinks he would be bought, when he told about his latest adventures with the police. But nothing had prepared him for what he was about to witness.

Mathew and Caleb walked to the front door. "Ready?" asked Mathew. Caleb nodded.

Taking hold of the door knocker, Mathew hit the door loudly. He continued for several seconds.

Redman opened the door, appalled that anyone should make so much noise, even more so when the master was believed to be dying upstairs. He found a stern faced Mathew and Caleb on the doorstep, and noticed the cab still waiting by the kerbside, with its driver staring at the three of them.

"We need to see Mrs Waldren," announced Mathew, officially and without any preamble.

"That's not possible, gentlemen." Redman made the word *gentlemen*, almost sound insulting.

"I said we need to see Mrs Waldren, now! So get her, please." There was nothing polite about Mathew's use of the word *please.*

"I will not. She's with the master who's dying," protested Redman.

"Then we will," snapped Mathew, and pushed his way into the house, brushing the butler aside. He led the way upstairs accompanied by Caleb and a protesting Redman.

They met Sarah just coming out of Thomas's bedroom.

"Are you Mrs Sarah Waldren?" said Mathew sharply.

"You know full well I am. What's this all about?"

"Sarah Waldren, I have a warrant for your arrest for the attempted murder of your husband, Dr Thomas Waldren."

"**NO! NO!**" she screamed. "Where's Mayfield? Is this his doing? And to think we gave him our friendship." Sarah made to go back into Thomas's room. But Mathew caught her left arm.

Immediately she swung her right fist at his face, catching him in the eye. Mathew caught this arm. Caleb joined in the scrap but Sarah began screaming with all her might, and kicking both men. It took them several seconds before they could put some manacles on her wrists.

At last they had her subdued, and started to go down the stairs. In the hallway, they found their path blocked by Redman and all the servants, most of whom held heavy saucepans and pokers. They obviously had no intention of letting them through.

"What the devil's going on here?" came a new voice.

The servants turned and saw Richard.

"They're trying to take the mistress away and we won't let them," replied an angry Redman.

"Is this true sergeant?"

"Yes doctor, I'm afraid it is."

"Where's Mayfield?"

"Waiting for us back at the station. He didn't think it was right, given their previous friendship, that he should make the arrest." Mathew made no attempt to disguise his disapproval.

"Let them pass, Redman," instructed Richard. The servants reluctantly moved aside. "Don't worry, Sarah. I've two more patients to see, then I'll check on Thomas and come to you."

"Thank you," called Sarah, her eyes blazing hatred at the policemen. "At least there's one gentleman here this evening." She allowed herself to be pulled towards the front door.

Looking up to the landing, Mathew saw Margaret. "Go home, now!" he instructed.

"You bastard!" she shouted.

But she made no attempt to leave.

* * *

Several minutes after the house had become quiet again, Thomas saw his bedroom door open and a familiar figure enter.

"What a bonus, eh Thomas?" The figure chuckled malevolently. "What an unexpected piece of luck."

Thomas struggled to sit up, but his visitor pushed him back on to the bed. "Just think. The mistress of the house will be topped for your murder and I'll be well in the clear. What's that you say?"

He gloated again, as Thomas made a faint gurgling sound. "Still alive eh? Well not for very much longer."

Lying still, Thomas's breath came in gasps. He looked up at his tormentor. "Why?" he gasped.

"I suppose you have a right to know. Quite simply… revenge."

"But....but.....what...have...I....done....to...you?" His words came out weakly.

"You? Nothing. In fact you're a very good doctor. But," his voice hardened. "I hate all doctors. They failed me when I needed one once. And as a result, my darling wife died. We hadn't been married very long. The drunken Dr Boyd died just a few days later. He'd been too drunk to help my darling wife, but he was very sober when I killed him. There have been, oh let me see, several others since then."

"Who?"

"Never you mind. They're not important. I'll give you a clue though. Did you like my references? I wrote them myself. I am quite a specialist in the art of forgery. Make the most of your last few minutes. You'll soon be gone, and dear Sarah will take the blame. That fool Hopper always suspected her. And so did Mayfield. He's not as clever as everybody thinks. Pity, though, because I quite liked him."

"How did you do it?"

"That was simple and it fooled the great Dr Hopper. He was so fixated in looking for poison, that he forgot the obvious. Not really a poison, but a high powered purgative. Even with an autopsy, at the most it would have looked like a tragic mistake, and Hopper would have been blamed. Once I discovered he was looking for poison, and suspected Sarah, the rest was simple."

The figure laughed mirthlessly. "And when that idiot Perkins began asking questions about some missing poisons in the house, the rest was easy. It's been very successful. Even better than I dared to hope."

"Don't bank on it," said Thomas in a much stronger voice. "Once we worked out that it wasn't my food being poisoned, it only left the medicine. That was quite clever, giving me a potent purgative instead of poison. It would have looked like natural causes. However, I'm now well on the road to recovery."

"Possibly you might have been. But I feel a relapse coming on. Everyone's expecting you to die tonight, so when it happens, nobody will take that much notice. Your dear Sarah has her own problems, and will soon be joining you. I'll stay on until after she keeps her appointment with the hangman. When's she topped, I'll be there."

"You fiend! You'll never get away with this."

"A word of advice, Thomas. Don't struggle. It'll be much quicker and less painful, when I smother you."

As he finished speaking, the man pushed Thomas down onto his back, and at the same time, pulled out the pillow from under his head. Thomas struggled, but he was still too weak to put up much resistance. He felt the pillow being pushed down onto his face and it became difficult to breathe.

There was an almighty crash, as the wooden screen in the room, was pushed over to reveal John and Robert Andrew standing there.

"Dr Gilson, or is it Godwin or even Gittings, or whatever your name is, I am arresting you for the attempted murder of Dr Thomas Waldren," John announced.

Richard released the pillow on Thomas's face and stood up as Robert approached him with his manacles. Suddenly he moved quicker than they had anticipated.

A lancet appeared in his clenched fist, which he used with devastating effect to stab through Robert's left hand, and pinned him to the wooden bed head. Robert cried out in pain, and dropped the manacles and went to pull it out.

"Leave it," instructed Thomas. "It'll help control the bleeding." At the same time he started to sit up.

Meanwhile John had his staff in his hand and was advancing on Richard. Another lancet appeared in the doctor's hand, and just at that moment, the door opened and Margaret came in.

* * *

She had not gone home as her husband had instructed, but stayed on, in case she could be of some assistance. Much relieved, she had seen Richard go into Thomas's room. But then she thought about it and remembered how he was smiling, which did not seem to be right in the circumstances.

She had tiptoed to Thomas's bedroom door, where she stopped and listened. Appalled, she had heard Richard's confessions, and realized Sarah had been wrongly arrested. Then all went quiet in the room, and it had taken her several seconds to realize what was happening.

When she did so, Margaret went to scream for help, but at that moment, John had knocked the screen over. She was so relieved to hear his voice and wondered what he was doing in there.

Then came Robert's cry as he was stabbed, and unable to contain her curiosity any longer, she went in to see for herself what was happening. Margaret could not have timed her entrance at a worse possible moment.

* * *

Sensing the door open, Richard spun around and caught hold of her. Wrapping one arm round her, he held her tightly to him, whilst holding his lancet to her throat.

"Get back, Mayfield!" he instructed. "And drop your staff." John hesitated. **"NOW!"** snapped Richard and pushed the tip of his lancet into Margaret's neck, where it drew blood.

"NOW!" he repeated. "Or I'll kill her."

"Don't do it, John," Margaret cried bravely, but he could see the fear in her eyes. He knew Richard would not hesitate to kill her, if he had to, and he could not let that happen. He let his staff fall to the floor.

"That's better," said Richard. "Now, you walk out of here in front of us. You tell any of your men who are hanging around, and any of the servants, to let us through. If they don't, then she dies. Understood?"

"Yes. But, let her go. If you want a hostage, then take me."

Richard gave a cruel laugh. "Not a chance, matey. Not a chance."

Thomas had now freed Robert's hand, and was binding it up. Robert looked for guidance from John, who shook his head. Margaret's life was not worth the risk. Possibly, if Robert had not been injured, they might have tried something, but not now. At least Sam and Ben were still outside somewhere.

Keeping a wary eye on Richard, John moved carefully past him to the door. He slowly opened it, and was not surprised to find Redman, and a group of servants, standing on the landing. They moved to stop Richard passing through.

"Redman," said John. "Please let us through. I'm afraid he'll kill Mrs Harrison if anyone tries to stop him." For a moment he thought the butler was not going to obey.

"What's going on Mr Mayfield?"

"Dr Gilson here has tried to murder your master, but he has failed, thanks to Mrs Harrison and Mrs Waldren. Now please stand back and let us through. Go to your master."

"NO! You stay here!" instructed Richard. "I want you all where I can see you. You all go down the stairs first."

Redman instructed the other servants to go downstairs, and he followed. They were clearly most unhappy with Richard, and radiated hostility towards him. John knew, if he was not very careful, Margaret or one or more of the servants could still lose their lives here tonight.

* * *

Back in the police station, Sarah sat drinking tea with Caleb, Mathew and Julius. Having attended to Caleb's bruised shins, he turned his attention to Mathew's black eye and shins.

"I'd loved to have seen it," he smiled. "I've no doubt it's all over the town by now. From what I hear, Sarah, you've missed your true vocation, as an actress, and the stage is the poorer for it."

"Actually, I think being a prize fighter would have been more to the point," replied Mathew. "I really think you could teach Ma Morgan a few things."

They all laughed nervously.

"I'm sorry Mathew," said Sarah, holding his arm. "I was told to make it look as realistic as possible, and I got carried away. Do you think Margaret will ever forgive me?"

"I'm more concerned about her forgiving me."

"Will Thomas be alright though?" asked Sarah.

"I think so," replied Julius, with more confidence than he felt. "Mayfield knows what he's doing. And there are two of them to protect him. And we really needed the evidence to convict Gilson, otherwise he'll get away. I appreciate we would have saved Thomas, but how many others would have been put at risk?"

"What made you suspect him, Mathew?"

"You'll have to ask young Sam Perkins about that. It was his idea and he acted on his own initiative."

"Don't forget though, it was your wife, sergeant, who thought to stop giving Thomas his medicine and that put us on the right track," added Julius.

"I wish I knew what was happening back at the house," sighed Sarah. "I really had hoped to have heard something by now."

So had the others.

CHAPTER TWENTY

Later on Monday

Back in the house, John, Richard and Margaret had reached the foot of the stairs. Richard stopped and looked at Redman.

"Go and get the carriage ready, and be quick about it. There's just about enough time for us to catch the Birmingham train. I don't doubt for a moment, that one of Mayfield's lackeys is out the back. Have him bring the carriage round the front, the moment it's ready."

Richard paused. "But warn him, any tricks and she dies."

He nudged Margaret's throat again with the lancet, and made it bleed in a different place. Redman did not move, but looked at John.

"Best do as he says, Redman."

The butler went off reluctantly. Meanwhile, Richard, still holding the lancet to Margaret's throat, instructed everyone to sit down. It was a long tense wait. At last Redman re-appeared and announced the carriage was on its way round to High Street.

Richard moved towards the front door still holding onto Margaret. "You drive, Mayfield," he instructed, and indicated to John to open the door. John did so, hoping Ben would have told Sam what was happening, and between them they would be able to disarm Richard.

He opened the door and his heart sank.

"Hello John," said Laura Grant. "Fancy meeting you here. You don't look very pleased......" She broke off as her eyes took in the drama inside the hallway.

"What a stroke of luck," interrupted Richard. Pushing Margaret to one side, he transferred his grip to Laura and pushed the lancet onto her throat.

"The same rules apply, Any tricks....from anyone.....and she dies. And that includes you, darling."

He pricked Laura's throat with the lancet, making it bleed. There was a tinge of bitterness in his use of the word *darling.*

Moments later, Ben Underwood appeared leading the carriage horse. John moved forward helplessly. Where the hell was Sam? He could do nothing without him.

Taking the reins helplessly from Ben Underwood, he shook his head slightly. "Don't try anything, Ben. He'll kill her at the slightest suggestion of a trick. As soon as you can, let Sergeant Harrison know what's happened."

Ben nodded unhappily.

John climbed into the carriage driving seat, still holding onto the reins. Richard forced Laura into the carriage, behind John, and followed her.

"To the station Mayfield and no tricks," Richard hissed.

They arrived at the station with several minutes to spare. Richard tossed some coins to John. "You get me two tickets to Curzon Street. If she's good, I'll let her go there. If not....well who knows? And no tricks as I'll be watching you the whole time. Understand?"

"Yes," John replied miserably. "Do as he says, Laura."

John bought the tickets, gave them to Richard, and all three waited anxiously in the carriage, for the train for Birmingham to appear. When it arrived, he was forced to wait and watch, whilst Richard bundled Laura into the last carriage. After a few minutes, the train drew out of the station. As it did so, Richard leaned out of the carriage, and blew a kiss to John.

"Nice knowing you. Shame about Laura." He laughed mirthlessly.

Watching the train move slowly out of the station, John cursed his helplessness. There was nothing he could do. Whilst there was a telegraph system in operation in some parts of the country, it had not yet arrived in Warwick. In any case, it only operated in daylight, and it was now quite dark. The quickest he could get a message to Birmingham was by horse, and the train would be there before the rider.

He had saved Thomas's life, but at what a cost. In spite of Richard's promises, John very much doubted if he would let Laura go. The last despairing look on her face showed him she understood that only too well.

Where on earth was Sam? It was not like him to be missing when he was needed. He had better have a damn good excuse if he wanted to keep his job. John turned away in total despair.

As he did so, there was a tug at his sleeve. Turning he found Redman standing behind him, holding the reins of two horses.

"The master says to take Midnight."

The horse, Midnight, was Thomas's pride and joy. She was a powerful black mare with immense stamina.

John shook his head. "It's a kind gesture, but I'll never get to Birmingham before the train. And even if I did, I'd probably kill Midnight in the process."

"No sir! Not to Birmingham!" interrupted Redman angrily, which was quite unlike him. "The train's got a long haul up Hatton Bank, and it has to use another engine. When it gets up to Hatton station the other engine has be unhitched, whilst the first one takes on water. It's a moonlit night and on Midnight you should get to Hatton Station before the train."

Spurred into action, John was already mounting the black mare.

"Leave her tied by the water tower," instructed Redman. "I'll be close behind you."

John urged Midnight into a gallop straight up the Coventry Road and then onto the canal towpath. Here he was obliged to slow to a canter, because of the uneven ground.

The ride brought back memories of that night, not so long ago, when he had ridden along here after Charles Pearson, who had taken Kate as his hostage. How ironic, he thought! Here he was, again, riding after a felon who had just abducted the woman he loved. Only this time it was much more serious.

Last year he had not been on his own, knowing help was close at hand. But this time he was alone. He had relied so much on Sam, who was nowhere to be found. When he was, he would have some explaining to do. And it had better be good.

By now he had reached the Birmingham Road Bridge, where he pulled off the towpath and onto the road. As if sensing his urgency, Midnight broke into a gallop.

Somewhere towards the top of Hatton Hill, he passed the train, which was still labouring up the bank. Nevertheless, although there were trees on both sides of the road, he took no chances, but kept to the far side whilst he passed the train. It was doubtful if Richard, even if he was expecting a pursuit, would have been able to see him. But it was not worth the risk.

John arrived at the water tower about three minutes before the engines lumbered into the station, steaming and smoking heavily. Several men rushed out to connect the hose to the second engine's boiler, whilst the lead one was unhitched. A quick look had told him tying Midnight to the tower was not a good idea, as she could be seen from the train. Swiftly he tethered her by the station entrance. Stripping off his coat, which he placed over the saddle, he ran out to the engine, as if he was part of the crew filling it up with water.

When it was full, he left the other men and climbed on board the engine. Fortunately, the rear carriages were round a slight bend, and he could not be seen by anybody in them.

"Who the hell are you?" snarled the large engine driver.

"I'm a police officer from Warwick and I've no time to explain. I just need to get to Birmingham, without being seen by a felon already on this train."

"So what! You pays yer money same as everyone else, policeman or not."

"Will this do?" John handed him a crown, although he had doubts the man would actually hand it over to his employers.

The engine driver took the coin and held it close to the fire in the cab. Seemingly satisfied, he nodded. "But you'll have to shovel," he instructed. "My mate's had to go off, and it'll save me having to do it. But first, get the kettle boiling so we can 'ave some tea. It's thirsty work in here."

By the time they arrived at Curzon Street Station, John's back ached: his hands were blistered, and he had singed his hair. The good thing was, with his face covered in soot, like the rest of his clothes, he would be extremely difficult to recognise. And, if the truth was known, apart from his concern for Laura, he had actually quite enjoyed the journey.

"Will you do something for me now, please?" he asked.

The driver looked at him, and then nodded suspiciously.

"In a moment I'm going to get down and follow a man. He will be holding a young woman very close to him. When I do so, will you please go and find the nearest policemen, and bring them towards me. But, on no account must they make a move or acknowledge me until I say so. Do you understand?"

The man nodded.

"If they do," stressed John. "The man will kill the woman before any of us can help her. I cannot stress enough just how dangerous he is."

As he finished speaking, John saw Richard walking past the engine. His eyes were continually looking around him, and he held Laura very tightly with his left hand. Although, as John expected, the lancet was not immediately to be seen, he saw Richard still had his right hand in his pocket. No doubt, he guessed correctly, that was where it probably was. Laura looked exhausted and terrified, but otherwise, she seemed to be unharmed. She was being made to walk quickly to keep up with her captor.

Richard was wary and kept looking around him. Knowing how quickly he could react, even when not expecting trouble, John had no doubt he would move even quicker when he was fully alert. Getting Laura away from him would not be easy. He just had to hope the policemen, when the driver found them, would keep calm, and not make matters worse.

Having killed before, there was little doubt in John's mind, Richard would kill again. He had nothing to lose by doing so.

John let them pass, indicated them to the engine driver and quietly climbed down on to the platform. All was going well until Laura looked behind, and recognized him.

"**JOHN!**" she cried, before he could stop her.

"**DAMN YOU MAYFIELD!**" shouted Richard, spinning round. "She dies now and it's all your fault."

Suddenly the lancet appeared in his hand, and he pulled it back for a strike. Other people had seen what was happening, and two women screamed. John began to run towards Laura, but knew he would never get there in time.

"**DON'T DO IT, RICHARD!**" he called. "We can sort this out."

At the same time, he heard the sound of raised voices from behind him.

"**HEY....THAT'S MY CASE!**" one of them shouted.

"**GILSON!**" shouted another voice, which John immediately recognised. Nobody was ever quite sure what happened next.

John was aware of a small shape flying by his ear. Richard saw it coming, and thrust Laura away, whilst his arm moved forward to protect his face. She staggered but quickly regained her balance.

"**LAURA!   THIS WAY!**" shouted John. But, she hesitated, unable to believe she was free. "**THIS WAY!**" John shouted again. He was relieved to see her start moving towards him, but Richard was already running towards her.

Richard had fended off the case that had been thrown at him, and lunged after Laura with the lancet. It only just missed her back. Then he was on her, caught hold of her dress, and raised the lancet to stab at her throat. John knew he was still too far away to help her, but he kept on running.

He was aware of another figure hurtling by him. This figure blocked Richard's downward thrust with the lancet. Before Richard could react, his wrist had been grasped, and at the same time, his feet were kicked away from under him. Richard fell heavily onto the platform and screamed, as his arm was twisted high up his back. His assailant knelt on him, boring hard with his knees. The lancet fell out of his grip, and it was kicked away by one of the other passengers on the platform.

"Please struggle you bastard. Please. Dr Waldren saved my mam's life, and mine. To say nothing of your abducting Miss Laura and trying to seduce my Lucy," snarled Sam Perkins. "Please struggle, and give me an excuse to really hurt you."

Richard lay still. All the fight had been knocked out of him by Sam's threats and the sudden, unexpected viciousness of the policeman's attack. He could not believe his misfortune. Of all the policemen he had ever known, this one scared him the most, and he knew he could expect no mercy. He relaxed and remained still, whilst Sam put manacles on him.

"Easy Sam," said John, touching him gratefully on the shoulder. "Am I glad to see you?"

Moments later, two railway policemen arrived, with a pair of manacles. Quickly John explained what had happened.

"Leave him to us, mate, until you can get cleaned up, and then you can have him back."

"Mate? Mate?" asked Sam in disdain. "Since when do you address my superintendent as mate?"

Sobbing with relief, Laura was being tended to by another female passenger. But when John went across to her, she flung herself, sobbing, into his arms. For a while he said nothing, but just held her tightly, before they both sat down on a trolley. Sam stood by, obtaining details from those people who had seen what had happened.

"What the deuce is going on here?"

John looked up and saw a police inspector stood alongside him. The man had a red face, and he was waving a silver topped cane about officiously.

"We have just explained to your......" began John.

"Stand to attention when you speak to me? Don't they teach you how to address your superior officers in whatever organisation you're from. And you," he broke off and pointed to Sam, with his cane. "How dare you come here so improperly dressed? I'll have you put on a charge."

"I'm sorry, sir," replied Sam, quietly. "I considered preventing a felony to more important than how I looked."

"Preventing a crime? You don't know what crime is. Where is it you're from? Oh yes: Warwick. What have you had in the last few days eh? A bit of larceny and poaching, eh?"

"Actually," said John very quietly. "In the past few days we have had one suspicious death, three murders, a bank robbery, one attempted murder and two abductions. Kindly don't lecture us on what crime is." He handed Laura to Sam, who had already recognized the danger signs, and had difficulty in keeping his face straight. Life would soon get very entertaining.

"Stand to attention when you address me. What's your name and rank? And stand up when you speak to me." He began jabbing John, in the chest, with his cane.

A crowd of passengers had gathered to watch the incident. Some of them had seen the way Sam had saved Laura's life, and were muttering about the way he was now being treated. The inspector was unaware of his two grinning policemen standing behind him.

They were the same two who had been reprimanded by Sam for not addressing John properly. As their inspector was not a popular man, they were thoroughly enjoying the drama, and had a good idea what would be coming next.

Without any effort, and still whilst sitting down, John caught hold of the cane, and twisted it out of the other man's hand. The inspector gaped in disbelief, and the crowd cheered. John stood up, and put one foot onto the trolley. Without any further words, he broke the cane over his knee and handed the pieces back to the Inspector.

"Don't you ever dare hit me again." His voice was icily quiet.

The inspector turned to look for his own constables and was relieved to see two of them stood behind him. "Arrest that man!" he ordered. Neither of them moved.

"Did you hear what I said?" he roared.

One of the constables whispered something in his ear and the inspector went white with shock. "Superintendent? Superintendent?" he gasped, and stood to attention.

"Correct," came John's quiet reply.

"My deepest apologies sir, I had no idea. You're not in uniform."

"Correct. I have just helped bring the train into here from Warwick, in order to effect this young lady's rescue, so I'm sorry my standard of dress bothers you."

"Sir! Can I suggest you bring the young lady, and your constable to my office, where you can get cleaned up and explain what is going on. Obviously all my facilities are at your disposal. It'll be more private there and I dare say you could all do with some tea."

They followed the, now very chastened, inspector. The crowd cheered them on their way. Sam and Laura waved to them.

Several minutes later, they were sat in the inspector's office drinking tea. Laura had calmed down, but she still held on to John. He was only just starting to relax himself, and was already regretting having doubted Sam, after what had just happened.

* * *

Sam had watched as Sarah was taken kicking and screaming from the house, and settled back to wait. He had been concerned as the time passed, and there was no signal from the guv'nor. Then, to his horror, he had seen Laura walk up High Street and go to the surgery door. Even as he climbed down from the cab, he saw he was too late to warn her. The front door opened and Laura was pulled inside the house, and the door slammed loudly behind her.

In the brief moment the door had been open, Sam had seen a group of servants sitting on the floor of the hallway, and he knew something had gone terribly wrong.

He had thought about going to the door and see if he could hear anything, but decided against it. Gilson was clearly in control of what was happening inside the house, and now had Laura as a hostage. The problem was what to do?

If necessary, he could get into the rear of the house with Ben, but would that help? An attempt at a frontal assault on Richard, as he left the house was probably his best choice. But, he decided to wait for a while longer and see what developed.

Several minutes later, he saw Ben coming from Back Lane leading a carriage. Sam quickly went to meet him. "What's happening?" he whispered.

"It's all gone wrong. Gilson had Margaret Harrison as a hostage, but now he's changed her for Laura Grant. He's got a lancet at her throat and is promising to kill her if there are any tricks. They're going to catch the Birmingham train and the guv'nor is going to take them to the station."

"Is there any chance of us jumping him when he comes out to the carriage?"

Ben shook his head miserably. "No. He's instructed that I'm to stand well away or he'll kill Miss Grant."

"Are you certain it's the Birmingham train they're catching?"

"That what Redman said."

"Can you delay taking the carriage to the front door for a few more minutes, and give me a head start?" Sam had the beginnings of a plan.

"What are you going to do?"

"Get on the same train and take it from there."

Moments later, his friendly cab driver was taking him to Warwick railway station, at a fast trot.

* * *

"Bless you, dear Sam," said Laura, gripping his arm, as he finished his tale.

Then John took up his side of the story.

It was close on midnight when they returned to Warwick. John was relieved to find Mathew and Caleb waiting for them, complete with a spare pair of manacles, and a cab.

"Thank God you're all safe and you've got him as a bonus." Mathew indicated Richard. "I brought these, just in case he was playing up. I'd have enjoyed putting another set on him."

He glowered at Richard, who found he was unable to meet the big man's gaze.

"How's Margaret?" asked John.

"She's getting over it. Its lucky that I didn't arrest him. He would have known about it."

"I can assure you," chuckled John. "He did not have an easy time with Sam."

They took Richard to the police station, formally charged him with the attempted murder of Thomas Waldren, and the abduction of Margaret Harrison and Laura Grant. Then they escorted him to the cells.

"A question, Mayfield, please? How did you get on to me?" Richard asked.

"I didn't. Tell him Sam."

"The main reason, I suppose, was the incident with the arrow heads, and the so-called missing poisons. Somehow, it seemed too contrived. It was just too coincidental and I don't believe in coincidences, especially when I asked a few questions of the servants. None of them had seen any of your poisons."

"You said the main reason. What was the other?"

"I decided to check you out, after seeing you with Miss Grant."

"So that's why you wanted all my qualifications?"

"Not really. It's what the guv'nor insists we do, whenever we take a statement from a witness. After that, I made my own enquiries and we discovered quite a lot about you."

"What would you have done, Mayfield, if I hadn't been away from the house, all this afternoon? You'd never have got into the house unnoticed."

"Bella Carson did a good job. She knew just how long to keep you, so you could arrive back at the house, at the same time as Sarah and Redman, to be greeted by Dr Hopper, with his bad news. I hope you enjoyed your last afternoon of freedom. I'm told she's very good at what she does."

Gilson was stunned. "You arranged my visit to Bella Carson?"

"Yes. She's a whore, albeit a high class one, who owed Sergeant Harrison a big favour. This was her way of repaying the debt. If you had only left women alone, especially those who were already spoken for, and had refrained from being too clever with the arrowheads, you might have got away with it."

He said nothing more, and Sam locked the cell door. The other formalities could be attended to later in the morning. Laura had stayed in John's office whilst Richard had been charged and locked up. She had found a note on John's desk urging him to call on Sarah, regardless of what time he got back. Laura and Sam went with him.

Sarah was overjoyed to see them all safe and well, and hugged each one of them in turn. "Laura," she said. "I owe you a most sincere apology."

Laura looked at her.

"Yes," Sarah continued. "I had completely forgotten to cancel you coming for supper until the action all started. By then it was too late. I never dreamt you would have been put in any danger. Can you ever forgive me?"

"Of course I can." She released her hold on John's arm and hugged Sarah, before she returned to holding John's arm. It was an action that did not go unnoticed by Sarah.

"Talking of supper," Sarah continued, "I have no doubt you are all very hungry. So I've had a late supper prepared, and I will not take no for an answer." She led them into the dining room, where they were joined soon afterwards by Thomas.

When they left the house, sometime later, John said. "May I escort you home Miss Grant?"

"I can think of nobody else I'd rather be with right now."

When they arrived at her school, John stood aside to let her enter.

"No John," she said, gripping his arm tighter. "Please come in with me. Stay with me tonight."

The door closed behind them.

* * *

A few evenings later, Thomas and Sarah held a small informal *thank you* supper to celebrate her husband's recovery. Their guests were John and Laura, Mathew and Margaret, Sam and Lucy and Julius Hopper.

Thomas was now well on the road to recovery, and Mathew's black eye was fading. There was still some concern regarding Robert's hand, which had been stabbed, although it seemed to be healing now. Acting on Thomas's advice, John had sent him home to Aylesbury, for a few days convalescence.

"However," said Thomas in a serious tone. "I am not sure when he will be declared fit enough to resume active duty. I fear it could be some weeks and, I am concerned he may never regain the full use of that hand." He paused, aware the others were listening intently.

"I am aware how he only just manages to get by, financially," he continued. "I know he sends money to his mother on a regular basis. So he will soon be back, but on light duties. Is that alright with you John?"

"Absolutely. It's not his writing hand and there will be plenty for him to do, but, will the Watch Committee agree?"

"After you've just saved the life of their chairman, probably not." Everyone laughed. "But, as you've recovered most of their stolen property, they'll do as I say. Also, I've set the scene for you to recruit another constable, regardless of whether or not Robert ever comes back to full fitness.

He did not tell them how he had discussed Robert's case with Sarah. They had agreed, if there was any problem, then he would pay Robert to act as John's clerk.

Sam explained how he had decided to check up on Richard's background, with amazing results. None of the towns, where he had supposedly worked, knew of a doctor by the name of Richard Gilson. However, they could remember a Roger Godwin, Robert Gittings and Roland Grant, whose former medical employers had all died, apparently from natural causes, albeit unexpectedly. Another doctor who answered Richard's description, was wanted by the police, in one town, for rape and indecent assault, on one of his female patients.

Dr Richard Grant, who had been employed as a ship's doctor, was a slightly different case. A female passenger had died on the ship, after having been operated on by him. Her relatives had complained to the shipping company, who in turn, had tried to find Grant. But he had disappeared.

Further checks revealed no such Richard Grant had ever qualified as a doctor, at the places and times he said he had. No doctor answering to the other names and descriptions had ever qualified as such. All his references, from former employers, had been written after their deaths. Other references were from people who did not exist. Now other references were being checked out.

"Yet, medically, he seemed to know what he was doing," commented Thomas.

"I have to agree," added John. "Certainly what he discovered on Harding's body, as to the correct entry wound, was excellent. In fact it was the only solid evidence we have against him."

"And that, my friend, is a big problem," commented Julius. "I think it is highly unlikely Gilson or whatever his name is, will ever testify for you in court."

"Actually, I've studied his report, and the body," said Thomas. "And I totally agree with his findings."

"I've spoken to a barrister," added John. "He is of the opinion we can use his report and statement. You see, this is why it's so important to write all the evidence down."

As the party was breaking up, Sarah held up her hand for everyone's attention. "John, be honest with me. Was Richard your only suspect for trying to murder Thomas?"

"Of course," he replied after, only a slight hesitation.

Sarah punched him playfully on his arm. "You always were a poor liar."

"I must confess, Sarah," said Julius, with a reddening face. "You were my main suspect. But Mayfield here never really agreed. He genuinely believed in you and, I have to say, I was delighted to find you were totally innocent."

"Bless you, John," said Sarah and kissed him.

CHAPTER TWENTY-ONE

Eighteen months later

Mrs Laura Mayfield winced slightly, and gently held her swelling belly. "He's kicking me again," she complained laughingly, putting down her knife and fork.

"Are you sure it's a boy?" asked John, as he did on a regular basis, and continued eating his supper.

"So Thomas tells me, and he ought to know."

The couple laughed. It had not been the easiest of pregnancies for Laura, especially after two earlier miscarriages. Thomas fussed over her, as if she was his own daughter.

Deep down he was concerned this might be her last chance to conceive. He knew, only too well, the heartbreak of not having any children of his own. And after Harriet's loss, he and Sarah had no other family. John and Laura were family to them.

* * *

Thomas had been delighted when John and Laura announced they were to be married. Sarah was not quite so sure. Soon after their wedding, John had gone to London for a trial, and seemed different when he returned. He had been restless before he went, and was even more so on his return. Something had happened to him whilst he was away, but he would not talk about it.

Finally Sarah gave up trying to find out what it was. She presumed he had been tempted to go back to work in London. Since the eventful time of his first few months in office, nothing much had happened to break the monotony of fairly minor, routine matters. And, she thought he missed the more hectic way of life he had experienced in London. After Laura had told him she was pregnant, John changed again, and seemed to settle down.

Sarah had watched him carefully, after Laura had her first miscarriage, but it only served to make him much more attentive towards her. It was a similar situation with the second miscarriage. She just hoped now that all would now be well, not just for the couple's sake, but she relished the idea of being able to spoil a baby, just as she would have done with her own children and grandchildren, had there been any.

Laura had settled down to being both the police superintendent's wife, and running her own school. As a general rule, Watch Committees did not approve of policemen's wives working. However, Laura's teaching occupation was considered to be acceptable, and in her case they raised no objections.

And it paved the way for Sam's Lucy to start up her own business, as an artist and plan drawer. Her application was helped by the numerous times her plans had been, and continued to be used at the Quarter Sessions and the Assizes, not only in Warwick, but also elsewhere on the Midland Circuit.

It had been a tense time for them all after Richard's arrest. In the end, he had not been hanged, but had committed suicide in his cell, on the eve of his trial. In many ways Laura felt sorry for him, and thought this was a kinder way for him to die, rather than be hanged in public. He had left various notes, which were not found until after his death.

In one, addressed to John, he had made a full confession, not only about his attempting to murder Thomas, but also another seven doctors he had killed, including a Dr William Boyd. He had even given details of the dates and places and methods used.

As it was suspected, he had never qualified as a doctor, but had learned his trade as an apprentice to various doctors, and apothecaries. At no time did he ever admit his true identity, so he was always referred to as Richard Gilson.

He explained how his young wife had died, because the same Dr Boyd had been too drunk to save her. Boyd's murder had soon followed, and Gilson was well on his trail of revenge. It made no difference how his victims were strangers to him, and in most cases, like Thomas, had been good at their profession.

Another note had been addressed to Laura, in which he asked for her forgiveness for trying to seduce her, abducting her and trying to murder her. Unbeknown to John, she had made a special visit to St Nicholas church and said a prayer for him, when his death was announced.

Richard's written evidence, supported by Thomas, had been enough to convict Giles Bradford of the murder of Jacob Harding. He too had made a full confession, on the eve of his execution, which included the murders of Bernard Hamlyn and Billy Beech, and robbing *Jersey's Bank*. Bradford steadfastly denied being involved in the bank manager's death, and he explained about the fight between Quinn and Hamlyn.

It was reported how he had died well on the gallows, which was an expression John loathed. How could anybody die well in such circumstances? However, he confirmed Bradford had died in a very penitent frame of mind. John had been there, in his official capacity, and Bradford had insisted on shaking hands with him, before being pinioned.

Laura was a little envious of Lucy Perkins, who already had twin boys, and had taken to pregnancy like a duck to water. She was now expecting her third child. Both women had become good friends. Sam had taken to fatherhood, and maintained he was training his sons already to become policemen. Lucy wanted them to become artists, and follow in her footsteps, and it all led to good humoured banter between them.

* * *

"Have you got to go out this evening?" asked John.

"I'm afraid so. I'm speaking at Leamington, on the subject of education for the poor. As you know, it's something I feel very strongly about. I shouldn't be too late back. And you?"

"I need to brief the night men, especially as Mathew is away, and one of them is new. But I don't intend staying there too long."

Robert had never fully recovered the use of his hand, and the Watch Committee had been obliged, albeit reluctantly, to terminate his employment as a constable. However, with a little bit of persuasion from Thomas, they agreed to his full time employment as a clerk for John. With his writing skills, fortunately not affected by the injury, coupled with his filing systems and retentive memory, he had quickly proved himself to be a tremendous asset to the Borough Police.

William Robinson had been appointed to replace him, but it had not been a sound appointment. The man was later dismissed for drunkenness. His replacement, Simon Palmer was starting that night, and Caleb was to show him around.

John nodded his agreement as Laura finished speaking. Although she ran a private school, she devoted some of her time to providing free lessons for the poor and underprivileged: and he supported her in this work. She was trying to extend the idea into Leamington.

Their thoughts were interrupted by a knock at the door. John went to answer it as Abbie was away. Although she had arranged for a Mrs Skinner to come in her place, John did not recognize the woman standing there.

"Mr Mayfield? I'm sorry to call so late, but my sister only just asked me to come." The woman looked to be on her late 40s with straggly greyish hair. She was quite slender and wore poor quality clothes. John looked puzzled.

"Oh, I'm sorry," she smiled. "I thought you knew. Mrs Skinner, my sister, has had a bad turn, and she can't come to clean and cook for you tomorrow. So, she's asked me to come in her stead." The woman paused, as John smiled and nodded.

"Of course," he said.

"I'm Mary Pegg," she continued. "I just thought I'd come and introduce myself, and see what needs doing tomorrow. And I've brought a present for Mrs Mayfield. It's beef tea which I believe is her favourite at the moment. Or so my sister tells me."

John smiled and invited her into the house.

She was so right about Laura liking beef tea. Thomas had said it was something to do with her pregnancy. And, if he was honest, John had developed a liking for it as well.

"I like beef tea too," he said jokingly.

Mary Pegg looked at him, half-seriously and half-mockingly.

"Mr Mayfield! It's for your wife, not you." She emphasized by wagging her finger at him, still smiling. "If you really want some, I'll bring some with me tomorrow. But this is for Mrs Mayfield."

Whilst Laura showed Mary Pegg round the house and explained what needed doing, John went and changed into his uniform, prior to going on duty. Whilst the women were out of sight, he poured some of the beef tea into a bottle, corked it and slipped it quietly into his pocket. He would heat it up at the station.

Laura said farewell to Mrs Pegg, and came back into their dining room. "I've got to go now my love," said John. "But I don't intend being too late home. Take care and don't overdo it."

"Don't worry! As you know I'm going with the Reverend Stephen Darnley and he fusses round me worse than you do," she laughed. "Off you go and enjoy the beef tea I've no doubt you've put on one side to take with you." Laura raised her eyebrows.

The couple laughed. John kissed her and went to the police station. Laura watched him go. Once he was out of sight, she heated up the beef tea and drank it. She had to admit it tasted a bit different to any other she'd drunk, but it was still good. Soon afterwards, Stephen Darnley arrived in his carriage and took her to Leamington.

They reached Leamington after an uneventful journey, but she was dismayed to find herself feeling a little nauseous by the time they arrived. She put it down to the journey and her pregnancy. As she sat waiting for her turn to speak, the waves of nausea began to spread over her.

For a few moments she thought it might have been a late session of morning sickness, but quickly dismissed that idea. Then it was her turn to speak. She took a deep breath, gathered her papers together, and breathed deeply again.

Slowly Laura stood up, only to find the room swimming before her eyes, and she was conscious of sweating profusely. Undecided, whether to speak or not, she saw several anxious pairs of eyes looking at her. The room began to swim faster in front of her eyes, and she felt for the edge of the table to put her hands on to steady herself. At the same time she looked at the vicar.

"Stephen....." was all she was able to gasp.

He stood up and went to help her. Laura opened her mouth to speak, but only a great fountain of vomit erupted from it. Only vaguely aware of the sudden screams, coming from the audience, Laura fell forwards. Everything was going black and there was a harsh roaring in her ears.

And then nothing.

Nobody moved for a moment.

"She's pregnant, so I expect it's something to do with that," Stephen announced lamely, to nobody in particular.

Several women from the audience ignored him, rushed onto the stage and looked at her. Laura's breathing was very shallow and laboured. **"For God's sake, someone get a doctor!"** one of the women shouted. **"NOW!"**

It was several minutes before a doctor arrived. He knelt beside the stricken woman and felt for her pulse.

"Take her to my surgery," he instructed.

* * *

John arrived at the police station, where he spoke to Caleb and the new constable just before they went on duty. Once they had gone, John heated up the beef tea and took a sip. It was too hot, so he took it back into his office, and began looking through some paperwork. From time to time he took a sip of the beef tea, but he soon began to feel nauseous, and left the rest of it. Not only did he feel sick, but he had a sudden urge to use the privy. As he stood up, the room began to swim, and he vomited violently. Moments later he collapsed onto his desk.

* * *

Caleb had not been on duty very long, before his lantern began to flicker and go out. He tried several times to get it going, but without success. Cursing, he and Simon returned to the station, to find another one. As he opened the door, he heard a crash from John's office, accompanied by groaning. Quickly he ran to the office and saw John just falling off his desk, into a pile of slimy smelly vomit.

Instantly recognizing the need for medical help, he ran back to the door of the station, where Simon was waiting.

"**QUICKLY MAN!**" he shouted. "**GET A CAB AND FETCH Dr WALDREN. I THINK Mr MAYFIELD'S DYING!**"

Caleb ran back into the office, his mind in a whirl. He was no stranger to people vomiting, but what John had fetched up reminded him of a time, when he was on a building site, when one of his fellow workers had accidentally taken some poison. They had saved his life by giving him a salt drink, and making him vomit. Running into the kitchen, he found some warm water in the kettle, which he poured into a mug.

Next he stirred in copious amounts of salt. Running back to John's office, he forced the mixture down the superintendent's throat. Moments later, John was violently sick again, all over Caleb's uniform. Although it still smelled vile, the vomit did not seem quite as intense as the first lot. He forced some more of the salty water down John's throat.

* * *

In High Street, the Waldrens were having a late supper, as Thomas had been delayed visiting a patient. They had only just sat down, when there came a furious, urgent knocking at the door, and Thomas cursed. Redman was in the act of serving the soup, so he instructed Sally, one of the house maids, to answer the summons.

It was Simon.

"**Dr. Waldren!**" he shouted, rushing into the house, and ignoring Sally. "**Can you come quickly? We think Mr Mayfield's dying.**"

Thomas pushed his chair back, stood up, collected his bag, and with, his mind in a whirl, rushed out of the house, ignoring another unexpected visitor, who had just arrived and was standing on the doorstep.

"Get a bed ready and see who's at the door," he instructed over his shoulder to nobody in particular, as he followed Simon into the waiting cab.

Sally had only just returned to the dining room, and, after looking at Redman, went to the door again, in response to Thomas's instructions.

"Can I help.........**NO!**"

Her voice tailed off, and she gave a long piercing scream, as she stared, in disbelief and horror, at the figure standing on the doorstep.

Hearing her scream Redman sighed, put down the soup tureen, and went out into the hallway. He stopped dead, and the colour left his face, when he saw the figure standing in the hallway. Already other servants were appearing, having heard Sally's scream. They too stopped dead in their tracks, and some of the maids screamed.

Redman was the first to react, and he returned, ashen faced, to the dining-room. But before he could speak, the visitor followed him.

Sarah had already been walking towards the door, when Redman came in. "What's going.......?" Sarah's voice faltered. Her hands went over her mouth as she gasped, in shock when she saw the figure standing behind Redman.

Unaware of the drama unfolding at his home, Thomas was questioning Simon about John, as the cab raced back to the police station.

* * *

John was exhausted, as yet again he climbed down the steps into *Bradford & Harding's* cellar. As he walked across the floor, the flagstones began to move and Harding's corpse climbed out of its temporary grave. Barely waiting a moment, John fled up the stairs, through the yard and into Old Square, where Albert Quinn stood smiling, with blood dripping from his head. In his hand he held a glass inkwell.

Screaming, John headed to St Mary's church, only to find Bernard Hamlyn standing there, pointing towards the churchyard. Still screaming, John ran inside the churchyard, where he fell into an open grave. Even as he struggled to climb out of it, Giles Bradford appeared and started to cover him with earth.

As the last clods of earth fell over him, John panted and struggled for breath. He became incredibly hot and thought he would dry up. Then he was lying in the coolness of the River Avon, with James Cooper continually holding his head under the water. He closed his eyes and all went black for a few seconds.

When he opened his eyes, John found himself in the *White House*, fighting with Charles Pearson again, only this time it was with axes. Pearson, who now had a very bloated and almost unrecognizable face, was putting up very stiff resistance. He laughed at John, and pointed to Kate Whiting's dismembered body lying by the stairs. John flew at him and severed Pearson's hand, which held his axe.

But Pearson only laughed louder, as another hand grew in its place. Meanwhile, the severed hand still attacked John on its own accord. Again and again John attacked Pearson, and severed various limbs, from the man's body. But they all grew again.

When Kate's dismembered body and limbs, joined in the attack on him, John screamed, threw down his axe and fled out of the house. The phantom limbs and Pearson's mocking laughter followed him. On his way up towards the town centre he was offered a lift, in a glowing carriage, driven by a grinning Richard Gilson.

He ran all the way to *Bradford & Harding's* office and hid in the cellar. But even as he did so, the nightmare started all over again, and again, and again.

*   *   *

Suddenly John's eyes opened, and he found himself lying in a strange bed. For once he did not feel frightened, and saw there was a lantern glowing on a nearby table. Strangely he felt completely at peace, although totally exhausted. He was aware too of a female figure, sitting by his bed, reading a book by the lamplight.

"Laura?" he croaked.

The female figure looked up and smiled at him. It was a face he knew so well, yet it was not Laura sitting there. And he knew he must be dead.

The woman was Harriet.

Leaping to her feet, Harriet ran across the room, opened the bedroom door and shouted. **"UNCLE THOMAS! UNCLE THOMAS!"**

Moments later a worried looking Thomas, followed by a just as anxious Sarah, both still tying their dressing gown cords, rushed in. Their concerned looks quickly faded into smiles, when they saw look of happiness on Harriet's face.

"John's back with us," was all she could say.

It was too much for John to take in, and he slipped back into unconsciousness.

Thomas checked John's pulse, felt his forehead and nodded satisfactorily. "I'm certain the crisis is over. He'll sleep now. And so should you, my dear."

He addressed the last remark to Harriet.

It was morning before John awoke again, and was able to take in his surroundings. Slowly Harriet told him how he had been ill for nearly ten days, during which time she had nursed him continually. Gently she broke the news to him about Laura's death and that of their unborn child, then held him tightly in her arms, as he wept.

She could not believe how John had nearly died on the very night she had arrived back in Warwick. Neither could she believe how she had survived in that dreadful desert in Africa.

CHAPTER TWENTY-TWO

Harriet's Tale

H arriet had slowly opened her eyes, and found she was lying on a sandy shore. However, she could see nothing for a dense fog which swirled around her. Lying there exhausted, she tried to work out if she was alive or dead. In the distance, she could hear the gentle lapping of the sea. Otherwise it was deathly quiet. When the sun slowly burnt through the fog, Harriet was left in no doubt. Somehow she was alive, but she wondered, for how much longer?

Getting stiffly to her feet, she looked about her, and was not filled with much hope. Everywhere she looked there were sand dunes and desert. Perhaps it would have been better if she had drowned, rather than face death from thirst and starvation. These thoughts reminded her of how she was thirsty. Uncorking one of her water containers, she took a few gentle swallows, and re-corked it. The water would not last for ever, and she sank miserably to her knees. She also knew the chances of rescue were so remote, as to be non-existent.

Looking around, her confidence rose when she saw several other people lying on the sand. However, these hopes were soon dashed, when she discovered they were all dead. She was very much on her own, in one of the most inhospitable parts of the World, with little or no chance of surviving. Taking out her revolver, Harriet prepared to shoot herself and end it all.

But, as she did so, she felt something rub against her left breast. Reaching inside, she found the letter she had written to John, before the ship had been wrecked. It stirred her into action. "No," she resolved. "I'm going to fight this. If I don't survive, then it will not be for the want of trying."

Putting her revolver away, she went across to the other bodies. By now the sun had become quite hot: reflecting off the sand and sea, made it even hotter. She knew, from travelling in the Australian Outback with friendly Aborigines, how her best chance of survival had to be by getting under cover during the day, and only moving at night. But, the tide had turned and was now coming in, so she needed to move quickly.

A search of the bodies produced some useful items. Amongst the seamen's knives, she chose the longest and sharpest one to carry, and put another two on one side. One of them could be used to make a spear, and she would keep the other for culinary use. The thoughts made her chuckle wryly. Just where would she acquire such food out here, for culinary use?

An examination of the captain's body produced a revolver and spare ammunition. Luckily it was the same calibre as her own, so she just kept the ammunition, and ignored everything else. Another man had a length of twine on him, and another body gave her a small box of dried meat and two more water containers. From three women, she removed their skirts, which would help provide a cover, to shade her from the sun. She was already grateful for her own hat.

After Harriet had cut some laths from driftwood, she pushed some of them through the skirts, and inserted the others into the sand. Using some of the twine, she made a passable tent, and piled her treasures into it. Remembering too how hot sand could get, and she was starting to feel it under her feet already, she removed the thickest coats she could find, and lay them down to act as ground insulation. Having checked all the hats, she found, none of them fitted her any better, than the one she had brought with her from the ship.

From a washed up trunk, she found two pairs of half boots, slightly larger than her size. But with extra stockings on her feet, they fitted fairly well. She knew how walking around in bare feet was a recipe for disaster. Not only would she be burnt, but there was a very real risk of being stung by scorpions on land: and other stinging creatures, if she had to cross any water. Her own boots, although well made, were designed for town living, not desert walking. At least these other boots were more robust, and should last much longer.

As she looked at the last body, Harriet gave a slight smile. It was one of her would be suitors, and he had tied his spectacles round his head. She had not known he was that short sighted. After saying a short prayer over the bodies, and asking their forgiveness for not burying them, she went to move away, then stopped and went back to the man with the spectacles. Stooping, she removed them, and found they folded up. Now she had a source of fire with both the sun and the spectacles.

Harriet spent the remainder of the day lying under her sunshade, taking the occasional sips of water, and moving as little as possible. Once night fell, she gathered up her few belongings, tied them in one of the skirts, shouldered the bundle and set off in a Southerly direction. The captain had said to keep the land to her left and the sea to her right. As the night progressed, it became deliciously cool before it went cold. Now she was glad of one of the heavy coats to wear. Long before dawn, it had become foggy again and she was forced to camp early.

By the fourth day, Harriet had used up all the dried meat, and she was starting to get hungry. To add to the problems, her drinking water was disappearing at a quicker rate than she had hoped. Two of the containers were now empty.

She had found one or two nut plants, but they had not provided much food. Bird life, for the most part, was too small and not worth wasting precious bullets on, although she knew that time might well come. Harriet had no idea just how far away Walvis Bay was. All she knew was it had been annexed by the British in 1795. It was the only settlement for hundreds of miles and represented her only hope.

So far she had not seen any other signs of human life.

She was now used to sounds of the dunes, and actually enjoyed watching the colours of the desert change. But, it was early days in her trek, and they still had a novelty value. Slowly she was conscious of another sound, and on further investigating, found it came from hundreds of seals basking on the shore. This had to be a source of food. She decided to rest for a day, have something to eat and hopefully find some water.

After looking around for some time, as she had learnt to do in the Outback, Harriet found a small depression in the sand, somewhat inland from the shore. Very conscious of the dangers of losing her sense of direction, she marked her path with several pieces of driftwood, onto which she had tied pieces of ribbon, from her hat. Getting down to her knees, Harriet began to dig into the sand, with a piece of driftwood. After digging down about eighteen inches, she was beginning to have doubts, when the sand became less dry. Six inches later, it was positively damp. Having widened the sides, she left it to fill.

Her next job was to gather plenty of driftwood and some thorn scrub, which she piled up into a cone shape, fairly close to her shelter. Judging by the heat, she guessed it must be about midday, and so she rested for while. When she awoke, Harriet went to look at her makeshift well, and was overjoyed to see it contained several inches of water. But it would take a long time to fill. And now, she steeled herself for the task she had been putting off doing.

Checking her revolver was loaded, Harriet walked quietly on to the beach, where she selected a small seal at random, and with tears in her eyes, shot it. The creature died instantly. Harriet wept, but she knew it had to be its life or hers. She found dragging it back to her shelter was harder work than she had anticipated, and it was not the best of ideas in the heat. Taking one of her smaller knives, she gutted and skinned the animal. Knowing it be impossible for her to joint, she contented herself by cutting off several slices to cook.

Next she used the spectacles to focus the sun's rays onto her prepared fire, and soon had it burning. She had already speared some of the meat onto driftwood, which she now propped up, close to the fire. With the meat cooking, she returned to her well and was able to refill one of her water containers. The water was a little brackish, and would have been better for filtering, but she found it tasted excellent.

Returning to the fire, Harriet tasted her first ever piece of seal meat, and found it delicious. She ate slowly, and cooked other strips of meat, which she could eat later. And, she decided to cook some more tomorrow, before it became too hot. As a bonus, she had rubbed some of the seal fat onto her wind burned face, and found it to be most beneficial. For the first time since beginning her trek, Harriet ate and slept well.

When she awoke in the morning, the first thing she noticed was the uncooked seal had vanished. At first she thought jackals had taken it, but could not see any obvious signs of them. Then she noticed an ostrich egg close to where the seal had been. On closer inspection she saw it was stood upright, and had a small twig bung in the top, obviously acting as a stopper.

Picking the egg up, she shook it gently, and heard liquid sloshing around inside. She took out the stopper and poured out some of the liquid into her hand. It was pure clear fresh water. Whoever had taken her uncooked seal had left the water in payment. Although she looked about her, Harriet could see nobody, but she now knew she was not alone. Her visitors had to be natives, and so far they had been friendly.

In the following days, whenever she left unused food out, it was always exchanged for water. During this time, she had steeled herself to killing seals with her makeshift spear, in order to conserve her bullets. If she had no food to leave, the egg was left out instead, and it was always replenished

Harriet tried to keep a tally of the passing days, but she lost the count. Finding the task depressing, she quickly abandoned the idea. Consequently, she had no idea just when she came across the wreck of a large wooden ship on the beach. It was not the first she had seen, but this one appeared to be fairly intact. However a search of it revealed nothing that could be of any use to her, as scavengers had clearly been there before.

Just as she was leaving, Harriet saw a small cloth bag lying, half in and half out, of a cupboard. On opening it, she saw it only contained stones. Disappointed, she tossed them down, but then she had second thoughts. Why should anyone store a bag of pebbles?

Taking one of the stones in her hand, she rubbed it down part of a window, which had not broken. The stone easily scratched the glass. Excited, she tried the others: all with the same effect. She laughed aloud at the thought they might be uncut diamonds.

Here she was, marooned somewhere in Africa, with a possible fortune in uncut diamonds! How ironic! Nevertheless, she collected them all up, and tied them in a spare stocking, which she attached to her belt. "Who knows?" She mused aloud. "I might just get out of here some day."

One afternoon, Harriet woke up feeling excessively hot.

Her skin was dry and hot, and she had a raging thirst. She tried rationing her water, but found she was unable to do so. When she tried to stand, she felt giddy and everything spun before her eyes. At first she thought she had been affected by the sun, and fell into a troubled sleep.

At one stage she was vaguely aware of people standing around her, all making strange clicking sounds with their tongues. Later, she would liken their clicking to the sound of a cork being pulled out of a bottle, or the encouragement one gave to a horse. On another occasion she was aware of being undressed and having her body washed with cool water, which was a lovely sensation. She was also very conscious of the way many of the visitors touched her red hair, with a degree of awe.

When she finally woke, Harriet found herself in a small native settlement and had no idea where she was. All she knew was she was nowhere near the coast. As she recovered, she found the natives were friendly and very respectful. She also found a small scar on her arm and discovered she had been stung by a scorpion, which had led to her fever.

In time, she learned to communicate with her rescuers, albeit mainly by drawings in the sand. Yet, they always ignored her pictures of men riding horses, which was the only means she could find to explain where she wanted to go. Much later she discovered how they were frightened of white men and had only helped her because she was a woman, on her own: fairly capable, and with a head of wondrous red hair.

Harriet felt strangely at peace with these people. From them she learned more survival tricks and which desert plants could be eaten safely. Meanwhile, she never gave up her attempts to persuade them to take her to a white man's settlement, and hopefully, re-unite her with John. But her pleas were all in vain. Her only alternative was to move out, on her own, into the desert, which was not an option. So, she stayed with them.

* * *

One morning, several months later, she woke up to find they had all gone. In the distance she could see the sand moving, and knew it had to be a party of mounted men. Initially the knowledge thrilled her, but then she wondered what would happen if they were Arabs, or slave traders? She had no intention of living the rest of her life in a harem.

If they were Arabs, she would definitely kill herself this time, but would sell her life dearly. She took out her revolver, checked it and ran her other hand through her hair, only to find it had been cut short during the night. Was that a good sign or a bad one? Crouching in one of the native's temporary shelters, she waited.

The sound of horses drew nearer, as their riders searched the deserted campsite. Two of them made their way to Harriet's shelter, where they dismounted. She lay still in the forlorn hope they might think she was dead. Through her partly closed eyelids, she saw the flap open and the large silhouette of a man, in uniform enter.

"Sergeant! Come here quick!"

On hearing the English voice, Harriet burst into tears. "Oh thank God," she sobbed.

The soldier took off his shako and put his arms round her. "It's alright now missy. You're safe now."

Moments later Sergeant Willie McEwan came into the shelter, and looked puzzled, as he saw his man holding the sobbing Harriet.

"She's English," came the soldier's simple reply. "You'd better get the officer." His voice held the faintest note of contempt.

Minutes later a young lieutenant arrived, and was clearly surprised by finding Harriet. "Oh this is a surprise. But, I don't suppose you've got any water have you? Only we're very short of it and the last water hole has gone dry. And I fear we are not going to make it back to Walvis."

Coming to her senses, Harriet heard his words.

"I doubt there's any here. They would have taken it with them when they left."

"We'll go after them. They can't take a white woman prisoner just like that. They'll have to be taught a lesson."

"NO! You can't do that," insisted Harriet. "Firstly, I was not their prisoner." She stressed. "In fact, they saved my life and treated me with the utmost respect and kindness."

The lieutenant looked at her, clearly wondering about the morals of a white woman living with a tribe of natives.

"Don't you dare to even think it: let alone accuse me of anything," hissed Harriet. "They treated me with the utmost respect and kindness. I had my own shelter and no one forced themselves on me. Get that quite clear."

The lieutenant was quite taken aback by her vehemence, and he could feel Sergeant McEwan and some of the others soldiers grinning behind his back. He was not a popular or respected soldier. When he spun round to confront them, they were straight faced once more.

"As for getting water from them, you can forget that idea. You'd never find them. But if it's water you want, let us go and find some."

Harriet led them to a small depression in the sand, where she knew water existed. "Get your men to dig here," she said. "They'll have to go down about a yard, and make it as wide across as they can."

He reluctantly ordered some of men to do as she said. They were led by Sergeant McEwan. The officer watched on disbelievingly. When they reached the suggested depth, McEwan cried. "The sand's damp here."

"You'll have to let it alone now for a few hours and wait for the water to rise," she instructed.

"This is a waste of time," sneered the lieutenant. "We need to move now if we're to stand any chance of getting back to Walvis. Sergeant, instruct the men to mount up. As for you, miss whatever your name is, you can come with us or stay for your native friends to come back to you. It's your choice! Carry on sergeant!"

But McEwan made no move to obey. Instead, he looked down into the make shift well once again. "I think you ought to have a look at this sir."

"I've given you an order, now obey it!"

"Even if you don't believe me, sir, then look at the horses."

The lieutenant did not have to, as his own horse, like the others had become excited and restless.

"They can smell the water," continued McEwan. "And there is some now in this hole."

Reluctantly the lieutenant looked into the hole and was surprised to see water beginning to soak through the sand. "I owe you an apology, Miss ....?" He said, very formally and stiffly.

"Actually it's Mrs Foxton. Harriet Foxton."

* * *

Without Harriet none of the patrol would have survived to reach Walvis Bay. Yet, in spite of her actions, she found herself shunned by most of the other women in the settlement. They believed she had gone native, after hearing the tales of her finding water and other foodstuffs in the desert. It was convenient for them to forget how she had saved lives. The Governor's wife gave her some cast off, worn out dresses, but it was only as an act of charity, not friendship.

For her part, Harriet found it difficult to readjust to a civilized way of life, all of which added to the contempt the other women had for her. Harriet ignored them. She had done something they never could: survived both the Skeleton Coast and the desert. Where she found friendship was amongst the womenfolk of the ordinary soldiers, in particular of those who had been on the patrol, which found her. They appreciated how she had saved their men's lives, and were grateful.

When a ship called in, on its way to Europe, Harriet could not wait to board it. The problem was she had no money, and was unwilling to disclose anything about the possible diamonds she had. Finally the captain agreed to take her wedding ring as security for her passage, although she would have to earn her keep. She agreed and became their cook.

As Harriet made her way to the docks to board the ship, before it sailed, she was suddenly aware of Sergeant McEwan and his men, marching alongside her. "Just wanted to make sure you got to the boat safely, miss," he smiled.

He carried her pitifully few possessions on board ship, and stood with her for a moment.

"I just want to thank you again, Mrs Foxton, on behalf of all the men. We owe you our lives and will always be forever in your debt." He paused, clearly embarrassed. "And so, we would like you to have this. One good turn deserves another." He put a small packet in her hand. "But don't let the captain see what you've got."

Before she could say anything else, he had gone. Minutes later the ship cast off, and Harriet waved farewell to McEwan and his men. At his command they all stood to attention and saluted her. Then they did an about turn and marched away.

With tears in her eyes, Harriet went down to the tiny cabin she had managed to arrange for herself. She would never forget the kindness she had received from Willie McEwan and his men.

Having closed the cabin door behind her, she opened the package Willie had given her. She gasped both in amazement and pleasure as she looked at the object enclosed in it.

It was her wedding ring.

EPILOGUE

John recovered slowly, but it was another six weeks before he was fit enough to resume his duties. Meanwhile he had learned all about Laura's death, and was sad to have missed her funeral.

The coroner's inquest had returned a verdict of murder by person or persons unknown. Thomas explained how he had analyzed the beef tea and found it contained a little known, but deadly poison. Had Laura been treated immediately, there might have been a chance of saving her life, but help for her had come too late.

Mrs Skinner had been found lying in a drugged state in her lodgings. When she had recovered, she was unable to help. All she could remember was opening her door to a strange woman, and nothing else.

John owed his life to having drunk less of the tea, and his being found so quickly by Caleb, whose drastic first aid treatment, had worked. Harriet would always be grateful to him. This was followed by Thomas and Harriet's loving care, which ensured he recovered.

Slowly he began to come to terms both with Laura's death and that of their unborn child, plus Harriet's miraculous return. At the same time, he felt twinges of guilt for not having waited for her.

On his first day back on duty, John was only too aware he had a murder enquiry on his hands, which he was determined to solve, regardless of how long it took him. He was still wondering whether he or Laura, had been the intended victim, when he found a letter marked *personal* and addressed to him.

John opened it and read:

Dear Mayfield

Welcome back to the land of the living. I really did try to stop you drinking that beef tea, but, silly man you did it all the same. Your man did well to save you. Yet you won't have cause to thank him.

You destroyed the love of my life, and now you can discover just what it feels like to lose yours, just as the Whiting bitch has discovered, having lost her husband and son. You've lost your Laura.

I doubt we'll ever meet again, but rest assured how I curse you for what you've done to me, and now you can suffer for it, just as I've done.

See you in hell.

Mary Anne Peters alias Mary Pegg.
PS You never told me how you enjoyed the play that night.

HISTORICAL NOTE

Mayfield's Law is not, and is never intended to be a history of the Warwick Borough Police. It is a work of fiction, although set in a real town. All the characters are fictitious.

The Warwick Borough Police started in 1846, and not in 1840, as in this story. I have had to change the date because I needed a certain time line for the trilogy.

Life for early policemen was exceptionally hard, by today's standards. Discipline was harsh, with most supervisors coming from the Army and Navy, and bringing with them their own exacting standards. There were all manner of restrictions placed on both the working and private lives of officers, some of which still exist today. They were not permitted to marry without permission, and with very few exceptions, their wives were not permitted to work. Considerate officers, such as John Mayfield, were very few and far between.

Promotion within a small force was very slow, if ever! It was literally a case of waiting for dead men's shoes. Warwick was no exception.

Whilst all the main locations still exist today, you will not find the house where Thomas and Sarah lived, nor the location of Laura's school.

The original police station in the Holloway is now used for a different purpose. *The Green Dragon* is now the *Tilted Wig*. Although the buildings which once housed the *Woolpack* and the *Bull's Head*, still stand, they are now in private occupation or used for other business purposes. Eastgate House is now divided into apartments. *The Rose and Crown* still operates as licensed premises. At the time of writing (September 2010) *The Globe* is undergoing refurbishment, but will remain as licensed premises.

There never was a *Jersey's Bank*.

Finally, I have taken another liberty with history, for the sake of the story. Warwick Railway station opened in 1852, not in 1841. The early trains had difficulty in going up Hatton Bank, and it was necessary for them to utilize the services of a second locomotive.

Electric telegraphs first appeared in England in 1838, but did not catch on immediately. Also they depended on someone being at the other end to read the message, when it came through. In the 1870's it was quite usual for many such offices not to be staffed 24 hours a day.

Police chiefs such as John Mayfield, had no clear guidance or instruction on how to investigate crimes. For many it was a case of trial and error. However they set the scene for future generations of police officers to follow. There was no special detective force in the 1840s, and all crimes were investigated by the police officers who were available at the time.

Likewise, although postmortems were performed, what they revealed was not always appreciated or even understood by the authorities. However, forensic science was growing, albeit slowly. John Mayfield was fortunate in having Dr Thomas Waldren's expertise to assist him.

John Mayfield and his men still have long rocky road ahead of them.

Extract from Mayfield's Last Case
(The final part of the trilogy)

C harlotte Goodwin, always known as Lottie, was not having a good night. There had been a race meeting in the town, that afternoon, which should have resulted in her getting some trade. But, for some reason, it never happened. In some respects, Lottie was grateful, as she did not desperately enjoy being a whore, but she had to live. Although, with luck, she hoped she would not need to sell her body for very much longer.

She had made the acquaintance of a young stranger, soon after he had arrived in town, and he had taken an interest in her. Whilst she attended to his sexual needs, from time to time, he was encouraging her to give up whoring, and get some proper employment elsewhere. To help, he had started teaching her to read and write. Now, whenever they met, he continued with her lessons.

As her education was greatly improving, Lottie was coming quite close to abandoning the street life, although it was with mixed feelings. For the most part, her clients were reasonably well behaved. She especially liked the young man who was giving her lessons, and she would have liked to have known him better. But she knew that could never happen, no matter how much the idea appealed to her.

He more than made up for the occasional man, who preferred to give her a good beating, rather than pay. Whilst she would miss some of her regulars, there were others she would not.

Lottie had been with her tutor that evening, for another lesson. He had his own rooms now, close to the Harriet Foxton Hospital, and was impressed by the way her reading and writing was improving. As she had left him, although it was only late summer, the evening had gone a little chilly, which was probably deterring her customers, and he had lent her his scarf. She promised to return it to him, on her next visit.

Lottie now moved up to her normal area, by St Mary's church. Meanwhile, the only men she had seen were already accompanied by women, some of whom Lottie knew. Such was life!

It was also becoming a little foggy, as happens sometimes on a summer's evening, so Lottie decided to call it a day, and she moved slowly down Church Street. Walking by the edge of the churchyard, she stopped and listened.

"Pst! Pst!" The sound came again from behind her: actually in the churchyard.

She turned, and could just make out a figure, wearing a top hat, who beckoned to her. Clearly he wanted what she had on offer. Happily she went into the churchyard, and followed him into the shadows. Then she stopped. It was dark in the churchyard, and she did not know who she was going to meet in there. But, it was where she often took her customers: and she needed some money.

No doubt had she asked her tutor, he would have given it to her: but that would have seemed like begging. So she decided to take a chance. Lifting her skirts, she followed the figure onto the grass, and going under the trees, Lottie went further into the depths of the churchyard.

* * *

Joseph Garner, the gravedigger, known to all as Joe, did not feel very well. He knew it was his own fault. If only he had not decided to go out, for a few drinks with some old friends, the previous night: but he had.

It had started off reasonably, but all four of them were former soldiers, and they began reminiscing about their time in the Crimean War. After that, one drink led to another, as they re-fought old battles.

They had finished so late, that Joe was too scared to return home and face his formidable wife's wrath. There had only been one place where he dared go: and so he made his way into St Mary's churchyard. He had decided to sleep in his hut, for what remained of the night. In any case, he had to dig a grave later that morning, and he convinced himself he had a good excuse for not going home.

Now, as he shouldered his spade, and made his way, blinking, into the sunlight, Joe cursed the drinks he had had the previous night. Whistling tunelessly, he made his way to where he had already marked where to dig the grave.

Passing a small clump of trees, near the path, he saw what looked like a female's shoe lying by a tombstone. Curious he went to take a closer look. It was then he saw another shoe nearby, poking out of a bush. He picked up the first shoe, and then went to pick up the second one. Using his spade to push the bush aside, he took a closer look at the shoe, and soon wished he had not done so.

He saw there was a foot still in the shoe. Investigating further, he discovered, as he now expected, the body of a young woman. Going further into the bushes, he saw the area was covered in blood, as was the dead woman.

Joe took a closer look at her, and immediately regretted it. Although he was no stranger to death, both in his current occupation and his earlier military service, he was not prepared for what he saw, on this particularly pleasant and sunny morning.

Her body had been ripped open, along with a huge gaping wound in her throat. She reminded him of some of the bodies he had seen on battlefields. But, never in his worst nightmares, did he ever expect to see such a sight in Warwick. It was too much for his already weak and suffering stomach.

Leaning over another tombstone, he was violently sick.

* * *

John was in his office, trying to concentrate on some reports, which needed his attention. He was now spending very little time in his office, normally only an hour or so each day, before returning to be with Harriet.

She was weakening by the day, if not by the hour. Silas and Thomas had done all they could to make her as comfortable as possible. But they all knew she only had hours left to live.

As he stood up and prepared to go home, John heard running feet, followed by the station door being thrust open. Instinctively he knew it could only mean trouble. He waited patiently as a babble of voices came from the front counter. Soon Constable Harry Barlow appeared at his office door.

"Guv'nor," he announced without any preamble. "It seems we've got a murder in the churchyard."

"Which one?"

"St Mary's."

"Right. I'm on my way. Get Dr Waldren, then find Inspector Harrison and Sergeants Perkins and Young, and have them meet me there."

Stopping only to collect his uniform kepi, John followed Joe Garner into the churchyard. Although Joe had warned him she was not a pretty sight, John was aghast when he saw how Lottie had been killed. As he stood there, Thomas Waldren arrived.

"Dear God!" he breathed. "What sort of person could do this?" Thomas shook his head in disbelief, as he knelt beside her body, on a patch of grass which was relatively blood free.

"I don't suppose it could have been an animal, could it?" John asked forlornly.

Thomas peeled back part of the girl's dress, and shook his head. "No. These injuries have been caused by a very sharp instrument, such as a scalpel. Oh no! Look!"

He pointed to the heavily bloodstained scalpel lying nearby. Turning back to the body, he looked closer at the injuries. John said nothing, as he had an idea the way Thomas's mind was working. At length the doctor stood up.

"I hate to say this, John. But I think you are looking for someone with medical knowledge. The only good thing is that she doesn't appear to have been raped. As you can see, her skirts do not appear to have been lifted. And provided her throat was cut fairly early on in the attack, she wouldn't have suffered very much."

"What's that" asked John pointing downwards.

Thomas knelt down again and studied the girl's right hand. Clutched in it was a piece of material.

"It looks like she might have pulled this from her attacker." Thomas hesitated.

"Why do you hesitate?"

"If she died almost instantaneously, I don't see how she would have the time to pull this material away."

John felt a gentle tug on his sleeve.

Lightning Source UK Ltd.
Milton Keynes UK
UKOW051319021211

183049UK00001B/18/P